Dressing
the
Countess

Dressing
the
Countess

RACHEL BRIMBLE

HARPETH ROAD
PRESS®
Nashville

HARPETH ROAD PRESS

Published by Harpeth Road Press (USA)
P.O. Box 158184
Nashville, TN 37215

Paperback: 979-8-9887744-5-7
eBook: 979-8-9887744-4-0

Dressing the Countess: A Sweeping, Captivating Victorian Romance

Cover design by Kristen Ingebretson
Cover images © Shutterstock

First printing: May, 2024

For my dear, beautiful writer friend, Teri Wilson—there is no one I love talking about British royalty or visiting London with more than you and only wish I could transport us for a walk around in Victorian times! I am eternally grateful for your friendship, love, and support... mwah!

Chapter One

Rose Watson tightened her hold on her sketchbook and walked in a slow circle around the mannequin in front of her, her head tilted and eyes narrowed. A dart of hazy sunshine streaming through the shop window lit her work in a delicate glow, heartening Rose's hope that the lady's dresser—Mrs. Hayworth, who had ordered the dress—would be delighted with it. Despite her trepidation, the longer Rose stared at her creation, the more persistently a smile pulled at her lips. There could be no denying it. The dress was a triumph. Her best yet.

She lightly ran her hand over the emerald-green velvet of the embroidered bodice, her fingertips tracing the whorls and swirls of intertwined vines and the shimmering silver thread edging the butterflies' wings as they frolicked from waist to décolletage. The jet beading on the sash, as well as trimming the cuffs and hem glinted, the delicate black overlay falling perfectly over the skirt, making the stiffness and aches Rose had suffered in her knuckles and back during the stitching worth every uncomfortable minute.

Oh, how desperate she was to know the identity of the woman who would wear it! Mrs. Hayworth had been so reticent, so discreet about her mistress, it was impossible to guess. Whoever she might be, her dimensions proved her fortunate enough to possess a perfectly proportioned figure and, although unusually tall, Rose had no doubt the woman's height would only make her more striking. Mrs. Hayworth had shared with Rose's father that her mistress had light-brown hair, blue eyes, an olive complexion, and a deep love of nature, especially of the world's creatures. All details Rose had kept at the forefront of her mind while designing and making the dress.

She glanced at the wall clock and drew in a long, calming breath. Mrs. Hayworth was due at any moment for a final viewing and—fingers crossed—a concluding endorsement. If she approved…Rose closed her eyes. *Please let her approve.* Only then would Rose carefully remove the dress from its mannequin and prepare it for delivery.

"Oh, Rose. It's marvelous." Florence Davis, Rose's friend and fellow seamstress, entered the shop from the back room and slid her arm around Rose's waist, hugging her close. "Whoever this dress belongs to owes you a hundred thank-yous."

Rare nerves took flight in Rose's stomach as her confidence faltered. "Do you really believe it will meet her expectations?"

Florence laughed. "How could it not? It's beautiful."

"I am certainly proud of it, but…" Rose eased out of her friend's embrace and circled the mannequin again, the heels of her shoes tapping the floorboards. "It doesn't matter how much I believe this dress is my finest work. Not knowing who will wear it makes me uneasy. She could be anyone. Her taste a million miles from mine. Mrs. Hayworth was so very vague with her brief, leaving all to me and my imagination."

"Which is a good sign. You have only just turned one and twenty and already your work is gaining recognition. If this Mrs. Hayworth is who I think she is, she has been studying your work for a while."

Rose stopped walking. "What?"

"She's been coming into the shop for at least two or three months. At least, she has if I am thinking of the right woman."

"You're not sure?"

"No, but from what you've told me of her manner and looks, I am almost certain I know who she is, and she was already familiar with your work when she commissioned this dress. I'm sure she bought one of the jackets you created. One of those your father finally agreed to display in the window a while ago."

Rose glanced toward the front of the shop, excitement churning in her stomach. Florence walked behind one of the shop's counters and splayed her hands on the top. "And then she came back and spoke to your father about something or other. What, I don't know."

"Are you quite certain?"

"Absolutely."

"But one garment would not be enough for a lady's dresser to commission an outfit as expensive as this one, surely. And from a clothes maker she's never met?"

Florence lifted her shoulders. "I don't see why not. Anyway, can't you just enjoy that it's happened? You are outstanding at what you do, Rose. It's about time you had some proper recognition."

Hope swelled inside Rose as she turned back to the mannequin. "If what you say about Mrs. Hayworth is true, then it certainly helps settle my nerves."

Rose adjusted the dress's shoulder and smoothed her hand over the hump of the bustle as she pondered the events that had led to this moment. She had been working in the back room on what she had believed was Mrs. Hayworth's first time entering the Watsons' small, family-run shop six weeks before when, unbeknownst to her, Mrs. Hayworth told Rose's father she would like to commission a dress of original design and using materials of the finest quality, specifically requesting that the unexpected task be given to "the young lady with the dark hair and lovely eyes."

Her father had been somewhat taken aback by the request, considering he had only allowed his daughter to design and create five dresses to sell in the shop so far. Despite their immediate popularity and the fact that they sold within a day or two of their unveilings, Rose's parents had not been impressed. Instead, her success made them increasingly nervous that Rose might come to think too highly of herself. They told her as much again and again.

"Good lord, whatever are you thinking about?" Florence asked, her eyebrows raised. "Your face tells me that whoever or whatever it is, you are not at all happy."

Rose looked at the door again. "Oh, I am. Just nervous. I can't help feeling at a disadvantage. I want to make something of myself, but my parents do not see my work as remarkable, although it seems Mrs. Hayworth did."

"Which is all that matters."

"But after all the free time I've spent making clothes I love rather than those my parents consider acceptable, the sacrifices I have made by not seeing friends because making clothes means so much to me…" Frustrated, Rose shook her head. "I just think it's time my parents gave me the chance to shine a little. Instead, they keep me in this shop making boring designs they believe people will buy." She sighed. "They can be so narrow-minded. It's maddening!"

Florence sneaked a glance at the curtain behind her and lowered her voice. "Shh, they will hear you!"

Rose continued in a whisper, "Worse, they often imply people like us should not expect too much from life, that we should keep to convention. Lord knows they've made it perfectly clear they wish me to spend less time dreaming about my designs and instead pursue finding a husband and starting a family... all while working in the shop."

Florence gave an inelegant sniff and strode to one of the glass counters. "Ignore them. Your parents say much the same to me. You know as well as I do that life is what we make of it, and you, Rose Watson, are brimming with talent. You cannot fail to make a success of yourself one day."

Rose's heart filled with love for her loyal, optimistic friend. "You're very sweet, Flo, but sometimes I fear my parents will never be swayed, and I'll end my days within these four walls."

"That's absolute rubbish and you know it."

Exhaling a shaky breath, Rose looked through the shop's front window where two women stood on the other side of the leaded glass, their fingers pointing at the prominent hat display in the center.

"Well, rubbish or not, if you are right, my father met Mrs. Hayworth quite a few times before she commissioned this dress, and still he has not introduced us."

"But why agree to the commission if he didn't want you involved?"

"Because..." Rose narrowed her eyes. "When Mrs. Hayworth did not balk at his overpricing, he was overjoyed."

"Ah, I see." Florence grinned. "Well, your designs are magnificent and that's all that matters." She walked to the front door and opened it. A billow of wintery wind swept inside, lifting the ribbons and feathers donning the hats inside the bay window as the two women outside moved on. "Mark my words, your name will be on the lips of every lady in town one day."

"What are you doing, Florence?"

"Seeing if I can spot Mrs. Hayworth. Shouldn't she be here by now?"

Nerves tightened Rose's stomach, and she again looked at the wall clock. "It's a few more minutes until three o'clock."

Florence stepped back inside and closed the door. "We're as good as anyone else, Rose, and you will be a success one day. I know it."

Rose smiled, loving Florence even more than she already did if that was possible. Her friend was right. She needed to think positively and not let her fears about Mrs. Hayworth hating her design override her desire for a more dynamic future than simply working in her parents' shop.

"Fine. I'll say no more about it for the time being," Rose said firmly. "Now, later this afternoon I think we should start on—"

The bell above the front door tinkled and an older, smartly dressed woman entered the shop. Rose's heart picked up speed. The woman's brown hair was twisted into a thick rope over one shoulder, and her maroon-colored hat was pinned just so at her crown. She had to be Mrs. Hayworth.

Rose stood a little straighter and walked forward. "Good afternoon. Might you be Mrs. Hayworth?"

The woman smiled. "I am, indeed."

"It's a pleasure to finally meet you. I'm Rose Watson."

"Oh, I know who you are, dear. A while ago I asked your father who had worked on a jacket I purchased, and he told me his daughter, Rose. And then I came back on another occasion, and you were serving someone else and wearing the most wonderful ensemble. I could tell it was of your design and knew you must be the daughter. That ensemble led me to ask your father to allow you to make this special commission."

Frustration with her father knotted Rose's stomach as she struggled to maintain her smile. "Then I can only assume my father was trying to prevent my nerves when he decided I shouldn't meet you."

Mrs. Hayworth seemed to assess Rose for a moment before her eyes filled with kindness. "Yes, I'm sure that's what it must have been. Now…" She looked around the shop. "Is the dress ready?"

"It is, yes." Rose glanced at the back-room curtain. "I hope it fits with what you envisioned." Holding out her hand toward the mannequin, Rose purposefully pressed her lips together, trapping in any further words. She must appear confident in her work and not blabber aimlessly as she was so sorely tempted to do.

"Well…" Mrs. Hayworth drew in an audible breath. "It is quite a sight, Miss Watson. Quite a sight indeed."

Dread dropped into Rose's stomach, and she quickly looked at Florence, who was staring wide-eyed at Mrs. Hayworth, the woman's self-assured presence clearly discombobulating her friend, who was rarely affected by anything or anyone. Rose's parents had urged her to lessen her zeal. They believed the money she had spent on luxurious materials for the dress was exorbitant and even reckless since they did not know the identity of the woman who would wear it. Mrs. Hayworth's mistress was clearly wealthy, considering the agreeable deposit, but what if she did not like the dress?

Forcing herself to stand tall, Rose clenched her hands in front of her as Mrs. Hayworth scrutinized the dress. This was the start of something bigger, and the need to grab even the smallest opportunity for something more for herself and her family had overtaken Rose in a wild swirl of creativity. She would entertain no regrets.

"Yes, this is most satisfactory," Mrs. Hayworth murmured as she slowly walked around the mannequin in one direction, before circling back the opposite way. "This will suit my mistress quite beautifully."

Relief mixed with pride as Rose released the breath she'd been holding. "Well, that is most welcome news, Mrs. Hayworth. I have done my very best work with this dress, and I hope it shows."

"You are a most capable seamstress, Miss Watson." Mrs. Hayworth put her purse on the counter next to Rose's sketchpad, her brow furrowed. "It is quite a feat to have completed the dress in such a short time, considering you must have had other work as well."

Mrs. Hayworth's observations were laced with a questioning insinuation. Unsure how to respond, Rose glanced at Florence, who lifted her shoulders, indicating she was none the wiser than Rose as to what Mrs. Hayworth wanted or needed to hear.

"I did have other work for the shop, as well as what I enjoy making for myself and others to wear." Rose grimaced. "Pieces my parents do not wish to show in the shop as they feel they are too elaborate or visionary."

Mrs. Hayworth raised her eyebrows. "Is that so?"

Rose's cheeks warmed. She should not speak about her parents in any way but complimentary in front of a customer… any customer. She cleared her throat. "Creating a dress of this magnitude was a dream. I wanted to include every detail you specified as well as a few I thought would complement and escalate the serenity you said your mistress is so fond of. The colors were carefully selected, considering both the wearer's complexion and her—"

"It is perfect, Miss Watson."

"In addition, I have used—" Rose stopped. "Perfect?"

"Yes, my dear." Mrs. Hayworth's kindly brown eyes shone with amusement. "I do believe my mistress will be overjoyed, enthralled. Even captivated."

Rose grinned. "I don't know what to say."

"You say, 'I am very pleased you like it, Mrs. Hayworth, as I have other designs I am sure your mistress would like to see.'"

Rose stilled, her heart beating faster. "Pardon?"

Mrs. Hayworth lifted her eyebrows. "Do you have other designs? Would you like to work on another dress equally as elaborate as this one?"

"Well, I—"

"Or might it be that this commission stretched your extraordinary talent to its limit for the time being? Or maybe in making this dress you realized its detail and originality equate to a one-time creation and to make something similar would actually be beyond the scope of your family's shop?"

Rose held the dresser's stare and the warm, good-natured challenge she saw in her eyes sparked a determination in Rose that obliterated the need to defend the shop she loved.

Rose lifted her chin. "No, I wouldn't say that at all."

Mrs. Hayworth smiled. "Good, because this dress is for the Countess of Bath, Miss Watson, and I'm sure Her Ladyship will request more from you once she sees this."

Rose's breath lodged in her throat. She could not speak, was unable to breathe... even as Florence's delighted squeal pierced the silence.

Chapter Two

Henlow House, St. James's, London

The chilly March wind blew the stench of hay, straw, and manure into a nauseating aroma as Henry Ward swiped a soft brush against the flank of the Earl of Bath's favorite horse. Drawing the brush back and forth in long arcs, the muscles in Henry's arm strained from the work he'd done since rising at six that morning, when darkness had lingered for a couple of hours before giving way to dawn and the remainder of his ten-hour day.

The habitual suffocation that had steadily grown worse in recent years pressed down on him as he glared blindly, following the brushstrokes with his eyes, if not his mind. It meant little to him that he was a saddler for a member of the British nobility; it also meant little to him that his place of work happened to be in the stables of Henlow House. What did matter was that he was only able to train the earl's horses sporadically, whenever the establishment was a trainer short. What he really wanted was to be training horses every day, all over the world, and making his damn fortune while doing it.

Henry pulled loose hair from the brush before walking around the horse, pausing to rub his hand over its velvet-smooth muzzle and look into its eyes. "I won't be here forever, my friend. This is just a temporary situation until I am on a ship across the Channel. Mark my—"

"I wouldn't be so sure about that."

Muttering a curse, Henry closed his eyes. "How long have you been standing there, Uncle?"

"Long enough to hear you telling that horse your fanciful plans." Charles Summers strode into the stable and dumped a bale of straw in the far corner, then swiped his hands over the front of the leather apron covering his gray trousers and white shirt. "And long enough to know you need to get a move on. You've still got that saddle to finish by the end of the week."

"I'm just about done here, and the saddle is close to finished so there's no need for you to burst a blood vessel."

His uncle glowered. "Your aunt kindly informed me this morning with a sharp elbow to the ribs—damn near pushing me out of the bed—that she heard you whistling your way down the street past eleven o'clock last night."

Henry gave the horse's neck a final swipe of the brush before tossing it into the wooden box at his feet. "And I was up and out of my lodgings by half five. More than that, I even made sure I had time to nip out as soon as the shops opened to purchase the supplies Aunt Elizabeth has been fretting over. She'll be pleased as punch when I bring them to her later."

Charles sniffed and crossed his arms. "Maybe she will, but your late-night shenanigans are showing in the bags under your eyes and the paleness of your face. You look a sight, son." His uncle turned away and picked up a bedding fork from the straw-laden floor. He leaned it up against the stable wall and stood there, his back turned and his knuckles sharp as he tightly clenched the fork's wooden handle. "I don't suppose you're any better off than you were yesterday?"

Tension inched across Henry's shoulders. "Let's not do this again."

"You're heading down a very shaky path, my boy."

Henry picked up the tack box and strode past him into the long avenue that ran the length of the ten stable doors. "I just want to build a life of my own making. Follow my dream of training horses overseas. Nothing more, nothing less."

"You already get the chance to train horses here alongside your saddle making. Why can't that satisfy you?"

"Because I don't want to be a saddler." Henry sighed. "And the amount of time I spend training is not enough. I want to train day in, day out."

"And you think doing that overseas will make you happy."

It wasn't a question. Why would it be when Henry gave his uncle the same answer every time Charles challenged his dreams?

"You could do a lot worse than continuing to work in one of London's finest houses—"

"For the love of God, Uncle!" Henry shoved the box into a cupboard at the far end of the stables and slammed the door. "I am not you. This is not the life I want. I am twenty-four years old—old enough to make my own decisions. Why has this become such a problem between us?"

"It's the gambling, Henry. That's my problem with you over the last twelve months. It's a mug's game, and I love you too much to stand by and watch you throw your life away." Charles's cheeks mottled, his brown eyes darkening. "Your aunt and I have given you a good life. A life many others would give their eyeteeth for."

"I know, and I'm grateful." Henry briefly closed his eyes. "Truly I am, but I'm not you, Uncle, I'm me and, for all my faults, my passion lies in horses, not saddles. I'll be on the first boat out of here once I manage to get the money together."

"I see." His uncle's bottom lip protruded, and he nodded as if he was thinking over Henry's words. "And visiting gambling houses and brothels is the way to get the money together, is it?"

Henry's defenses rose, and he glared. "I'll give you the gambling houses, but don't accuse me of using brothels because I damn well don't."

Charles shook his head. "When your poor, long-suffering mother became ill, we took her family into our home."

"I know you did, and I'll never forget that… wherever I am."

"And since your father left, I have done my best to give you all I can. Now I'm faced with a young man who refuses the opportunities given to him, refuses to appreciate the good life he has, and worse, doesn't realize the miserable life he could have had."

Shame burned in Henry's chest, but his pride was also aflame. "Uncle, please. This bad feeling between us is not doing either of us any good. I've never known us to argue as much as we have over the last few months. Is that really what we want?"

Their gazes locked before his uncle slumped his shoulders. "You're right, son. The last thing I want is this bad blood between us."

"Then, let's—"

"Just promise me something."

Unease tiptoed along Henry's spine. "What?"

"That you'll be careful not to lose everything." Charles's gaze bore into Henry's. "I don't just mean money."

"What do you mean?"

"Love, friendship, family. All those things mean so much more than money in this life."

"Right."

"There's no 'right' about it, son. It's the damn truth."

Claustrophobia pressed down on Henry as Charles turned away. There was so much he wanted to see and do. He could not falter and give his uncle hope that he might succumb to his wishes. Unable to bear the concern he saw more and more frequently in Charles's eyes, Henry brushed past him and returned to the stable where he'd been working. He snatched his jacket from a brass hook and reached into his pocket. Withdrawing a pamphlet that showed a ship bound for America, he strode back to his uncle, opened it, and pointed to the picture.

"That's what I want, Uncle." A deep yearning stirred inside him. "I know you don't want to accept it, but I want to sail away and train horses amid sea and sand, sun and excitement. London is enough for most, but it's not for me."

Charles shook his head, defeat clouding his gaze. "One day you will see that you have all you need here. There is nothing worse than loneliness, Henry. Nothing worse than passing through this world without someone special who truly cares about you and your happiness."

"Who says I'll be alone?" Henry smiled, trying to ease the tension enveloping them. "I'm as partial to finding myself a wife one day as the next man. Just not yet."

"Well, that's something, I suppose."

His uncle stared at him for so long and with such skepticism, Henry looked away, all too aware of the heat that rose up his neck and along his jaw. He hated disappointing Charles, but he would never lie to him either.

"Fine." His uncle raised his hands in surrender. "I'll leave you to your plans. But know this: while you are here and continue to work for His Lordship, you will toe the line and do as I say. Whatever might or might not happen in the future."

Henry pulled back his shoulders. "Have I ever let you down?"

"In your work? No, and for that I am grateful." His uncle walked to the huge wooden doors at the stable's entrance and turned. "I love you, Henry. Your aunt loves you. Your cousins love you. I just wish that love and working for the earl was enough for you, but I'm starting to see it never will be."

His uncle walked into the stable yard and Henry dropped his head as a heavy sadness crept over him.

Chapter Three

"We cannot even be sure this woman is who she says she is."

"Oh, Mama." Rose put down her glass of water lest her frustration cause her to spill it. "You are being entirely unfair. Papa has met Mrs. Hayworth before, has he not?"

"Yes, and he was duly suspicious of her motives." Rose's mother glanced at her husband, who nodded before returning his attention to his plate. "See? Why would the Countess of Bath be interested in a small backstreet shop in London when she can have the pick of garment makers the world over?"

"I have explained why Mrs. Hayworth chose me, Mama. Her visits to the shop, my designs, and what I was wearing were enough to catch her interest." Pride knotted Rose's stomach, her smile stretching wide. "The countess wishes to sponsor a local artisan and, at least for now, I am someone she is considering. It's exciting. Why can you not see that?"

"Considering? That is not enough to hang our hats on, Rose."

"Well, even if Mrs. Hayworth's employer isn't the Countess of Bath, although why you think she would lie about that is beyond me, she is wealthy and paid the full amount due for the dress."

Her mother sniffed and then stabbed at the cut of mutton on her plate. "So what next? You no doubt see yourself working for the aristocracy or even royalty."

"Yes, that's exactly what I envision."

Her mother's eyes widened with incredulity. "Who in heaven's name do you think you are?"

Rose fought against the shame burning in her cheeks. "Why shouldn't I dream of a life making clothes of my own creation for someone important? Is that really such a bad virtue?"

"It is to your father and me."

"But why?"

"You…" Her mother glanced at her husband, before snapping her gaze back to Rose, her cheeks mottled. "You don't understand anything, Rose."

"Then explain it to me, Mama. Because you are right, I don't understand this resistance to such an opportunity. Your protestations make no sense."

Her mother's gaze darted over Rose's face, deepening Rose's suspicion that her outburst was about something more than her daughter's work, more than the possibility of her working for someone of a higher class.

Her mother blew out an exasperated breath. "And what of the rumors?"

"What?"

"The rumors, Rose. Lord above, surely you have heard tales of what goes on behind the walls of Henlow House as much as we have. I don't want you exposed to debauchery and goodness knows what else!"

"Debauchery?" Rose laughed even though she'd had fleeting reservations about what she might witness at the house if its reputation proved true. "That is mere speculation by the papers and gossipmongers. How would anyone of our class really know what goes on there? I'm sure everything that happens inside that house is suitably prim and proper."

"And what if it isn't?"

"Mama, please." Rose turned to her father. "Papa, do you agree with what Mama is saying?"

Her father continued to eat his food, but something about the hunch of his shoulders, the crease of his brow, told Rose he was not happy. Far from it.

She faced her mother, guilt that she was distressing her parents twisting inside her. "You and Papa mean the world to me; I hate that my wishes are upsetting you this way."

"You… can't do this, Rose. I won't allow it," her mother said, with anger in her voice.

Rose stared at her, entirely flummoxed. "You are not being fair. I—"

"Fair? I'll tell you what isn't fair, young lady. That your father and I were clearly mistaken to assume your duty would always be to us and the future of the shop we have worked so hard to make a success. *That* is unfair. Heavens above, child, I had believed we could rely on you to marry, and you and your husband would ensure our comfort in our old age."

"You can rely on me. Regardless of *if* I marry. These things are never guaranteed, but whether I marry or not you have nothing to fear."

"How can you say that when—"

"When what, Mama?" Rose frowned, praying she hadn't unwittingly brought her dead brother to her mother's consciousness by talking about her aspirations.

Her mother impatiently flapped her hand, her eyes dark with irritation. "When we have primed you, trained you to take over the business in our old age."

Relieved that Gideon, and the gap his absence had left in her parents' future security, wasn't the concern her mother battled with in that moment, Rose sighed. "Mama, looking after you both ultimately requires money and security, and I strive for both. I will look after you and Papa, whether I am here in the shop or sending you funds from elsewhere."

Her mother groaned before facing Rose's father. "Will you not say anything, Harold?"

"Oh, Mama." Rose closed her eyes and tried to stem the rapid beating of her heart, a sure sign she was close to losing her temper completely. She opened her eyes and pinned her mother with a glare. "Why can't you be happy that such good fortune has come to our door?" Rose looked at her father, the only person capable of calming her mother's hysterics. "Papa, please. It is not…"

She stopped talking. It was almost eerie the way he continued staring at her above the glass of ale that hovered at his lips, not having said a solitary word since her mother started her tirade ten minutes before. Their maid, Sarah, had managed to find herself extraordinarily busy in the kitchen next door throughout their meal.

Slowly, Papa lowered his glass to the table, a muscle tensing and relaxing in his jaw.

Rose fought to hold her tongue and not blurt how ridiculous she found her parents' reservations and how disappointing their lack of excitement and vision was. Why couldn't they imagine how happy it would make her to create clothes for a lady who could afford such grandeur? Why couldn't they be proud at the mere possibility? The material alone had cost more than the shop had ever spent on a single ensemble. If the price of the beading and thread was also considered, its purchase was a triumph. The dress had been an indulgence for her as much as the woman who would wear it, and she would not apologize for feeling proud of herself.

Her father picked up his glass again, looked at Rose and then his wife, and swallowed a hefty draft. Slowly, he returned the glass to the table and nodded at Sarah, who had just walked into the dining room, indicating he had finished. The young girl hurried forward and began to clear the plates. Rose and her mother followed her father's lead and lowered their knives and forks, the appetites around the table entirely depleted.

"Even if we cannot be entirely sure this dress is for the countess..." her father said before looking intensely at his wife, "or even what goes on at Henlow House, having met Mrs. Hayworth on three or four occasions now, I am more and more convinced she is who she claims to be. She is a good and honest woman who would hardly work at a place filled with immoral goings-on."

"Harold! Just the other night you said—"

He jabbed his hand in the air with such force his wife immediately snapped her mouth shut and Sarah, having returned for their glasses, emitted an audible squeak. Rose glared at her mother. Harold Watson may be stern at times, but he was always fair.

He focused his attention entirely on Rose. "I admire your ambition, Rose, but the simple truth is..." He cleared his throat and briefly dropped his gaze to the table as though he struggled to maintain looking at her. He lifted his gaze and tilted his chin. "We need your help if we are to continue to enjoy the level of income to which we've become accustomed."

"I would never abandon you, Papa. Either of you." Rose looked at her mother, her heart swelling with care for her parents despite the depth of her frustration. She sensed they were not telling her the full truth of their reservations, though. "I love you, but can we not grasp this opportunity with both hands? Can I not prepare my designs for Mrs. Hayworth as she has asked?"

Annoyance clouded her mother's eyes and she stood, snatching a dish from the table and causing Sarah, who stood nearby, to stumble backward before she beat a hasty retreat from the room.

"And if the dresses aren't commissioned?" her mother snapped. "What then, Rose?"

"There is no reason to think they won't be commissioned."

"But Mrs. Hayworth did not actually confirm there would be a commission, did she?"

"Well, no, but—"

"Then it is as I suspected." Her mother smirked. "We cannot live and plan on implications."

"Rose," her father said quietly. "Your mother and I have said our piece, but if you feel that strongly, then do what you must."

Rose's heart beat faster. "You mean—"

"I see no harm in you drawing up some designs, and then we'll take it from there."

"Oh, Papa! Thank you."

"Harold! How could you?" her mother's voice cracked.

Rose turned to her mother, distressed to see that her eyes shone with tears. "Mama, please. Let me do this, I beg you."

Her father abruptly stood, the legs of his chair scraping harshly over the stone floor. "I've had enough, Clementine." He looked at his wife and then Rose. "Mrs. Hayworth has explained the countess's interest in showing patronage to a local artisan. With that in mind, I suggest we all just wait and see what happens." He took his newspaper from the empty chair beside him before leaving the dining room.

Slightly trembling with the effort it took not to jump up and down, Rose picked up the remaining two dishes, catching her mother's eye as she threw Rose a final, disdainful look before following her husband out of the room.

Chapter Four

Legs firmly astride and reins tightly held, Henry sat upright in the smooth leather saddle as he trotted a young and rather beautiful thoroughbred around the grassland at the back of the Royal Mews. He had been breaking in the horse for several weeks and its progress had been noted, not only by Henry and his uncle, but also by the earl's groom who was assigned the task of deciding the horse's future role within the household.

Pleased and more than a little proud of himself and the animal, Henry slowed the horse to a walk and planted a few hefty pats on its strong neck. "You'll do as well as any that have gone before you, lad."

A chorus of male laughter drew Henry's attention toward the stables as his uncle left the group of smiling workers and strode purposefully in Henry's direction. He sat a little straighter in the saddle and tried to gauge his uncle's mood. Charles was a good man, his sense of humor and devotion to the earl and his family was appreciated by all who worked with him. Henry clenched his jaw, love and respect for his uncle prodding his conscience. Lately when they were together, he more often felt like a cad than a loving nephew.

Several days had passed since their most recent argument about the future Henry had planned for himself, and things remained strained between them. The atmosphere when he joined the family for breakfast each day continued to stretch thin. This morning his aunt had taken him aside, stood on her tiptoes and clipped his ear as though he were fourteen again rather than twenty-four, telling him she would do a lot worse if he continued to upset her husband.

"Henry." Charles stopped beside the horse and tilted his head back, squinting one blue eye closed against the bright spring sunshine. "I have an errand for you."

Henry leaned over and patted the horse's neck. "I thought I had the whole afternoon to train this one."

"You do," his uncle said as he walked to the hind of the horse, his brow furrowed as he stood back and studied the animal's rump. "This errand involves a short ride across town. It will be good to try him outside again." He looked up at Henry, his face set in familiar concentration. "Have you stretched his legs outside since last week?"

"No, so a short ride is a good idea. What's the errand?"

"It's for the countess… or rather, for her dresser. Mrs. Hayworth sent a maid to the stables a short while ago. You are to take this note"—he handed Henry an envelope—"and go to that address. There, you need to find a Miss Watson. Deliver the note, allow her time to read it, and then await her response."

Henry looked at the address and his heart sank. "A clothes shop? This is all a little unusual, isn't it? Wouldn't Her Ladyship or her dresser usually send one of her ladies in a carriage? Why send someone from the stables?"

"I've no idea, and we're not in any position to question the countess's instructions." His uncle raised his eyebrows.

Message received, loud and clear. Henry nodded, glad he and Charles were talking civilly at least. "I'll get going then, shall I?"

"Now is as good a time as any. From what little I was told, the note contains important and specific instructions for Miss Watson's eyes only. Make sure you don't leave without a return message."

"Any idea what this message might be?"

"None, so don't waste your time speculating. It could even be that she gives you something for the countess. Who knows?"

"Gives me something?" *For the love of God.* "Are you telling me I could be carrying back some frocks, a hatbox, and God knows what else while steering a young horse? That's hardly a recipe for successfully completing the errand."

"I very much doubt it will be clothes." His uncle grinned, rare amusement shining in his eyes. "But I daresay it could be something similarly ladylike, so mind not to stare too hard at whatever it is you are given. I wouldn't want you going blind."

Henry opened his mouth to respond, but Charles was already walking away, quietly chuckling to himself.

Shaking his head, Henry glanced at the envelope again before pushing it into his shirt pocket. Clicking his tongue, he commanded the horse in the direction of the stables. He'd better put on a jacket and run a comb through his hair. He might have been charged with an errand like a good-for-nothing stable boy, but if there was the slightest chance of coming face-to-face with a pretty lady, he would be prepared.

He dismounted and tethered the horse outside the stables before entering and walking to the sink in the back room. Once he had swilled his face and hands, he patted his face dry just as fellow stable worker, Jeremiah Collins, entered, his shock of red hair sticking up in all directions as though he'd just removed the hat tucked under his arm.

Henry smiled. "And where have you been all day?"

"Just returned from Windsor. The earl wanted a horse brought over." Jeremiah sat down heavily and started to unbutton his boots. "You going somewhere?"

"An errand for the countess." Henry turned to the rudimentary looking glass above the sink and buttoned his collar before pulling a comb from his back pocket. "Have to go across town."

"Will you be back in time for the game tonight?"

Henry grinned at his reflection, a frisson of anticipation churning in his stomach. "Wouldn't miss it for the world. The stakes are high, but will undoubtedly turn in my favor, my friend."

"I bloody well hope so." Jeremiah laughed. "I would hate for you to risk losing the amount you lost last time. I'm surprised you've managed to get away with keeping it secret from your uncle, considering the way he's watching your every move these days."

Jeremiah's observation made it sound as though Henry was a child rather than a full-grown adult. He snatched his jacket from a peg beside him and shoved his arm into one of the sleeves.

"My uncle has nothing to do with what I get up to outside of these walls. He might be my boss here, but he isn't anywhere else."

"I agree, but I'm not sure he sees it that way. What's happened between you two? You used to get along well enough. These days, you're barely civil to each other."

The accurate summary of Henry and Charles's relationship of late irked him. His uncle needed to understand Henry was not his son to order about and beset with expectations.

"I'm my own man, Jeremiah, and I have the right to make plans of my own."

"What sort of plans?"

Henry slung his arm around Jeremiah's shoulders as they left the barn side by side. "Plans that will take me far away from London—far away from England—to do what I love."

"Then I hope your luck at the table changes soon, or else the farthest you'll be traveling is to debtor's prison."

Forcing a laugh, Henry shoved Jeremiah on his way, and his friend grinned as he walked backward a few steps along the gravel pathway before breaking into a jog. Henry watched Jeremiah until he disappeared, and then, shrugging off his irritation, remounted the young horse. He settled himself in the saddle where he knew he belonged. Clicking his tongue, he tugged on the reins and urged the horse into a trot through the back gates of Henlow House.

Chapter Five

Rose escorted Mrs. Tibbert and her three daughters to the shop door and pulled it open. "I hope the birthday party exceeds all your expectations, Mrs. Tibbert. You and your daughters will look wonderful."

The older woman looked down her nose at Rose, her daughters following suit as they flanked their mother. "As we should, considering your prices. I believe I have spent more money in your shop over the last few weeks than I have anywhere else in my lifetime."

"My family and I work hard to provide the best quality garments and service, Mrs. Tibbert," Rose said, holding the older woman's disdainful gaze. "We do not overcharge, but neither do we undercharge. We stand by our pricing. It is fair to our customers and to us."

"Hmm. Well, I will certainly be expecting my precious girls to shine at this party, Miss Watson. And I mean shine!" Mrs. Tibbert sharply turned to her daughters. "Come along now, my darlings, we have much to do."

Mrs. Tibbert led the way from the shop and Rose smiled sweetly, holding the disparaging gaze of each woman until the last had departed. Sighing, she was just about to shut the door when a beautiful chestnut horse drew to a stop at the roadside. Imposing and wholly magnificent, the beast's coat gleamed. This was no market dray or even a horse of ordinary standard. This was a horse belonging to someone of…

She drew her gaze upward.

The rider openly assessed her from head to toe—his study unapologetically brazen—before he looked at the sign above the shop, nodded, and looked back at her. He removed his hat in a theatrical sweep, revealing thick, dark-blond hair, some of the strands falling onto his brow.

"Good afternoon, miss."

Rose stood a little taller, determined to remain unaffected by his wide smile. "Good afternoon."

His mischievous gaze lingered on hers and she thought of the way her brother, whom she missed dreadfully, had often teased women. She fought her smile. Oh, how Gideon used to make them giggle! She tilted her chin. Although she suspected she might be blushing, she most certainly wouldn't be giggling. This handsome stranger might share Gideon's self-confidence, but he was dressed inexpensively—his jacket, trousers, and boots more suited to a groom than the monied owner of such a grand horse, which made his presence all the more curious.

Ignoring the stares directed to the man and horse from the people walking by, Rose cleared her throat. "Might I help you with something, sir?"

"Indeed, you can." His brilliant green eyes were bright as he swung his leg over the horse and smartly jumped to the ground. "Especially if you are Miss Rose Watson."

"You're looking for me?"

He lifted his eyebrows. "Are you Miss Watson?"

"Well, yes."

"Then it is you I am looking for." He reached into his inside pocket, removed an envelope, and held it out to her. "From Henlow House."

Rose's mouth dried and she stepped back, glancing over her shoulder into the shop. "Henlow House?"

"Yes. From the Countess of Bath's dresser, to be precise."

Rose dropped her gaze to the envelope, itching to take it, but disbelief held her back. "Mrs. Hayworth?"

"I believe so." His smile faltered, the amusement in his eyes dimming. "Is there a problem?"

Ripples of trepidation mixed with joy twisted through Rose's stomach. She peered through the shop's open doorway again and exhaled when she saw only Florence inside, her friend's eyes agog as she stared at the rider through the window. Flashing Florence a smile, Rose pulled the door until it stood slightly ajar and prayed her parents did not choose this moment to make an appearance. She had to read the letter without their knowledge. She suspected they would not jump for joy over its contents.

Forcing a smile, she accepted the envelope from the man's fingers. "Thank you. I will read it here."

"It's quite breezy, miss. Would you not prefer—"

"Here is fine." Rose quickly opened the envelope and extracted paper so much thicker than any she had ever written upon herself.

Dear Miss Watson,

I am writing with happy tidings.

The countess is overjoyed with the gown you made for her. She is especially delighted with the detailed work employed in ornamenting the bodice and the wonderful lacing at the hem. As I predicted, Her Ladyship wished to know all about you and what else you might be able to design for her. It seems her wish to support your creations is confirmed.

That, of course, is something for future discussion.

For now, I am writing in the hope that you might source some suitable gloves and a hat you feel would match the dress. I assume you will know a quality glove maker and milliner if you do not already have such items in your shop. Her Ladyship would prefer the entire ensemble be obtained from your shop, and your shop only, for ease of answering inevitable inquiries whenever she chooses to give the dress its debut.

Please confirm your ability to deliver the said items in the affirmative or negative to the messenger. If yes, the countess is most eager to make your acquaintance so I will send a carriage to collect you and the accessories at your earliest convenience.

Yours thankfully,
Mrs. E. Hayworth

Rose lifted her eyes to the rider's, pressing the letter to her breast. *For ease of answering inevitable inquiries…will send a carriage to collect you…*She swallowed.

"Goodness."

The young man smiled, his green eyes—eyes she found increasingly hard to ignore—lit with amusement.

"What is it? You look as though you might faint at any moment." He feigned panic and looked left and right along the street. "Please don't. I am not as strong as I look."

Rose laughed; her euphoria increasingly difficult to contain. "She wants accessories."

"What?"

"She wants to see me."

"Who?"

"Mrs. Hayworth. The countess. They want me to go to Henlow House."

"You're to meet the countess?"

"Yes!"

"My, my." He grinned. "Well, I assume that's a good thing?"

"Of course it is! I cannot believe it."

"Well, good, because your expression is bordering on hysterical."

"I *am* hysterical!" Rose looked again at the letter before slapping it to her chest once more. "But I can't possibly go. What would I wear? How can someone like me step inside Henlow House? It's beyond belief."

He frowned. "What do you mean, 'someone like you'? The earl and countess are only people, Miss Watson. There's nothing to be—"

"Only people? Are you mad?"

He shrugged. "Well, I suppose I have my moments the same as everyone else, but—"

"She wants gloves, a hat… the countess must genuinely like my dress." Rose's heart hammered as she snatched another look through the shop window. "My mother and father can't possibly have any more objections against me pursuing this once they learn the countess wishes to be my patron."

"She does?"

"Yes!" She laughed. "Stay there a moment if you will, mister—?"

"Ward. Henry Ward." He winked at her and smiled.

Inexplicable heat leaped into Rose's cheeks, but she would not give him the satisfaction of looking away. "Well, Mr. Ward, if you could wait here, I'll return shortly."

Rose strode inside the shop and closed the door, leaning her back against it. "Flo, you are not going to believe this."

Her friend rushed forward and gripped Rose's hand, her gaze flitting from Rose to the window. "Who is that? He must be the most handsome man ever to grace this street. Did you see his smile? My heart burst from my chest every time he flashed it."

"He's from Henlow House," Rose whispered urgently, pulling Florence away from the door and tugging her behind the counter. "The countess loved the dress so much she wants to be my patron."

Florence's shriek was cut off by Rose putting her hand over her friend's mouth. "Shh. I don't want Mama or Papa to hear. I want to keep this moment to myself a little while longer before I will undoubtedly have to endure another argument with Mama." Rose pressed the letter to her chest. "Oh, Flo. It's happening. It's really happening!"

Her friend laughed.

Rose glanced through the window as Mr. Ward pulled out his pocket watch, a frown creasing his brow. She looked to Florence. "Quickly. Go to the storeroom and make sure we still have the small black hat with the veil that comes just beneath the eyes and the black velvet gloves with the row of five jet buttons at each wrist. They will be perfect."

As Florence hurried to do her bidding, Rose pulled a sheet of paper and an envelope from beneath the counter and wrote her response, trying not to fret over the state of her hasty handwriting. She quickly sealed the letter and scribbled Mrs. Hayworth's name on the envelope.

Florence re-emerged. "The hat and gloves are both there. Shall I bring them to you?"

"Leave them where they are for the moment. I must get rid of that rider before Mama—"

"Before Mama what?"

Florence jumped and any response promptly lodged in Rose's throat.

"Well?" her mother demanded as she emerged from the back room, her eyes narrowed. "What are you two conspiring? Have you no work to be getting on with? Come out from behind that counter at once."

Rose held the opened envelope behind her back with one hand and snatched up her letter with the other before walking around the counter. She cast a furtive glance out the window. The rider stared back at her, his expression considerably more somber than when she'd been standing outside with him. It wouldn't be long before he lost his patience completely and left without her answer.

"Who is that?"

Her mother's voice snapped through the silence and Rose jumped.

"He's… he's…"

"He's what?" Her mother glared. "What is the matter with you? Is that gentleman the reason for your jitteriness?"

Drawing in a long breath, Rose lifted her chin. "He's from Henlow House, Mama. Mrs. Hayworth really is the Countess of Bath's dresser. What's more, Her Ladyship likes the dress I made, and…" Rose hesitated, clutching the envelope tighter behind her back, every instinct telling her not to reveal that the countess would like to make her acquaintance or show her mother her response. At least, not yet.

"And what?"

Rose met her mother's gaze. "And Mrs. Hayworth has sent the messenger out there with a letter asking that I supply her with a matching hat and gloves."

Her mother's eyes widened ever so slightly. The only show of surprise Rose could hope for. "She's written to you?"

"Yes. This is wonderful news, is it not? If Mrs. Hayworth intends to purchase even more from us, then—"

The bell above the door tinkled.

Rose, her mother, and Florence turned.

Mr. Ward's smile was downright devilish as he strode into the shop and held out his hand to Rose's mother. "Good afternoon, ma'am. Henry Ward, at your service."

Before her mother could emit a response from her open mouth, Mr. Ward continued, "Miss Watson is your daughter, I assume?"

"Well, yes," Rose's mother finally croaked. "But—"

"Then you must be mighty proud that she has been invited into the countess's company."

Ignoring Florence's giggle beside her, Rose snapped her gaze to her mother. To the contrary, her expression was the very antithesis of proud.

Chapter Six

Henry looked at the women's varied expressions of hostility, wariness, and delight and fought the urge to laugh. The atmosphere crackled with tension, each of them clearly wound as tight as harp strings. He had the distinct feeling he'd just walked straight into the middle of a situation that had the potential to evolve into a full-blown battle in fewer than ten seconds.

Miss Watson's mother narrowed her brown eyes. "My daughter tells me you are from Henlow House. Is that true?"

"I am, ma'am. I came here with a message for Miss Watson."

"Henlow House, indeed." The woman sniffed and raised her voice as she spoke over her shoulder. "Harold, will you please come out here? It seems we have a gentleman caller up to no good."

"Mama, that's not fair! Mr. Ward—"

"Clearly thinks himself amusing, but woe betide him if he grins at your father in such an over-familiar fashion."

Henry battled to suppress his smile. He coughed. "Mrs. Watson, I assure you I—"

"What is going on here?" asked the portly gentleman who entered from behind a curtain at the back of the shop, his graying hair sticking up in every direction as though he constantly pushed his fingers through it. He looked first at the older woman, then at Miss Watson and finally Henry, his expression somber as he nodded. "Good afternoon, sir."

Henry stole a glance at Miss Watson and ran his gaze over her dark, glossy hair, her fine jaw, and slender neck. She was indeed a beautiful woman. She briefly squeezed her eyes shut before opening them again and pulling back her shoulders, clearly bracing herself for whatever came next. She was a feisty one, he had no doubt.

Standing a little straighter, Henry faced the gentleman and dipped his head. "Good afternoon, sir."

"I'm Harold Watson, the proprietor of this shop. Can I help you?" Watson peered over his half-spectacles, his brown eyes marginally more amiable than his wife's.

"I am Henry Ward. I'm awaiting a response from your daughter to a letter from the Countess of Bath's dresser, sir."

"What?" Watson faced his daughter before returning his attention to Henry. "What are you talking about?"

"I came here with a message from Henlow House." He tilted his head in Miss Watson's direction and flashed her a brief smile. He was pleasantly satisfied when rewarded with a faint blush to her cheeks. "And from what I could gather from Miss Watson's exclamations, she is overjoyed to have received an invitation to visit with Mrs. Hayworth and the—"

"Does this young man speak the truth?" Watson turned to his daughter.

An immediate need to stand beside Miss Watson rose in Henry as she stepped forward, but he refrained. Something about the way she held her father's stare, the set of her shoulders, suggested that she was more than capable of handling this confrontation alone. Satisfaction wound tight in Henry's stomach as he waited.

"The countess likes the dress I made, Papa. So much so, Mrs. Hayworth infers the countess would like to be my patron."

"What?"

"Isn't it wonderful? She has asked for a hat and gloves that she might wear with the dress I made." Miss Watson grinned, her caramel-colored eyes lit with happiness as she held out the envelope to her father. "Here, read the letter for yourself."

Watson slowly drew the envelope from his daughter's fingers and looked first at his wife and then Henry. His scrutiny lingered, unreadable, yet intense enough that Henry respectfully lowered his gaze, the tension in the room growing as the seconds passed. He pursed his lips for fear of blurting something out to alleviate the friction. Lifting his eyes, Henry looked again at Miss Watson. The bright, enchanting smile that had captured his attention when he first arrived had vanished, the light that burned so brightly now dimmed to nothing.

Annoyance simmered inside him, and Henry looked at Mr. Watson. For all his uncle's mistaken assumptions and misplaced desires for him, Charles rarely managed to wither Henry's moments of happiness. Even the times when their origin was less than savory. Shouldn't Miss Watson's parents be pleased by her happiness? Even if they were more than a little shaken by the unexpected privilege of a deepening association with the countess and her household?

"Papa, please," Miss Watson whispered. "Surely this is a moment for celebration."

Henry shifted on his feet. He had to do something to alleviate the tension permeating the room. The crack in Miss Watson's voice had sparked a need to defend her. He didn't like to see any woman in distress, and it was clear the letter from Henlow House had evoked unease in all who stood in the room.

He addressed Mr. and Mrs. Watson. "Madam, sir, whatever Miss Watson has done for the countess has been noted and her attendance requested at Henlow House. Moreover, if the news has made your daughter smile so beautifully, it is indeed a time for celebration." Henry put on his hat and dipped his head. "I will wait outside for further instruction."

Turning on his heel, Henry paused in front of Miss Watson and bowed again before heading for the door. After striding outside, he untethered his horse from the lamppost and swung into the saddle. If the Watson family trouble continued, he would have to leave without a return message, which would undoubtedly set his uncle after him. Again. Henry took another glance at the shop, only to be startled by the sight of Miss Watson marching through the door, her eyes focused entirely on him.

"Mr. Ward, wait, please. Will you…" She held up a small envelope, her caramel eyes brimming with tears, but her jaw tight with determination. "Please give this to Mrs. Hayworth. I am sorry you had to witness such unforgiveable tension between my parents and me."

Henry's heart flickered. He could not remember a woman ever looking so lovely, and he was ashamed to feel that way when her gaze was so shadowed with anxiety and apology, the tremor in her fingers strong enough that the paper trembled.

Blinking to clear his sensibilities, he leaned down to take the letter. "You do not have to apologize, Miss Watson." He put the message in his inside jacket pocket. "Although I must admit it was a shame to see you so deflated after witnessing such joy in your eyes."

A speck of light returned to her gaze and a tentative smile pulled at her lips. "You are very kind. I'm sure my parents will see this is a monumental moment in time. They are good people, and they only want the best for me."

"I'm sure they do, but that does not mean—"

"Do you not care what people who love you ask of you, Mr. Ward?" she asked, as she glanced at the shop window. "Or your responsibility to others? I'm afraid both mean so much to me."

Henry shrugged, willing her to look at him with those wonderful eyes again. "Not always, and neither should you."

She faced him, and an uncomfortable sensation twisted in his chest as Henry was caught in the intensity of her stare. The warmth he had seen in her eyes before had darkened, grown colder. He searched for the right words to respond. He suspected if she learned of his wish to leave the family who raised him, it would be met with disdain. Why he cared what she thought of him, he had no idea, but he had no wish to further upset her.

"I shall bid you goodbye, Mr. Ward. Please ensure Mrs. Hayworth receives my response." She returned to the shop, closing the door behind her.

Henry heeled his horse forward, wondering if—or maybe hoping—he might see Miss Watson again. Not that such a thing was likely in usual circumstances. If he threw in the fact that he had clearly annoyed her, the likelihood of her wanting to see him again was highly improbable.

Chapter Seven

Rose stood in the shop's bay window and looked along the street in both directions, her nerves jumping. Why she continued looking for her ride when it was not due for another thirty minutes at least, she had no idea.

It had been two days since she had received Mrs. Hayworth's second letter, which was delivered much more discreetly by a foot messenger. Rose assumed Mr. Ward might've had a hand in that, but who knew? What she did know was that she was grateful the messenger had given the delivery to Florence and not one of her parents. Another family argument was the last thing any of them needed. Now she waited anxiously for her transport to Henlow House to arrive, and she still had not told her parents what she was up to.

The tension the day Mr. Ward arrived at the shop had continued into the evening, with her mother continuing to present a dozen and one unmerited reasons why Rose needed to stay working at the shop. Much to Rose's sorrow, her mother had even briefly mentioned Gideon and how, when he'd been alive, his antics had caused her to fret, and now Rose was doing the same. She had scowled at the blatant and entirely excessive excuses; her brother had never showed Rose's ambition, and she had never displayed his good-natured carelessness. However, she had tried to allay her mother's fears and give her all the love she possibly could. But her mother had then argued that if Rose took the position at Henlow House, it would be all-consuming and prevent her from finding a husband with whom she could settle down. That, of course, had been the final push she needed to engage in today's subterfuge.

The tap of her mother's shoes on the floor tiles brought Rose quickly away from the window to kneel in front of a dressed mannequin. She lifted the hem of the long purple skirt she was supposed to be altering. Her mother approached and walked back and forth, studying the back of the dress, her expression showing her dissatisfaction.

"Something is definitely missing," she murmured. "Maybe you're right, and it is the hem."

Rose sat back on her haunches as though this moment was not the same as a hundred others before. "I'm sure that's the problem, Mama."

"Hmm."

Taking some pins from the small wooden box beside her, Rose continued tacking the hem, her heart beating an unsteady tattoo.

"Yes, do as you think best," her mother said with a firm nod. "I will leave this one with you."

An unexpected sadness emanated from her mother and Rose slowly stood.

"Are you all right, Mama?"

Her mother cupped Rose's cheek and looked deep into her eyes before she softly smiled and retreated to the back room of the shop, the curtain falling closed behind her. Rose stared after her, concern and guilt curling into a horrible ball in the pit of her stomach. Did her mother know what she was up to? Was the sadness Rose had sensed actually disappointment?

Her father coughed from where he stood behind the counter and Rose turned, taking a slow, deliberate breath to calm the eddy of nerves reverberating through her. Her father leaned over the ledger in front of him, his habitual worry about money and supplies for the shop showing in the lines furrowing his brow.

Rose glanced through the window again. No sign of her ride yet. She swallowed and looked around the shop, thankfully empty of customers. Having witnesses to her imminent escape would only further anger her parents. From the busy window display, which Rose would have loved to make sparser, to the counters with their glass tops and wooden drawers, to the tallboy in the corner holding men's ties and handkerchiefs, to the stand displaying this season's hats and bonnets, the image might well have been imprinted on her brain, a banner running across the top saying, *This is your past, present, and future.*

Nothing ever changed. Everything stayed the same year after year, just as it undoubtedly would for the next twenty or thirty years. She could not bear it any longer. She would prove to her parents she was capable of so much more. She would make them proud of her, more so than if she managed to achieve all they had envisioned for her.

Refocusing on her task, Rose finished pinning the hem and soon the alteration was done and discreetly hidden within the drape of the material. She picked up her wooden sewing box and glanced at Florence. Her friend immediately gestured her over with a subtle tilt of her head. Joining her behind the counter, Rose picked up a folded shawl and held it up in front of them, high enough that their faces were hidden from Rose's father, but casually enough that he would assume they were discussing the item.

"How are you feeling?" Florence whispered, her green eyes glinting with undisguised excitement, her round cheeks pink. "I feel as if we're committing a crime, and any moment a constable will bang on the window demanding our arrest."

"Will you stop?" Rose lowered the shawl an inch or two, relieved her father still concentrated on his work. She lifted the material again. "I have never deceived my parents before. Ever. But this is too—"

"Too much of an opportunity to waste. Exactly." Florence gave Rose a pointed look. "Don't you dare regret giving that handsome Mr. Ward your message for one minute."

A pang of guilt still struck at Rose's conscience, and she lowered the shawl to the counter, knowing she had to speak to her father even if she couldn't bear facing her mother.

"Still, when my parents discover I put my desires before their concerns, it won't be a pretty scene."

"They have given you no choice. You have to do this. How could you have kept Mrs. Hayworth waiting while your parents dithered over the merits of you visiting with the countess? It's madness. You are too talented, too hardworking, and committed to let such a momentous opportunity drift by as though it never happened."

Rose exhaled a shaky breath. "I have done my duty by them all my life."

"And now it's your time."

The look in her mother's gaze from before appeared in Rose's mind, haunting her. "I should tell them I am going to Henlow House."

"What? When?"

"Now. I should tell them now."

She moved to walk from behind the counter when Florence gripped her elbow.

"Do what you must, but what if they refuse to see sense? Your ride will be here any minute. Do you really think you'll receive a second invitation? You are quite wonderful, Rose, but you're hardly a duchess to be invited hither and dither by nobility."

Indecision warred inside Rose, every second bringing the carriage due to take her to Henlow House ever closer. What choice did she have but to say something to her father before it arrived? It wasn't as though she could barrel past him and through the door without a word.

"Don't worry, Flo," she said, smoothing the front of her dress. "I will be leaving this shop this afternoon whether Father agrees or not."

"But, Rose, wait," her friend hissed.

Lifting her chin, Rose approached her father. "Papa, there's something I need to tell you. There is every chance it will upset you, but—"

"Well now, I wonder who that can be." Florence's sing-song voice carried across the shop. "They must be here to collect something… or someone."

Rose quickly faced the window. A shiny, black carriage with golden trim and lanterns stood at the roadside with two dappled horses in front and a hatted driver. A carriage that was clearly from Henlow House. Her mouth dried, but Rose stood tall, treacherous excitement churning inside her. There was no going back now.

She looked at her father.

He stared at her before closing his eyes. "Oh, Rose."

The bitter taste of guilt coated her mouth as Rose swallowed. "I'm sorry, Papa. I gave a message to Mr. Ward telling Mrs. Hayworth that I would bring the items she requested. I have to go, but please know how much I love you. There is nothing to fear, and I will be back before you know it."

She kissed his cheek, but when he opened his eyes, he looked deeply disappointed.

"Your mother—"

"Is standing right here."

Rose's mother walked closer, her eyes filled with more worry than Rose had ever seen in them before.

"I love you, Mama. So much. But I have to go."

She purposefully strode to the door where Florence stood holding a mint-green hat box and black velvet gloves wrapped in tissue paper. They exchanged a smile before Rose walked outside. This could be her first step to becoming a clothes designer, to becoming *someone*. She tamped down the urge to look back and forced a smile as the footman relieved her of her packages and put them inside the carriage before offering her his hand.

Rose climbed aboard and stared around the interior in wonder. It was grander than anything she had ever seen, the seats and walls upholstered in red velvet with golden trim and tassels framing the windows. Sitting back, she steadfastly battled her trepidation and stared resolutely ahead as the carriage jolted forward and began its journey to Henlow House.

Chapter Eight

Henry wiped his forearm across the sweat beading on his brow.

Although it was mid-March and the temperatures hovered around forty degrees outside the stables, the oppressive smell of burning charcoal, the weight of the leather across his lap, and the heat of the blacksmith's fires made the stone workshop behind the mews feel like a furnace. He moved the piece of leather he'd been working on to one side and glanced at Charles, who was standing at one of the work benches with a small hammer in his hand, his forehead furrowed as he finished work on his saddle. He didn't look far from wilting into a puddle either.

Henry stood and pressed his hand into the base of his spine, then stretched left and right to loosen the stiffness. "Drink, Uncle?"

"Yeah, go on then." Charles took a semi-clean rag from his waistcoat pocket and dabbed the back of his neck. "How are you getting on with that stitching?"

"Good," Henry said, lifting the empty water jug from a nearby table and walking to the workshop door. "I should be done with it today."

Once outside, he breathed in the refreshing afternoon air, enjoying the whisper of the wind over his face. He clasped the iron handle on the pump and half-filled the jar, taking a quick mouthful of water before returning the jug to the plentiful stream. The flowing water blurred in his vision as his mind wandered to Rose Watson.

Even though it had been three days since he'd been in her family's shop, the questions she'd asked him about care and responsibility to his loved ones continued to frustrate him. Worse, so did the undisguised disappointment in her expression when he'd made it obvious how little he considered people's feelings. And the truth was Henry *had* often solely, possibly selfishly, considered the pursuit of his path and finding somewhere he truly belonged above all else. He doubted he would ever become the same good, family-orientated man his uncle was, even though Charles refused to accept that.

Withdrawing the jug from the pump, Henry strolled back to the workshop accompanied by the habitual feeling of being torn between loyalty to Charles, and his desires for the life he dreamed of. But why shouldn't he go after what he wanted?

Pausing at the workshop doors, he looked at the heavy gray-white clouds. The threat of rain hung in the air, making him long for the sunnier climes of the continent more than ever. With another long English winter almost behind him, he could not be more incensed that he'd failed to make enough money to travel abroad this year as he'd promised himself he would. Culpability crept over Henry's shoulders like a heavy and uncomfortable cape. Fine, maybe he'd made some stupid decisions at the card table once or twice, but money was hard to come by.

"Do you intend to stand out here all day with that water?"

Henry started and turned, holding out the jug to his uncle. "Here. I was just thinking."

"Your mind has been elsewhere since you started work this morning," Charles said as he took the jug and lifted it to his mouth. "Want to tell me what's bothering you?"

"I'm all right."

Henry felt the weight of his uncle's stare on him before Charles sighed. "Come on, lad. Let's get back inside. Coming out here for a breather every now and then provides a welcome reprieve, but if we stand out here much longer, we won't be able to feel the leather between our fingers."

Henry followed his uncle inside and resumed his seat, pulling the length of leather onto his lap. A couple of silent seconds followed before his uncle blew out a breath.

"Your work hasn't been up to your usual standard for a while now. I'm becoming concerned."

"My work is just fine."

"You need to keep your mind on the job that pays, son," Charles continued. "Lay off the gambling that never will."

Henry stared hard at the needle in his hand. "Right."

"The pull of the gambling houses will never serve you, no matter what you might think. One night you win, the next you lose. That is no basis on which to build a life, start a fam—"

"You know starting a family is nowhere in my thoughts, Uncle, and unlikely to be for a long while yet. My first love is horses, and I want to spend the best years of my life training them. Nothing else matters more to me. Why can't you understand that?"

"Oh, I understand well enough," Charles said, leaving the workbench and standing next to him. "In fact, I am in complete comprehension of something that you are clearly not."

Henry held his uncle's glare, burning with frustration. "And what's that?"

"That you're chasing something to heal a hurt. Nothing more, nothing less."

Swift denial twisted inside Henry, and he turned back to his work. "Don't do this."

"Do what? I'm worried about you. Whether you realize it or not, gambling has got its claws into you good and proper."

"What are you talking about?"

"For the past couple of years, all you've talked about is training horses abroad, but all I see in the grand scheme of things is you trying to make that happen through winning a quick quid on the turn of a card. You and I both know that is not the way to make things happen in the world, Henry, and that is why I am telling you to focus on what you've got right in front of you."

"You don't know that the cards won't pay in time." Henry held his uncle's stare. "One big win, and I could be on a boat to the Mediterranean."

"You've won big before, son. I've spent enough nights at The Crown hearing all about it."

Henry stilled. "The Crown? You've been talking to Amos?"

Charles shrugged. "From time to time. What of it?"

"Amos is like a brother to me. I don't like to think of him talking behind my back."

"Amos doesn't gossip. You know that. He's merely passing on the latest news… of which you are sometimes the star as far as that pub is concerned." Charles's jaw tightened. "The fact of the matter is that your gambling is getting you nowhere or else you'd be out of here on the adventure you think will make you happy. Considering you're still sitting here at Henlow House in these stables is all the confirmation you should need about the profitability of your nightly pastime."

The tips of Henry's fingers pulsed from how hard he gripped his needle. "It's going to take time for me to save the fare for the boat and have enough in my pocket to find lodgings abroad. I have a plan, and it's coming along right on schedule."

"Is that so?"

Henry tried to focus on his stitching, but for some inexplicable reason all he could think about in that moment was the delight in Rose Watson's eyes that the countess had liked her dress. It had been pure, fiery passion. Unadulterated satisfaction. That was what made the world go round. Creativity. Fulfillment. Accomplishing something that set a person apart from the life their family had mapped out for them. Expressing himself through more than leather and errand-running. Living a life of his dreams.

He inhaled deeply. "That errand you sent me on the other day—the letter I took to the shop off Regent Street?"

"What about it?"

"The recipient was a young woman by the name of Rose Watson. A dressmaker. A woman who lit up like a gas lamp when she read that the countess's dresser would like her to come to the house with some added extras to go with the dress she made."

"What has a dressmaker and you spending your nights throwing good money after bad got to do with each other?" Charles shook his head and walked to one of the shelves lining the workshop walls. He perused some boxes.

Henry stared at his uncle's turned back. When Rose Watson had smiled after she'd first read Mrs. Hayworth's letter and then looked at him, eyes glittering and teeth shining, her beauty had damn near knocked him on his backside. But it had been the fervor, the satisfaction and hunger in her gaze, that stirred a deep yearning in him to get to know her better.

His uncle selected a box of copper rivets and turned, his eyebrows raised. "Well?"

Henry smiled. "She, like me, clearly believes she is destined for bigger and better things than she'll ever find in a backstreet shop.

Her smile was like a sun coming out from behind the clouds, her eyes as wide and bright as two full moons. She stared at me and—" Henry stopped, narrowed his eyes. "Why are you grinning like that?"

Charles chuckled. "Well, well, maybe there's hope you'll come to see what life's really about, after all." He walked back to his bench. "I'm not a gambling man, as you know, but I'd hedge a bet this woman has struck you right between the eyes."

"Struck me? Don't be daft." Henry turned back to his work, his chest tightening with an unfamiliar sensation. "I'm talking about her ambition. Her need and determination to do more, achieve more. She was—"

"A kindred spirit?" Charles arched an eyebrow. "Aye, maybe she was. Stranger things have happened. But I'll tell you again: people need people, and there is no shame in that. One day you will see how much you have been given and how you could build a good life here."

Henry's heart swelled with love for his family, but his determination to leave did not waver. Not for a moment. "I know what you've done for me, Uncle. Auntie and the little ones too. You all mean the world to me and always will."

Charles stared at him, his gaze unreadable. "Good. Then let's finish our work for the day so we can get ourselves back to them for tonight's meal, shall we?"

Turning back to the saddle he worked on, Henry released a heavy breath. He'd better forget his plans to go into town tonight. Keeping the peace for a night could mean the difference between his uncle digesting his dinner comfortably or suffering from indigestion until morning.

Chapter Nine

As the carriage entered through the gates of Henlow House, Rose peered through the window, her heart beating fast. The house was magnificent and one of London's finest. Built in the early 1700s, Henlow House had been in the earl's family for generations. As the horses trotted along the gravel pathways, Rose pressed her hand to her stomach to calm her increasing nerves even as she continued to stare wide-eyed at the red brick and white stone building, its countless windows dark except for lamplight dotted here and there across the four stories.

When the current earl took the title four years ago, Henlow House soon gained the reputation her mother so feared. Rumors of it being the party house of London's elite, on account of the earl's penchant for flamboyance and joviality, had run rife in the press and on the capital's streets. Rumor had it that the countess was equally keen on entertaining, but not to the extent of her husband's exuberance and over-indulgence. Her mother's concerns about what went on behind the high walls of this noble house poked at Rose's conscience, and she swallowed against her dry throat, praying nothing untoward would be revealed to her on this day or any other.

Eventually, the carriage came to a stop in a small courtyard at the back of the residence and the door was opened by a footman. Swallowing, Rose accepted his hand and stepped out.

"There you are!"

She barely had time to straighten her skirts before Mrs. Hayworth rushed forward and took her hands.

"I am so glad to see you again, Miss Watson." She beamed, her brown curls dancing under the brim of her cap, her blue eyes alight as she took the hatbox and gloves from the footman and pushed them into Rose's hands. "Now come along, dear. It won't do to keep Her Ladyship waiting."

"Yes," Rose stammered. "Of course."

Hurrying alongside Mrs. Hayworth, Rose tried her best not to stare at her surroundings, but utterly failed as she looked in awe at everything and everyone. She was led through what appeared to be a staff corridor before ascending a winding staircase. Holding her skirts and her packages became more and more perilous as Mrs. Hayworth strode forward with the brisk pace of one completely familiar with her surroundings.

Soon, stone floors gave way to highly polished floorboards and sumptuous carpets. It was only as they entered the more opulent area of the house that Mrs. Hayworth's chatter lost its jovial warmth and became decidedly more solemn. She gently cupped Rose's elbow and drew her to a stop in a discreet corner of the deserted hallway, the paintings on the walls and the ornaments atop the rich mahogany furniture leaving Rose in no doubt that they were now in the residence proper.

"Now, I need to make you aware of the protocol." Mrs. Hayworth frowned. "What you should and shouldn't do once you are in the countess's chambers and in audience with Lady Christina herself."

Rose nodded, any response lodging like a rock in her throat.

"Upon entering the countess's drawing room, you will see Her Ladyship and any number of her ladies keeping her company. Not to mention any number of dogs."

Rose stilled. "Dogs?"

"Yes, Her Ladyship's dogs." Concern shadowed Mrs. Hayworth's eyes. "You do like dogs?"

"Yes." Rose smiled as she glanced at the closed door beside them, suddenly eager to meet the canines. "I love dogs."

Mrs. Hayworth's shoulders dropped with obvious relief as she chuckled. "Thank goodness. If you did not, we would most certainly be faced with a problem. Good. Now, you are to stand behind me without a modicum of fidgeting while I introduce you, eyes to the floor, but your head not bowed so low as to indicate lethargy, your manner pleasant. I will announce you and when the countess looks at you, you will curtsy like so." Mrs. Hayworth dipped, one leg behind the other, knees bent, head slightly bowed. "Hover for a second or two and then rise, addressing the countess as 'Your Ladyship.' Is that clear?"

"I... yes."

"Good. Let me see your curtsy."

Rose did her best to copy Mrs. Hayworth's example and slowly rose.

The dresser beamed, her eyes glinting with pride. "Very good. You will do well enough. Now, do you have any questions before we enter the countess's apartments?"

Rose looked along the corridor, the fading light causing shadows to dance over the portraits lining the richly papered walls, candles in iron sconces in between, yet to be lit.

"I... cannot quite believe I am here."

"But you are. You must take ownership of your achievements, my dear. You produced an exquisitely made dress without knowledge of who would be wearing it. The attention to detail and your obvious care is testament to your work ethic when the dress could have been for anyone. You had no way of knowing if it would be worn by royalty, aristocracy, or gentry, yet you executed your skills to the best of your ability. I admire that very much, and I'm sure the countess appreciates it too."

Rose smiled, her confidence bolstered by the dresser's praise. "You're very kind. I just wish my parents felt the same way. They think I aim too high in my ambition. That I risk getting above myself." Rose hesitated. She couldn't possibly mention her mother's additional fears of debauchery in the house but felt the need to say something to ensure Mrs. Hayworth knew that the fault was not Rose's if her designing or making any future clothes for the countess was unceremoniously curbed. "At least, that's what I think is bothering them about me coming here."

"But you are not certain?"

"No." Rose shook her head, conscious that the curiosity in Mrs. Hayworth's eyes could also be disappointment. "I sometimes sense their protection of me is rooted in something I don't understand."

"I see. Well, you are an exceptionally talented young lady, and you deserve to enjoy this afternoon." She smiled. "And quite possibly many similar afternoons to come. If there is anything I can do with regard to your parents, I'd like to help. You have made my mistress very happy and that, in turn, makes me happy. I want you to do well here. I really do."

Mrs. Hayworth's sincerity was palpable, and Rose slumped, unable to contain her insecurities. She inhaled a deep breath, then shakily released it. "You are very kind." The need to share her concerns and frustrations about her parents danced on Rose's tongue. But how could she possibly talk so openly to Mrs. Hayworth, dresser to the Countess of Bath?

"Miss Watson?" Mrs. Hayworth gently laid her hand on Rose's arm. "If you want to take this opportunity with the countess, then bravery and determination must become your new and constant companions. Even with your parents."

Mrs. Hayworth was right. A moment like this might never come along again. Rose drew in a strengthening breath. She had to be strong.

She gave a firm nod. "I understand."

"Good. For the time being, you must put your parents to the back of your mind. Today is *your* day, Miss Watson. No one else's. I rose from working as an assistant to the royal housekeeper, to maid of the countess's bedchamber, to an assistant to her dresser, and then became her actual dresser when my predecessor married." Mrs. Hayworth smiled. "Opportunities arise when we least expect them, but when they come, we must grasp them and hold on with all our might. Today is your special day, and you must savor every moment. Now, let us go."

Rose stood tall and did her utmost to embrace Mrs. Hayworth's words, but her nerves only escalated as they walked along another corridor, then another and another, each more richly decorated than the last. The high, ornate ceilings; the thick, velvet drapery at tall windows; and the ornaments sparkling from every shelf and bureau all added to her trepidation.

At last, Mrs. Hayworth came to an abrupt halt. "This next door takes us inside the countess's quarters. Just remember, Her Ladyship has learned much from the Queen and shares Her Majesty's respect for England's people, whatever their station. She could have chosen anyone to champion, but she chose you."

Rose smiled, her fondness for the dresser growing. "On your encouragement, I'm sure. I'm so very grateful, Mrs. Hayworth."

"Now, now, you deserve it." The woman beamed. "The countess is keen to meet you and see the hat and gloves you recommend she wear with your creation. It is an exciting day!"

Rose grinned, the nerves swirling in her stomach becoming a little more akin to excitement.

A cacophony of barking and whining preceded their entrance into a huge sitting room grandly decorated in shades of peach and cream, every surface covered with ornaments and framed photographs, wooden and porcelain objects of infinite description. Yet, despite what could be considered a cluttered space, there was something wholly comfortable—almost homely—about it. And then there were the dogs. Of any number and every size. Joy squeezed Rose's heart as she fought to stem her smile and the urge to smooth the head of the beautiful brown-and-white spaniel that sniffed at her skirts.

Five exquisitely dressed women sat in a semi-circle around the fireplace, their jewels glinting beneath the flames crackling in the grate. Rose's heart pounded as her mind suddenly went blank, and she was unable to recollect what the countess looked like, despite poring over pictures of her in newspapers and magazines since discovering she was to wear one of her designs.

"Your Ladyship." Mrs. Hayworth raised her voice above the dogs' whimpers and the women's chatter. "I am sorry to disturb you, but Miss Rose Watson, the candidate for your patronage, has arrived with the accessories to accompany the wonderful dress she designed."

A rustle of silk and petticoats followed as Mrs. Hayworth stepped aside, and Rose quickly dropped into a curtsy, her eyes lowered and her heart threatening to break free of her chest.

"Miss Watson, I am delighted to finally meet you."

Slowly, Rose raised her eyes, her knees knocking against each other before she straightened and looked into the soft gaze of

Countess Christina. How could she not have remembered her? Only one countess in the whole world held such brown-haired, blue-eyed beauty, such kindness in her gaze and so genuine a smile.

An immediate and entirely unexpected ease whispered through Rose. "Your Ladyship, I cannot express how happy I am to be here."

The countess's smile widened as her gaze wandered over Rose's face, her fingers lightly touching the wide, diamond choker around her neck. "Oh, my child, I assure you the happiness is all mine."

Chapter Ten

The rapid clip-clop of several horses' hooves approached the court-yard outside the Henlow House mews at near six o' clock. Dusk was falling and the sky was thick with clouds. The earl's booming laughter joined his companions', their deep-voiced jests reverberating off the outbuildings. Henry shot a pointed look at his uncle, and Charles nodded before they both abandoned the tools they had been storing and strode outside.

His Lordship sat astride his handsome chestnut horse waiting for Henry and his uncle to come forward to attend him. Not that the man needed any help to dismount. Fit and robust, the earl's athletic stature drew attention wherever he went. Chitchat abounded of his popularity with certain ladies of society, and this was entirely justified—his brilliant blue eyes held many a woman captive.

Charles strode to His Lordship's horse and took the reins as Henry followed with the mounting block. One by one, more grooms joined them to assist with the earl's friends.

Henry quickly put the block by Lord Robert's horse and bowed. "Good evening, Your Lordship."

"Good evening." Lord Robert grinned, his gaze alight with mischief. "We have had quite a day."

"I can see you are in good spirits, sir."

"I am indeed." The earl plucked at the fingers of his soft leather gloves and nodded at Charles with a roguish smile. "My master saddler often seems to disapprove of my leisurely pursuits, but I guess you to be around my age. Am I right?"

"Three or four years younger, I believe, sir."

"Then I have no doubt you know what a man needs in this life. Drinking, gambling, and women—that's a young man's game, eh?"

Lord Robert's companions laughed along with him as they rallied around their most esteemed associate, outwardly adulating their noble patron, regardless of whether they concurred with His Lordship's views or not.

Henry smiled. "Is there any point to life without such things, sir?"

This blasé question was met with a resounding roar of laughter from Lord Robert before he approached his valet, who was patiently waiting at the edge of the courtyard. Henry was about to collect the mounting block when the earl abruptly turned, his smile dissolving.

"What's your name, young man?"

"Ward, sir."

The earl turned to Charles where he stood with his hand on the horse's bridle. "Your nephew, Summers. Is that right?"

"Yes, sir."

The earl gave a curt nod. "Very good." He smiled at Henry and said, "I'm sure you will continue to do well here. Keep up the good work."

Not wanting to look at his uncle and risk seeing the look of utter triumph on his face, Henry merely dipped his head. "Thank you, sir."

"Not at all. Come along, you fiends," the earl said, addressing his friends. "The evening has barely started. Let us seek out more food and drink!"

The gentlemen's laughter faded as they walked in the direction of the house. Henry picked up the mounting block, then walked alongside his uncle as Charles led His Lordship's horse to the barn.

"It's not just me who thinks your natural place is in the earl's service," Charles said smugly. "You can hardly dismiss a compliment from the man himself, son."

"A man who thinks nothing of drinking, gambling, and being unfaithful to his wife," Henry said stiffly as he replaced the block in its rightful place. "Earl or no earl, I would have thought you'd always disapprove of a man like that."

"I'm just pointing out further confirmation of what I know to be true: you belong here, getting better at saddling until you overtake me in experience and aptitude. You will be set in work for the rest of your life—your sons too."

Henry planted his hands on his hips, tiredness and frustration only adding to his gathering irritation. "The trouble is, I won't be here, will I? Can we just get his horse settled so I can head up west for the night?"

Charles slumped, annoyance in his eyes. "For the love of God."

"Tonight is my night." Henry smiled, his gut twisting with anticipation. "I can feel it in my blood."

His uncle's jaw tightened before he shook his head and led Lord Robert's horse to its stable, his reticence loud in the sudden silence.

Henry tossed the saddle over his shoulder and smiled. Something exciting hung in the air. Something deep and unseen, as though his fate was about to be sealed. He could not wait to get away from Henlow House.

Once he had wiped down and stored the saddle, Henry returned to the workshop to continue cleaning up. He had barely started when a liveried servant appeared in the workshop doorway.

"Excuse me, sir. Might you be Mr. Ward?"

"The one and only. What can I do for you?"

"I have a message from the countess's dresser, Mrs. Hayworth. I am to inform you that a Miss Watson, a visitor to the countess's apartments, will be escorted here within the hour and you are to ensure her safe return home."

Henry stared. Miss Watson was here? Now?

"Mrs. Hayworth wants me to take Miss Watson home?"

"Yes, sir. Mrs. Hayworth said you might be surprised." The man chuckled. "But apparently you are acquainted with Miss Watson and her parents?"

"Hardly acquainted," Henry protested, entirely flummoxed by what was unfolding. "I briefly met them a few days ago, and I can't say it was the best of meetings either."

The servant shrugged. "Well, I'm just passing on the message. Clearly whatever that meeting was qualifies you for the task of ensuring Miss Watson's safe journey home."

Unexpected pleasure clenched in the pit of Henry's stomach, but he kept his face impassive. "In that case, I'll prepare a curricle."

The man left and Henry stared after him before he grinned and hurried to finish tidying the workroom. A second meeting with Miss Watson, followed by a visit to the gambling house…. The day was turning out to be a very good one indeed.

Chapter Eleven

Rose could not stop staring at the countess or the beautiful sapphire-blue dress she wore as she placed her cup and saucer on a small side table. "You have the most extraordinary talent, Miss Watson. I am truly in awe of your work. Is what you're wearing one of your designs?"

Rose cleared her throat. "Yes, Your Ladyship. I spend almost every spare minute I have drawing and experimenting with designs, creating jackets, skirts, shawls, and scarves with different embellishments, materials, and patterns." She swallowed, knowing she was babbling. "I adore clothes, Your Ladyship. I really do."

Lady Christina picked up one of the three spaniels at her feet and placed it on her lap. "And your creations are displayed in your family's shop, I am told."

"Some are." Rose grimaced. "My father is finally allowing me to show some of my work, but…"

"But?"

"My parents are more traditional, Your Ladyship. They feel my designs will not sell and therefore are a waste of our resources."

"I see. Well, I'm sure your parents are right with regard to their own business, Miss Watson, but as I am now your patron, your resources will no longer be a problem, I assure you."

Rose's heart flipped. "You wish to be my patron?"

The countess grinned. "Yes. Very much so."

"Oh, Your Ladyship. I am thrilled." Rose smiled and blinked against the tears pricking her eyes. "Thank you. When I mentioned our resources a moment ago, I did not mean to suggest—"

"I know you didn't." The countess laughed. "I just want you to fully embrace your new good fortune, Miss Watson. I had every intention of seeking out a painter or photographer to sponsor, considering I have a keen interest in both arts, but Mrs. Hayworth's fervor for your talent was hard to ignore. Then I saw your creations…" She grinned. "I instantly made the decision to allow you this opportunity."

"I am so grateful, Your Ladyship." Rose set her teacup on the low table in front of her. "I am beyond delighted you think so highly of my work. I truly believe the dress I made for you is my finest work to date."

"Well, I'm pleased to tell you that I like that one and the others equally."

Rose froze. "Others?"

The countess smiled, her blue eyes sparkling with mischief. "My commission is not the first dress of yours I have seen, Miss Watson."

"I don't understand." Rose looked at Mrs. Hayworth, who sat on the opposite settee. "I understood that Mrs. Hayworth had been to the shop before, but I thought the commission was your first from our shop."

"It was." The countess smiled. "But Mrs. Hayworth admired others she had seen so much that she sent her assistant to purchase two of your dresses so I could see your talent for myself."

Mrs. Hayworth's eyes were kind and lit with more than a little amusement as she looked at Rose. "Didn't I tell you how and why I came to admire your work, Miss Watson?" Her smile faltered, and she widened her eyes seemingly in warning. "And how proud your parents are of you and your work?"

Rose swallowed, grateful Mrs. Hayworth was there to halt her foolish tongue. The worst possible thing she could do was blurt out something about her parents' reluctance for her to take this opportunity.

Rose forced a smile. "I had no idea all this had been going on while I continued my days as normal."

Lady Christina's eyes sparkled with delight. "Mrs. Hayworth loves to play her cards close to her chest."

"I do." Mrs. Hayworth nodded. "Because that is often the way things get done without fuss or faltering."

"Your parents are right to be proud of you, Miss Watson," the countess added quietly. "A parent's love is precious. Believe me, I long to be with my children more often than will ever be possible."

A quiet melancholy settled over the countess, and Rose shifted uncomfortably before purposefully pushing lightness into her voice in the hope of lifting Lady Christina's spirits. "Sitting here in such a grand house, having spent time with the Countess of Bath and her dresser, I fear I am surely in a dream."

Her Ladyship's eyes glinted with some of her previous happiness as she moved the dog on her lap to the floor and chose a second one to pet. "A dream that I would like to continue." She settled a black and tan King Charles spaniel on her lap and turned to Mrs. Hayworth. "Why don't you share our proposition with Miss Watson?"

"It would be my pleasure." The royal dresser's mouth twitched, her blue eyes gleaming with undisguised satisfaction. "Her Ladyship and I believe your work already competes with some established British designers. You are supremely talented, Miss Watson, and with the countess's sponsorship, you will become a valued member of her staff going forward."

Rose stilled. "The countess's staff? I don't—"

"Why, yes. You will have to reside here. The countess will need regular access to you."

"I don't know what to say." Rose looked between Mrs. Hayworth and the smiling countess. "This is beyond anything I could have imagined."

"And I'm sure…" Mrs. Hayworth pointedly raised her eyebrows. "Your parents will be equally thrilled by this unexpected elevation."

Rose's smile strained. "They will. Of course."

"You should also remember, Miss Watson, you are of age and do not need your parents' permission to work for the countess." She faced the countess. "Do you not agree, my lady?"

"I do, but their approval would be preferred." Lady Christina frowned as she looked at Rose. "However, I know all too well what it is to be directed in life, Miss Watson. To be told what one can or cannot do. But I also know about duty and respect to one's parents, so the last thing I would ask of you would be to defy them. Having said that…"

The countess's eyes flashed with determination. "Your circumstances are wholly different from mine in that you do not have noble blood to consider. You were not born with your life decided for you. You have choices. Your parents have choices, and I truly believe they will know the right one to make once they see your happiness and willingness to take on what will be a very busy future. You will be taken care of. Goodness knows, my parents had no such assurance when I married the earl."

Respecting the countess even more deeply now that she had shown a little of what she felt as a member of the British nobility, Rose wanted the countess to know that she, too, had strength when necessary. "Thank you, Your Ladyship. Despite my parents' not believing opportunities like this happen to people like us, I am determined to prove them wrong."

"Excellent," Mrs. Hayworth said firmly before the countess could respond. "Then we will assume you are entirely committed to the proposition set before you."

"Oh, I am most certainly committed, Mrs. Hayworth," Rose said firmly. "You have no need to doubt that."

"Good, because both the countess and I need to be certain you wish to learn all you need to know about working in the countess's household as well as being given the time to design and make Her Ladyship's clothes for the season. It will be hard and stressful work at times, Miss Watson, but it will also be fulfilling, exciting, and quite possibly the beginning of something spectacular for you."

Rose dropped her mouth open as she darted her gaze from Mrs. Hayworth to the countess. "You want me to design a wardrobe for the whole season?"

"Why, yes." The countess laughed. "But not all at once, of course."

Happiness and hope caught like fire in Rose's heart, her soul soaring. How in all things holy could this be happening?

"If you come to Henlow House and work as my wardrobe maid alongside Mrs. Hayworth," the countess continued, "you will learn from other designers' work and further enhance your remarkable talent. I will ensure you are given sufficient time to work on my wardrobe." Her Ladyship leaned closer and squeezed Rose's fingers. "This is the opportunity of a lifetime, Miss Watson, and I have every confidence of your success."

Dry-mouthed, trembling, and wanting to shout her joy from the rooftops, Rose feared she might burst.

Mrs. Hayworth smiled. "Speak to your mother and father. Tell them all that has happened and what you would like to do." She stood. "Now, it is time for you to bid farewell to Her Ladyship, and I will escort you to the mews where one of the grooms will take you home."

Rose stood, her mind reeling as she curtsied to the countess. "Your Ladyship."

Lady Christina smiled. "It's been a pleasure, Miss Watson. I will see you again soon."

Rose dipped her head and, unable to stop her smile, followed Mrs. Hayworth to the door.

Chapter Twelve

The sound of female voices snagged Henry's attention. The lamplight illuminating the Royal Mews cast Rose Watson in amber shadow, her teeth shining as she laughed at something her companion said. She was simply stunning. Her thick brown hair and big brown eyes…. His heart gave an unexpected jolt as she turned her attention in his direction, and their eyes locked for a heartbeat before she smiled.

"Good evening, Mr. Ward."

Henry touched his hand to the brim of his hat. "Miss Watson. It's a pleasure to see you again."

Absurdly pleased that she looked at him almost kindly, compared to the way she had looked at him when they last saw one another, Henry forced his attention to the woman beside her and met the hardened stare of the countess's dresser, Mrs. Hayworth.

He quickly dipped his head. "Ma'am."

"Mr. Ward." She narrowed her eyes as she looked at him and then Miss Watson, before facing him again. "There is no need to look quite so pleased with yourself. If Miss Watson is not returned to her parents in one piece, your head will be on the block. Do I make myself clear?"

"Yes, ma'am." He glanced at Rose and smiled. "It will be my pleasure to carry out the duty of ensuring Miss Watson's safety."

Rose's cheeks reddened before she dropped her gaze to the ground.

Entirely enchanted by her reaction, Henry momentarily forgot Mrs. Hayworth's presence until she pointedly cleared her throat. He quickly faced her. Her expression was not unlike that of a bulldog chewing a wasp.

"Miss Watson is a special guest of the countess, Mr. Ward." Her eyes flashed with clear warning. "I advise you to remember that when you are escorting her home." Before Henry could respond, Mrs. Hayworth faced Miss Watson. "Despite Mr. Ward's misplaced confidence in himself, I trust he will see you safely home, my dear. He is a valued member of the earl's household and would not dare to do anything that might threaten his position here." She faced Henry and raised her eyebrows. "Am I right?"

No, you're not right. Henry fought to bury his amusement. "Yes, ma'am."

"Very good." She addressed Miss Watson, "I'll be in touch again very soon."

"Thank you. I look forward to it."

Mrs. Hayworth gave a curt nod, threw a final warning glance at Henry, and then strode toward the house.

Henry turned, pleased that Rose's smile remained and hadn't vanished the moment they were alone. "She actually likes me, you know," he said with a wink.

"Who?"

He tilted his head in the direction the countess's dresser had walked. "Mrs. Hayworth."

"Oh, yes. Of course." Miss Watson's smile dissolved as she gazed at Mrs. Hayworth's diminishing figure. "I have no idea how I will explain all that has happened to my parents. No idea at all."

Henry stared at her turned cheek, not sure she was aware she had spoken aloud. "But it was all good, wasn't it?"

"What?"

"Your time at the house. It went well?" He shrugged to appear nonchalant even though her anxiety bothered him. "I'm just curious. It's no problem if you wish to keep your business to yourself, but if I can help…"

"You wouldn't believe me even if I told you."

"Why don't you try me?"

"I've just taken tea with the countess." She shook her head, her beautiful eyes on his as she waved her hand as though in disbelief. "Heavens above! I can barely believe such an event occurred. The whole scenario is preposterous!"

Torn between asking her to sit down so she might take a few calming breaths and his absolute relief that her previous disappointment with him seemed forgotten, he gently cupped her elbow.

"Then you must tell me all about it on the way home," he said with a smile, hoping to provoke at least a glimpse of the same in return. "Come on. Let's get you aboard."

Once she was sitting next to him, a thick blanket across her knees and a hot stone beneath her feet, Henry urged the horse forward with a click of his tongue. As they trotted along the road, he stole several glances at her, but she continuously stared ahead, her jaw rigid. Should he bother her? Or leave her to her obvious deliberation?

"You know," she murmured, "I am completely in my rights to expect my parents to listen to me. Not only am I one and twenty, but I have also just spent the last two hours with the Countess of Bath."

Henry bit back a smile. She sounded completely indignant, which he found wholly satisfying. "I couldn't agree more."

In his peripheral vision, he saw her snap her head around to face him.

"Good, because you should. Why? Because I am absolutely right."

"I have no doubt." Henry glanced at the passing houses as raindrops began to patter on the curricle's hood and people ducked under shop awnings to keep themselves dry. "Do you want to tell me what else happened?" The silence stretched until Henry faced her. "Miss Watson?"

Her eyes wandered over his face, pausing at his mouth before she lifted her gaze to his. "You really want to know?"

"Of course."

"Well, Mrs. Hayworth, and moreover, the countess, somehow decided to pluck a tailor's daughter from obscurity. From a small, side-street shop no less, to have her design and create the Countess of Bath's wardrobe for this year's season." She frowned as she lifted and dropped her hands. "See? Complete and utter madness."

"That's what happened?" Henry faced her, shocked yet supremely happy for her. "God above, woman, you should be shouting this achievement from the rooftops. That's astounding. Incredible."

"I know! Which is why I cannot believe it to be true."

"Rubbish." Henry grinned and stared out into the street, the gaslight glinting yellow in the puddles on the wet cobblestones. "You must believe it. Am I not taking you home from Henlow House? Have you not just been inside areas of the house very few people ever go? You have been found like a nugget of gold among a coal pit of a thousand ordinary people, Rose. Don't you dare dismiss this. This is your chance."

Silence fell again and Henry inwardly grimaced. Not only had he been overly enthusiastic, but he'd also used her Christian name. He cleared his throat. "Look, maybe I shouldn't be so—"

"You called me Rose."

"I'm sorry if I caused offen—"

"No, it's nice." She smiled. "Might I call you Henry?"

He stared into her beautiful eyes as attraction like he had never known twisted deep in his gut. "Course you can." Henry silently willed her to look away before he added kissing her to his long list of impulsive decisions that had landed him in trouble in the past.

Finally, she looked off to the side. "The countess wishes to employ me as her wardrobe maid, but also said she will give me ample time to work on my designs. It is like a dream come true."

"Then you must accept."

"But my parents—"

"What about them? How can they not be happy about this? There is every chance this could be your ticket out of here."

Damnation. Why did you say that? She's not you, you fool.

The heat of her stare burned into his temple, but Henry refused to face her.

"Out of where, Henry?" she asked quietly.

He pulled lightly on the reins as they entered Regent Street, not far from her family's shop. "England. There's no saying where this could lead you. You could become a renowned garment maker, known throughout the country, throughout Europe. You might be a millionairess this time next year."

She gave a rather inelegant snort. "Oh, yes. There is that to consider, of course."

He glanced at her, annoyed that she mocked him. "I know you feel a lot for your family, Rose, but this extraordinary request from the countess is real and pretty spectacular. You have to do this, regardless of what your parents might say. You will have days off to visit. I imagine you'll be free to come and go as you please whenever the earl and countess are away."

"You don't know that any more than I do."

"Maybe not, but you must rouse the courage to discover what this could mean for you. Accept the position and take it from there. If you become rich"—he nudged her shoulder and winked, earning a raised eyebrow—"and I genuinely believe you will, then you can hire people to help your parents in the shop, if that's what they want. Or maybe they will want to retire. Who knows? Either way, you cannot dither about this. Who knows what the future might hold? What if you get to travel the world? How wonderful would that be?"

She stared at him before looking at her clenched hands in her lap. "Is that *your* dream? To travel the world?"

Henry smiled as the usual tingle in his gut erupted whenever he imagined his future. "Yes."

"And how do you mean to make that happen?"

The question was a simple one, but it struck deep, highlighting the flimsiness of his plans. He swallowed, refusing to look at her and have her eyes draw a confession from him about his cycle of saving, then gambling, and how—at least so far—it was proving entirely unfruitful.

He cleared his throat. "I have the steps in place. Don't worry."

"And how are they coming along?"

"Well enough."

They lapsed into silence again. What would she think of him if she knew how he spent most of his evenings? If she knew where he was headed once he'd dropped her safely home and returned the curricle to the mews?

"Mrs. Hayworth said you are a valued member of the earl's household," she said quietly. "Are you his groom?"

"No. I'm a saddler and horse trainer." He blew out a heavy breath. "I wish I was more the latter, but I fear that will never be the case while I remain working with my uncle."

"Why not?"

"He believes my future is here, following in his footsteps as the earl's master saddler."

"And you don't want that?"

"No. My passion lies with horses and always will." He clenched his jaw as he stared ahead. "I want to train horses and travel the world, Rose. I feel deep in my gut that is what I was put on this earth to do."

"Then you, too, are fortunate."

He glanced at her. "I am?"

She smiled. "If a person finds their calling, they are fortunate, Henry. I love clothes—designing them, creating them. That's my calling. It's funny that you know about stitching, too, though. Albeit in an entirely different way."

Henry relaxed his shoulders, relieved the conversation had moved on. "Yes, I'd say we have that in common."

"You make saddles for nobility, Henry Ward, you are no less talented than me. Could that not add to your income while you travel the world? I imagine there will be much demand for a saddlemaker of your status abroad."

He shook his head. "Saddling and working for one of England's nobles is an inherited position from my family, taught and passed down to my uncle from his father and his father before him. It's not what I want to do. Nothing burns inside me like training horses. Nothing."

"Does your uncle not have a son? Is that why he taught you saddle work?"

"He only has daughters." He smiled, his heart warming with love for his young cousins. "Martha and Maud, who are beyond fantastic, but yes, he most definitely considers me his surrogate son."

"Then you must feel truly grateful." There was a smile in her voice. "Clearly, your uncle loves you very much, or else he would not entrust you with such a legacy."

Guilt slithered like a snake into Henry's stomach, but he lifted his chin. "I *am* grateful, and always will be, but it's time for me to seek out a life of my own, and if I can center that around horse training, I will."

What he hoped was companionable silence fell, and Henry urged on the horse to her family's shop. Once they arrived, he drew the horse to a stop, hooked the reins, and dropped down onto the cobbled street. He jogged around to the other side and offered his hand to her. She studied him for a long moment, her gaze unreadable and her brow slightly creased before she slipped her hand into his. Henry dipped his head before relishing how easily her gloved hand slid into his and the beauty of her profile as she stepped down beside him.

Reluctantly, he released her hand and she smiled.

"Thank you for bringing me safely home, Henry. It has been interesting getting to know you a little better."

He flitted his gaze from her eyes to her mouth and back again, his hand itching to take hers a second time. "Likewise." He touched the brim of his hat. "You take care now."

"You too."

Henry watched her enter the darkened shop and lock the door. She didn't meet his eyes through the glass nor acknowledge him further. Turning, he climbed aboard and clicked the horse on, a strange melancholy whispering through him. He clenched his jaw against it. He would not linger on Rose Watson a moment longer. He had a card game to win. Women had never been part of his plan… and that wouldn't change now.

Henry cursed as he surrendered to a final look along the street toward Rose's family shop and saw only darkness.

Chapter Thirteen

"It's impossible, Rose. You must see that we need you here."

"No, Mama, I do not see that at all. You have Florence. You will be fine." She closed her eyes against the anguish in her mother's gaze. "I would be foolish to reject such an opportunity. Please." She opened her eyes. "I must do this."

Her father stood from his armchair and walked to the fireplace. He stared into the flames. "The Countess of Bath... I cannot fathom it."

"Neither can I, Papa, but the opportunity has arisen all the same."

Her mother's eyes glistened with tears in the lamplight. "You could be eaten alive behind nine-foot walls, forced to do something against your will or values, and we'd have no idea. Aren't you afraid?"

"Well, yes, a little when you put it like that, but..." Rose tightened her fingers around her mother's as they sat side by side on the sofa. "The countess is lovely, and I have no doubt she will be kind to me. Mrs. Hayworth will look after me, too, I'm sure. There is nothing to fear."

"Nothing to fear, she says. Nothing to fear!"

"Clementine... calm yourself," her father said. "Everything will be all right."

As Rose looked at each of her parents, her suspicion that her mother's resistance was about something more than a potential royal appointment rose again.

"Mama, please tell me what bothers you so."

"I…" Her cheeks darkened and the sadness in her eyes swiftly changed to irritation. "You are too trusting, Rose. How are we to keep you safe if you are living and working at Henlow House? A place that stands behind locked gates?"

The agony in her mother's eyes cut deep into Rose's heart as suffocation and lost opportunity edged into her soul. Why did she feel she was being cruel by pursuing this? That her dream was drenched in selfishness?

"… *rouse the courage to discover what this could mean for you…*"

Henry's words echoed in Rose's mind, sparking a deep desire that bolstered her determination.

"I must go. If I don't, there is every chance I will look back at this time with regret for the rest of my life. Despite Mrs. Hayworth's faith in me and the countess's kind words, I don't even know if I have the talent or capability to carry out all they expect of me, but I have to try." She looked at her parents' faces, trepidation for what lay ahead making flutters take flight in her stomach, yet her resolve burned ever brighter. "It might come that designing and making dresses for her is beyond me. But how can I not give this everything I have?"

When neither of her parents answered, Rose slumped.

"Are you concerned that our business will suffer financially without me? Is that it?"

"Of course not!" her father chided, as though she had slapped him. "This is not about money."

"Good," Rose retorted, pushing to her feet. "Because I will willingly send two-thirds of my earnings home. More, if that is what you wish."

Her mother looked at her husband, pleading in her eyes. "Tell her, Harold. Tell her once and for all we need her here, and there is to be no more discussion about her going away where goodness knows what could happen, and we'd know nothing about it until it was too late."

"Mama, you are being unreasonable!"

Her father walked to the settee and held out his hand. Her mother took it, tears in her eyes, and Rose suddenly saw the exhaustion in the lines on her face. When had she begun to gray? Rose could not remember. Guilt twisted inside her, yet she knew without a doubt that if she didn't go to Henlow House, she would be stuck in the same position for years, possibly forever. As much as she loved her parents, she wanted more than their shop in her future. Yet, that did not mean she would not always return when and if her mother and father needed her.

"I will visit as much as I can, Mama," she said softly. "And you have Florence to help you. Everything will be all right."

Her mother sniffed, pressing a cotton handkerchief to her nose. "You do twice as much work as Florence. She is competent, yes, but she is not you."

"Then help her become more like me. Give her more responsibility. More opportunity."

Rose faced her father, and he stared back at her, his brow furrowed, but there seemed at least to be consideration in his eyes as opposed to her mother's stalwart determination not to relent.

"Florence is keen to work and loves her place here," Rose pressed. "With some encouragement and praise, she will flourish. This could be a chance for her elevation as much as mine."

The silence stretched as her parents turned to one another, their eyes flickering over each other's faces, until Rose could stand it no longer. She stood and walked to the tea tray she had set atop one of the dressers and lifted the near-empty pot.

"I'll make more tea, and we can keep talking. I know you are afraid, but I don't want you to go to bed assuming I will change my mind."

"Sit down," her mother said quietly, her gaze still on her husband. "There's something we should tell you."

Dread dropped like a stone into Rose's stomach as she slowly replaced the pot on the tray and returned to the settee, tentatively lowering herself onto the cushions. Her father had paled, whereas her mother's cheeks were pink, showing her discomfort.

Sickness coated Rose's throat. "What is it?"

Her father sat in his wing-backed chair and leaned forward, his elbows on his thighs, his head bowed as he stared at the rug. Rose glanced at her mother and her heart jolted as a single tear ran down her cheek.

"Mama? Please, whatever it is, just tell me. Papa?"

Her father raised his head and looked at his wife, holding his hand across the space between them so she might take it.

"This is about your brother, Rose."

Gideon? Was her mother's reaction to her going away connected to her grief over her son's sudden and tragic death? Shame flooded over Rose in a wave.

"Oh, Mama. I cannot imagine how it must feel to lose a child, but… Gideon's death was an accident. You cannot compare what happened to him to me working for Lady Christina." Tears burned her eyes. "I will be safe, Mama. I promise I will."

"Oh, Rose. You don't understand."

"Your brother has been gone seven years, my love," her father said, still tightly clutching his wife's hand. "But his death still affects your mother, and I suspect it always will. We couldn't protect him, and now your mother fears we will fail you too."

"Mama, no." Rose shook her head, her heart breaking all over again. "Gideon was killed by a falling beam. There was an investigation, and it was concluded that no one was to blame. You know this. There was nothing you or anyone else could have done to save him."

"You don't understand."

"I do, Mama."

"No, Rose, you don't!"

Rose stiffened, her mother's shouted protest piercing through her.

"It… it wasn't an accident," she cried. "At least not the accident we told you it was."

Ice-cold fingers tip-tapped along Rose's spine. "What do you mean?"

"You were so young, Rose," her father sighed, his eyes glassy with unshed tears. "We had no choice but to shield you from the truth. You looked up to your brother, loved him more than anything or anyone."

Rose looked between her mother and father, tears pricking the backs of her eyes. "What has that got to do with him dying? He was my brother. Of course I loved him."

"He wasn't the man you thought he was, Rose. Far from it."

She looked at her mother and asked quietly. "How did Gideon die, Mama?"

Her mother let out a strangled sob and her father leaped from his chair and pulled his wife from the settee into his tight embrace, his face anguished and his eyes glistening with tears.

"Gideon was a drinker, a gambler," her father said. "And a whole lot more we probably didn't know about."

"What?"

"To you, he was brave and wild, funny and rebellious, but that is not who he was to us. To us, he was a constant source of worry and distress. The reason your mother and I lay awake night after night, waiting to hear him come through the door. And then…" He briefly closed his eyes, opened them again. "Then the inevitable happened."

Rose swallowed the lump that had formed in her throat. "He…"

"Was killed, Rose. In a bar fight. One he provoked."

Rose fell back against the settee, lifting her hand to her mouth. "No."

"I'm sorry, my love, but it's the truth, and it's why your mother and I have kept you so close. You are the center of our lives, and always will be."

Memories of hushed conversations and arguments that silenced whenever she entered the room came rushing back to her. How she had amused herself, playing alone because her parents had been so wrapped up in Gideon and his future. The lack of importance she had felt in her family unit when she was young now made complete sense… and then how she became so very important after Gideon died even more so.

"He broke your heart," she whispered, "didn't he?"

Her father nodded. "More than once, but we never stopped loving him, Rose. Not ever."

Entirely unaware that she had wept, Rose swiped her trembling fingers over her damp cheeks and stood, then put her hand on her mother's back. "Well, now I know the truth, your care and love for me and the way you express it makes sense, and I only love you all the more for it." Her voice cracked, but a fire burned in her heart along with a new grief for the brother she had loved so dearly. "But now more than before, I am determined to pursue this position with the countess."

"Oh, Rose," her mother cried. "I'm so afraid for you. The thought of you being away from us where we cannot look after you and ensure your safety is an impossible ask."

"But I am asking you, Mama. Or rather, asking for your blessing." Rose took a deep breath. "I am going to Henlow House regardless, Mama, but it would be so much nicer with yours and Papa's good wishes." Tears burned Rose's eyes, her heart breaking for her mother's loss, but she would not falter.

"You are so precious to us," her mother said quietly as she leaned her cheek to her husband's chest.

"It is because of Gideon that your mother clings so hard to you, my love," her father whispered. "But… I see now that it is unfair to you."

"Harold, how could you?" Her mother stepped away from him and crossed her arms, hurt in her eyes. "Why would you say that?"

"Because it *is* unfair, sweetheart. Rose is a grown woman. She could be in a home of her own by now, have a husband… maybe even children. We cannot keep her here forever. Whatever the circumstances." He faced Rose, weariness deepening the aura of tiredness surrounding him. "Take the position. See where it leads. But promise me, promise your mother, that you will come back often and with love."

Guilt battered Rose's conscience as her mother seemed to visibly shrink, her shoulders dropping, her face etched with anguish.

"I am not leaving and never coming back, Mama." Rose stood in front of her mother, taking her hands in hers. "I will come back so often you will barely miss me, and I will bring extra money, which will help with the shop and lessen your burden. All will be well."

A soft sob escaped her mother before she stepped into Rose's arms and put her head upon her shoulder, her tears dampening Rose's dress. Rose stared over her mother's head at her father. He nodded and smiled softly, giving her his silent blessing.

Rose closed her eyes, willing her courage to the surface. Slowly, Henry Ward's face emerged in her mind. He, too, wanted freedom and flight, ambition and adventure. Was her need for more any different from his wish to travel the world training horses? She thought not. She squeezed her arms tighter around her mother's quaking body. Just as surely as Henry did, she must believe her dreams and aspirations would benefit her family in the end.

Chapter Fourteen

Henry hitched up his collar and ducked his head against the cold wind that swept along the busy thoroughfare in the very heart of London. He had stopped at several taverns on his way to his favored gambling haunt and was grateful his pockets weighed a little heavier and jangled a little louder than they had when he'd started out a couple of hours before. Dressed in his best coat and hat, his face and hands scrubbed clean—although no amount of soap and water would remove the black grit of his leather work—Henry headed for the West End. Once there, he would sit at a table with card players who had sufficient money to risk and carefree thrills to chase.

His gaming was supposed to be a means to an end, but the longer time wore on, the less the game seemed to be his assured route to liberty. A drunk, arm in arm with a garishly painted woman, bumped into him as they swayed past, and Henry scowled after them, yanking on the lapels of his coat.

"Cretins," he muttered.

Deep down, he knew he was no better than either of them and certainly had no right to feel superior to the people who drowned their sorrows or made their living amid the dirty, manured-lined streets of London. And it was that awareness—that truth—that drove at his heart and mind harder every day. Tonight, something had to happen to pave another step toward his ambitions. It just had to.

He reached The Crown and pushed open the door. The cacophony of yelling and shouting, jeering and jesting assaulted Henry like a slap in the face, the veil of pipe and cigar smoke eye-watering. Shouldering his way to the bar, he hissed a curse every time a splash of ale was spilled on his shoes, or a laugh roared in his face. How he longed to get out of this godforsaken city and bask in the sunny climes of the continent.

With a shove at a bloke beside him, who looked intoxicated enough that he might pass out, Henry finally reached the bar.

"Nice night for it, eh, Henry?" said his friend, Amos Brown, from where he stood behind the bar, his customary grin displaying his checkerboard teeth.

Henry rolled his eyes. "You think?"

Amos laughed. "Usual?"

"Yeah, go on then." Henry looked at the closed wooden door adjacent to the far right of the bar and nodded. "Many in tonight?"

Amos put a tankard under the tap. "Enough to make it worth your while. You looking for a seat at the table?"

Henry slid some coins across the bar. "I am indeed, my friend, and I won't be leaving until I'm considerably richer than I am right now."

Amos protruded his bottom lip as he picked up the coins. "Still itching to get away, then? I thought you might have changed your mind."

"Why would you think that? Have I ever given you the impression my mind has veered from my plan?"

"No, but your uncle has."

Henry hovered his tankard at his lips as irritation stirred in his gut. "Charles has been in here talking about me again?"

"Just last week." Amos's dark eyes shadowed with concern. "He's a good man, Henry. He only wants the best for you."

"Yes, I know."

Amos gave a curt nod and then walked along the bar to serve someone else. Henry blew out a slow breath, trying to hold on to the even temper he would need to play tonight. Being riled or tetchy did not serve a man well when he was at the table.

He took a hefty mouthful of his drink and set the tankard on the bar. It was important to get his head in the right place, his skill and intuition even more so. He stepped back and gripped the edge of the bar before dropping his gaze to the sticky floorboards. He closed his ears to the noise surrounding him. What had Rose Watson asked him? His mind scrambled for her words, his heart picking up speed as he pictured her eyes.

She had asked how his plans were coming along for working overseas, and his answer had been nonexistent. But what could he have said when his strategy remained little more than fantasy?

"You still here?"

Henry snapped up his head, heat leaping into his cheeks at being caught contemplating Rose Watson. He took another drink, licking the froth from his upper lip. "Not for much longer." He held Amos's gaze. "So, what did my uncle say exactly?"

His friend shrugged and turned his attention to the tankard he was drying with a scrap of rag. "Not much. I just got the feeling you're frustrating the hell out of the man, that's all."

"Maybe I am, but sooner or later he'll learn I know what's best for me. I hate to say it, but Charles is not my father, and I've no obligation to keep up his family's legacy. Not when I'm hell-bent on making my own."

"The trouble is, it's you Charles wants to pass on his knowledge to. No one else."

"Yeah, I know." Henry sighed. He drained his ale and held out his tankard for another. "I met someone the other day, and she challenged me to get my future decided once and for all. Turns out, her urging was just what I needed."

"She *challenged* you?" Amos raised his eyebrows as he picked up the tankard. "Well, that *is* interesting. I've never known you to think yourself challenged by anyone. What did she say exactly?"

"She asked me to tell her my plans." Henry glanced at the people lining the bar rather than meeting Amos's eyes. "And the fact that my plans aren't coming along as they should be has bothered me ever since."

"I see. What was this woman's name?" Amos grinned. "I think I'd like to meet her."

"The point is, she made me understand how much I could be hurting Charles, and he doesn't deserve that even if I don't agree with half of what comes out of his mouth. And I'm not sure what to do about that, but I do know I'll make him proud of me, and that I am perfectly capable of standing on my own two feet. What's more, I'll prove it to Rose Watson too."

"Rose Watson? That's the mystery woman's name?" Amos smiled. "Well, well. She's certainly put a firecracker up your backside, hasn't she?"

Henry looked at the door to the private gambling room. "You watch if I don't win big money tonight. That will soon wipe the smugness from your ugly mug."

"Yeah, all right, lad. We'll wait and see, shall we?"

Amos walked away and Henry scowled after him before draining his pint and heading for the room at the side of the bar.

Chapter Fifteen

Rose handed Mrs. Hayworth another pearl-tipped hairpin, and the dresser carefully pushed it into Lady Christina's splendid coiffure. Curls brushed her temples, but the rest of her tresses had been curled and gathered high on her head and strung with ropes of pearls that glinted in the candlelight.

"How are you enjoying working in my apartments so far, Watson?" the countess asked. "It has been a week now, has it not?"

"Yes, Your Ladyship." Rose blinked from her fascination and met the countess's smile in the mirror before handing another pin to Mrs. Hayworth. "I think I'm happier than I have ever been."

"And your designs? Have you had any time to work on them?"

"A little, and ideas are starting to take shape in my mind, so I intend to put pen to paper as soon as possible next week."

"Very good. I keep my promises, and I want to make certain you have time to work on your own. The earl and I will be visiting the Queen at Buckingham Palace for three nights next week"—she patted her hair—"you have my permission to stay behind. I will get along famously with just Mrs. Hayworth as I always have. Isn't that so, Mrs. Hayworth?"

"Indeed, Your Ladyship." Mrs. Hayworth stood back to study her work, her brow furrowed before she gave a curt nod of satisfaction. "I believe your hair is complete. Watson? Pass me the small hand mirror, please."

Rose quickly lifted the mirror from the dressing table and gave it to Mrs. Hayworth, who held it up behind the countess so Her Ladyship could inspect her dresser's beautiful hair styling.

Pleasure lit Lady Christina's eyes. "It's wonderful, Mrs. Hayworth. Thank you." She rose from the dressing table and walked to the center of the room, her hand gracefully lifting the side of her long skirt as the dogs who had been dozing at her feet scrambled to follow her.

Rose's heart filled with admiration. The countess looked so beautiful in a dark burgundy ensemble, the jacket and skirt hemmed with soft ivory lace, the silver thread decorating the bodice shimmering beneath the candlelight.

"Your selected jewels, Your Ladyship."

Mrs. Hayworth opened a black velvet box, and Rose barely managed to swallow her gasp. The diamonds glittered and the semi-precious garnet was a flawless match to the countess's dress. The five-band choker, earrings, and bracelet were undoubtedly worth more than half the city would earn in their entire lives.

"They are perfect." Lady Christina sighed. "And I haven't worn them in so long. It will be nice to give them a showing."

Mrs. Hayworth began arranging and securing the countess's jewels, not just the diamonds and garnet, but also lengths of pearls about her neck and wrists. Blinking from her stupor, Rose collected the discarded paraphernalia from the dressing table that hadn't been used in Mrs. Hayworth's endeavors, her mind drifting to her parents as it had a hundred times throughout the week.

The night she found out how Gideon had really died continued to pain her day and night, but the revelation also enhanced her desire to pursue her dreams of being a successful clothes designer and maker. It was almost as though she wanted to achieve her ambitions in her brother's memory.

Tears smarted her eyes and Rose quickly blinked them away, sliding a quick glance to the side to make sure neither the countess nor Mrs. Hayworth watched her. Thankfully, both were still too embroiled in the evening's preparations. She continued to put away the combs and pins, her fingers slightly trembling. With Gideon's true demise now revealed to her, she lingered on how alive and exciting he had always been, how full of fire and passion, teasing and fun… attributes that very much brought to mind Henry Ward. And although her thinking about him should be all the more worrying, she would be lying if she did not admit she would take Henry's flirtatious flare over the rather staid suitors she'd fleetingly engaged with in the past.

Closing the drawer containing the countess's hair accessories, Rose drew in a strengthening breath. At least with the truth about her brother shared, her mother had eventually given her reluctant blessing for Rose to go to Henlow House, and she had jumped at it before her mother had time to change her mind.

That had been eight days ago and, so far, she had not been able to visit her parents. She very much doubted she would have time over the next fortnight or so either. Shaking off her concerns, Rose moved about the room, rearranging and tidying discarded handkerchiefs, fans, and gloves. She could not allow herself to dwell on her parents' ongoing suffering and risk Mrs. Hayworth mistaking her concern for unhappiness over her new appointment.

A sharp, click-clack of shoes announced Lady Margaret Howard, the countess's favorite lady-in-waiting, as she entered the bedchamber. Rose immediately straightened and moved to the side, trying to remain inconspicuous. She had been intrigued by Lady Howard from the very first time she had seen her, even if she had yet to speak to her and was more than a little wary of her. With her dark hair severely parted at the center, pinned, plaited, and held in place with delicate lace netting at her nape, Lady Howard was an imposing figure. Pearls shone at her ears, throat, and wrists, a perfectly selected choice to wear with her midnight-blue dress. She was often smiling and always a comfort to the countess.

"Oh, Your Ladyship," Lady Howard exclaimed. "You look wonderful. Just wonderful."

"Thank you." The countess smiled at her confidante. "I need all the compliments possible to bolster me to face the earl tonight."

Rose's hand stilled on the handkerchief she folded. The countess was unhappy with her husband? They had seemed to be laughing or deep in conversation whenever Rose had seen them together so far. Unable to help herself, Rose strained her ears toward the conversation.

"Is something wrong, Christina?" Lady Howard frowned, her eyes darkening with concern. "Do you wish to speak to me privately? I'm sure Hayworth and her help won't mind leaving us."

"No, no," the countess said. "Both Hayworth and Watson can stay. Hayworth knows the earl well enough, and Watson will soon, no doubt. I trust them both to keep my confidence. His eye is wandering yet again, my darling, which I do not find particularly vexing or unusual, except this time the object of his desire is invited to dinner this evening. Albeit with her husband."

"So you must speak with her all evening? Oh, that is most unfair. Robert grows more insensitive with each passing day."

"Indeed, he does, but I will not be beaten."

Rose watched the countess in the dressing table mirror as Lady Howard stepped closer, her eyes bright with annoyance as she took Lady Christina's hand. They continued to talk quietly as Rose digested what had been said about the earl. Was she to understand this evening's guest was his lover? That he kept the company of other women? Married women? Or was it harmless flirtation? Could flirtation ever be harmless when it was a supposed respected member of the nobility who participated in it?

Carrying a box of pins to a bureau on the other side of the room, Rose furtively glanced at Her Ladyship as she passed her. Her wonderful smile had vanished, her cheeks paler than they had been all evening. Protectiveness grew inside Rose and mixed with a simmering hostility toward the earl, even though she had not yet met him.

Rose tightened her fingers around the box she held. The countess had given her an opportunity of such magnitude, she would have her allegiance and loyalty over the earl, whatever the circumstances. Lord Robert must be a fool of the highest order. How could he look elsewhere for companionship or beauty when the countess was the epitome of both?

"Watson, what are you doing?" Mrs. Hayworth's stern address made Rose jump as she swept up beside her. "Her Ladyship's conversation with her lady-in-waiting is none of your concern, and you certainly do not have time to be standing idly around," she whispered. "Now put those pins away and continue tidying up."

"I'm so sorry, Mrs. Hayworth."

"Is everything all right, Hayworth?"

Rose and Mrs. Hayworth faced the countess.

"Yes, Your Ladyship," Mrs. Hayworth said. "I was just giving Watson some instructions."

The countess smiled at Rose before walking to the full-length looking glass in the corner of the room. "If you were reprimanding

Watson for reacting to my chatter just now, it is misplaced. If my husband's activities and inclinations were anything of a secret within these apartments, I would not speak of them so openly. However..." She smoothed the front of her dress before tugging at the edges of her elbow-length gloves. "As his pursuits are public knowledge among most in this house, I have no issue with any of you present in this room knowing my feelings about my husband's lecherous activities... or how hurt I am by it. Besides—"

"Christina..." Lady Howard stared at Rose, her eyes darkening with mistrust. "I know you value your help, but I really don't think it appropriate that you—"

"Oh, Margaret..." The countess waved dismissively. "I am sure Watson will be as loyal to me as Hayworth. Isn't that right, Watson?"

Her knees slightly trembling from being singled out, Rose dipped her head. "Of course, Your Ladyship."

The countess's eyes sparkled with pleasure once more. "It is Watson who designed the dress you were exclaiming over last week, Margaret. She is to design more gowns for me. I have absolute confidence my wardrobe will be exceptional this season."

"Watson designed the dress? Well, I must say that is very impressive." Lady Howard came closer and stood in front of Rose, her gaze softening. "You are talented indeed, young lady. I look forward to seeing more of your designs."

"Thank you."

"Your family must be proud that you have found yourself working so closely with the countess."

"I... yes. They are very proud."

"As they should be." Lady Howard stepped back, her gaze gliding over Rose's face before she abruptly returned to the countess. "Once Her Ladyship trusts someone, she is loyal to that person's welfare beyond measure. You could do far worse than having the countess in your corner."

"Oh, Margaret." The countess laughed. "Why so serious? Leave poor Watson be." She sighed and looked at Rose, her eyes dimmed with defeat. "But you know, Watson, it is by no means a new phenomenon for a male member of the aristocracy or the royal family to take a mistress—or even three. In fact, the Queen herself took me aside before Lord Robert and I were wed and told me as much. What do you have to say about that?" The countess huffed a laugh. "Isn't it the most delightful thing for a young woman to come into one of the most renowned institutions in the world, entirely unsure of herself, and be warned by the Queen to expect infidelity from her husband in the future?"

Rose frowned as her indignation on the countess's behalf increased. "I can't imagine anything more undelightful, Your Ladyship."

The countess, Lady Howard, and Mrs. Hayworth all widened their eyes in surprise as they stared at her. Rose swallowed.

"You are absolutely right, darling girl, but the Queen is who she is, and what she expects for herself and what she expects for others are rarely the same."

The countess turned to speak with Lady Howard and Rose felt Mrs. Hayworth's hand on her lower back. "Have a care, Watson," she whispered. "We are servants. Don't make the mistake of ever thinking otherwise, no matter how kind the countess is to include us in conversation."

"Yes, Mrs. Hayworth."

The dresser retreated and Rose looked again at Lady Christina, vowing in that moment to do all she could to make her the most beautiful member of nobility Great Britain had ever seen.

Chapter Sixteen

Feet firmly planted, Henry whistled encouragement to the young colt circling the straw-strewn ground in a fenced area at the back of the mews.

"What is wrong with you?" he muttered as the horse executed the most insolent equine swagger he had ever seen. "For the love of God, you and I both know you are better than this."

Tugging on the lead rope, Henry's head ached, and his arms burned with fatigue. He was so tired he could not concentrate any more on training the horse than he could combing his hair that morning. It had been a long, mentally draining session at the card table the night before. To add insult to injury, he was almost six pounds down from what he had started with, meaning another few weeks of saving would be required before he'd have sufficient funds for an overseas passage.

The colt came to an abrupt stop, stubbornly flinging its head from left to right, snorting and hoofing the ground in defiance. Its saddle shifted as the animal's muscles tensed, the stirrups trembling against its sides.

"Think you're in charge here, do you?" Henry stormed forward. "Well, you're wrong, sunshine. Damn wrong." He tugged on the horse's halter so their eyes were level, their heated breaths mixing. "Now you listen to me, you good-for-nothing lump, you do as I have taught you or we are seriously going to fall out. That, my friend, is something you do *not* want to happen."

The horse snorted a rank cloud of hot breath into Henry's face before lifting its head, teeth showing, as though laughing uproariously.

"Right, that's it. You are in big—"

"Training going well, is it?" Charles entered the space, his smile wide. "I suspect that young whippersnapper thought you were of the mind to kiss him. Anyone faced with such a prospect is bound to rear and buck away. Wouldn't you say?"

Henry briefly closed his eyes and swallowed the choice words instructing his uncle to turn around and walk back to wherever he had come from. "Best you leave me to it, Uncle," he said firmly. "Me and His Lordship here are just getting a few things straightened out."

"I'll leave soon enough. I need a word with you first."

Biceps straining against the effort, Henry used both hands to grip the lead rope and once again pulled the horse's head down so they were eye to eye. The youngster fought and snorted, swishing its mane back and forth over its sleek black coat glistening with sweat. Sooner or later, he would understand who was in charge.

Charles cleared his throat. "So, this word…"

Henry focused on the horse, the hint of reproach in his uncle's voice worsening the state of Henry's already fragile temper.

"I gather from your landlady it was another late one last night."

"My God." Henry sighed. "I've got to contend with Mrs. Baxter telling tales on me now too? Give me strength."

"I bumped into her coming along the street. Unfortunately, your aunt was with me."

Henry closed his eyes.

"And you know I won't have you or your cousins upsetting my wife. No matter how old you might be. She worries about all you kids the same, and you have no idea what it's like to have an irate wife hissing in your ear into the early hours as she frets over every little thing the three of you are doing, day in, day out."

Henry avoided his uncle's accusatory stare as he strode to the side of the training ground. "Well, I'll do better ensuring Mrs. Baxter doesn't hear me come into the lodgings at the end of an evening."

"That, my boy, is beside the point."

The firm tone of Charles's voice drew Henry to a stop, and he turned.

His uncle pointed at him. "If you're so hell-bent on losing all your money over and over, that's your prerogative, but when it starts affecting my household, enough's enough."

Henry ignored the trickle of trepidation sliding down his spine. "Meaning?"

"It stops now, or you find somewhere else to live. Elizabeth loves having you so close by, but by God, having you a few doors down the road makes it damn hard to avoid her learning what you are up to."

"You want me to move lodgings?" Henry huffed a laugh. "It's not that easy, Uncle."

Charles's somber expression caused a deep hollowness in Henry's chest. His uncle was serious. Henry's lifestyle had finally pushed Charles to breaking point and there was little use in denying that his uncle, aunt, and cousins deserved better from him. Much better.

"Fine. I'll behave from now on, all right?" he said, holding his uncle's gaze. "Last night got a little messy, that's all."

As Henry untied the rope from the horse's halter, Charles's glare bore into his back. Tension stretched between them. A cruel, biting headache beat at Henry's temples, and his eyes watered with tiredness. He slowly coiled the rope, then hitched it over a post on the fence before working off the halter and hitching that over the post too.

"Your eyes are bloodshot, your clothes are a mess, you have less and less money—"

"All right, I get it," Henry retorted sharply as he spun around, squaring up to his uncle. "I'll sort myself out. If I'm going to be that late again, I'll find a pal to bunk down with so no one sees me coming back to my place. No problem."

"No problem?"

Charles's eyes blazed with anger. Worse, they glinted with disappointment and frustration, but Henry did not look away or step back, even as he trembled with suppressed frustration and self-disgust. Over and over again he failed Charles and himself, yet Henry's dream never changed, and neither did his uncle's wish for him to take over as the earl's master saddler. Therein lay the root of the problem between them, and Henry could see no end to it until he was gone.

"Do you know what?" Charles asked, stepping back and raising his hands in surrender. "I've had enough of trying to make you see sense. There is so much you don't appreciate about your life, Henry Ward. So much."

"And there are only so many times I can tell you I am grateful for what you and my aunt did for me, and what you still do for me, but staying here in a state of perpetual gratitude isn't fair to me, Uncle. Not by a long shot."

"Is that so?"

Henry's heart beat faster as the anger in his uncle's gaze grew more potent, his mouth drawn into a thin line.

"I don't know what else you want me to say," Henry said, shaking his head and grabbing a bridle from the fence, starting the task of putting it on the colt. "But that's the way it is."

"'That's the way it is?'" Charles's voice was ice-cold. "Are you serious?"

Henry lifted his shoulders, thinking it best not to respond, considering the color that had risen in his uncle's face.

"My God, Henry, you can be a real piece of work. Your craftmanship is exceptional and when you love someone, you love unconditionally, but God above, sometimes I see parts of your father in you."

Henry's defenses slammed into place, one by one like pieces of armor. He retrieved a set of reins from beside him and snapped them to the bit, thankful his young trainee had decided not to fight him for once.

"I know how you feel about my father. There's no need—"

"There's every bloody need when you are a son to me. Stop throwing your future away at the gaming tables. Don't end up in debt and owing money left, right, and center to people who won't accept you messing them about like he did."

"I don't borrow. I lose what is mine to lose, not a penny more."

"For now, but you're already caught up in what you're doing, and this path could lead you anywhere. Your father ended up losing everything, Henry, and you're headed the same way. Why do you think you, your ma, and her sluggard of a husband came to live with us, eh?"

Henry swallowed, the hairs on his nape prickling with warning. "My ma was ill. She needed her sister to care for her."

"That's what it came to in the end, son, but that is not where it started."

"What are you talking about?"

"I'm talking about your father."

"What about him?"

"Once he was married and your ma was expecting you, your aunt couldn't stand him continuing to gamble as he had when he was young, free, and single. Your ma knew how far into the game he was, but she married him anyway. She and your aunt fell out over your father and didn't speak for years. *Years*. And their estrangement suited your father just fine because it meant he could keep your mother and you as he saw fit."

"Isn't that what any husband wants to do for his family?" Henry tried to sound unimpressed, but his heart hammered with the knowledge that Charles hadn't finished what he wanted to say, that the contempt he felt for Henry's father was as raw today as it had always been. "Just let it lie, Uncle. Whatever my father was, he left years ago."

"Yes, he did... after he'd spent every damn penny he had, and his family was living on the streets!"

"What?"

"You heard me. The families you help across town whenever you're feeling flush? Well, those cobbles were home to you for a few weeks until your mother got ill, and your father finally gave in and allowed her to ask my Elizabeth for help." Charles's eyes bulged with anger and frustration. "Your mother came to her sister's home to die, Henry, and your father let it happen because his love for the tables was more important than his own damn family."

Henry swallowed against the bile that rose in his throat, his mind reeling.

"And," Charles continued, his finger pointed at Henry, "you've got the same hunger for risk, the same hunger for an easy quid or two as he had. God help you if you go the same route as him and kick all I'm offering you back in my face."

Disgust and disappointment filled Henry. "I don't believe you."

"Then don't, but deep down you know I'd never lie to you."

Anger at his father, anger at Charles, anger at himself pulsed inside Henry.

"Maybe you're right and it is for the best that you leave Henlow House," his uncle said quietly. "Leave London. The last thing I want is for Elizabeth to have another man who supposedly loved her sister spiral into the bloody abyss."

Retaliating words flailed like knife blades on Henry's tongue. He wanted to lash out, to hurt Charles as his words had hurt him, but to do that Henry would have to pull a lie from somewhere, while his uncle had only spoken the truth.

"Damn it," Henry growled, humiliation igniting pathetic insolence. "I don't need this." He thrust his foot into the stirrup and flung himself astride the horse, desperate to feel in control, to feel speed, to feel the power and muscle of a truly magnificent beast as it galloped around the track without heed or thought.

The horse took off, kicking up sand, dirt, and straw as his uncle leaped backward.

"For the love of God, man! What are you doing?"

Faster and faster, Henry urged the horse on. Around and around the training circle, kicking in his heels and urging the fiery horse onward. Charles stood at the fence, now a blur in Henry's peripheral vision as he ignored his uncle's frantic waving. It was too late. Everything was too late. He was nothing more than a wastrel just as his father had been before him.

He hated himself, hated his father. On and on, faster and faster. He had to outrun his anger, his failures.

Without warning, the colt let out a bloodcurdling scream, stopped, and reared, its front legs clawing at the air, its ears flat. Henry gritted his teeth and fought to regain control, the muscles in his arms and thighs burning.

The horse dropped and then reared again.

As Henry slid from the saddle, he grasped the reins, but it was useless. He fell, pulling the horse with him. A gigantic thud reverberated through his body and slammed his teeth together. His shoulder hit the ground first, followed by a blinding pain in his leg as he landed on straw, the horse collapsing onto his lower half and winding him.

Somewhere in the distance he thought he heard breaking bone. Then the world went black.

Chapter Seventeen

Rose carefully hung one of the countess's dresses in her wardrobe and shut the door. She glanced at the clock above the mantel. Her duties were almost done for the afternoon, and then she would have the rest of the day and evening to work on the dress design she hoped Lady Christina would think perfect for an upcoming garden party at Henlow House.

"Ah, there you are." Mrs. Hayworth hurried into the dressing room, looking more than a little harried. "Rose, I'm sorry, I know I promised you some time to yourself this afternoon, but the mother-of-pearl buttons I was expecting to be delivered have not arrived. I need you to go into town and collect them."

"Of course." Rose followed Mrs. Hayworth from the room into the countess's bedchamber. "Where do I need to go?"

"Here. I've written down the address for you." Mrs. Hayworth handed her two pieces of paper. "And this is the order. It is all paid for, so you should have no problems. Go to the mews where I have arranged for a gig to be waiting for you. Whichever groom or stable hand drives you, give him the address. He is sure to know the shop."

Rose nodded, her stomach filling with treacherous butterflies at the possibility of seeing Henry again. She had no idea why the thought of him caused her spirits to lift, but he had not drifted far from her mind these last few days. She had recollected his startling green eyes, and his dark-blond hair combed back from his ridiculously chiseled face—

"Off you go, then, my dear," Mrs. Hayworth said. "I'm sorry to do this to you at such short notice, but I will find a way to ensure you have ample time to work on your designs. Don't you worry. Now, make sure you wrap up warmly. It's deceptively chilly outside."

Rose left the apartments, smiling over her growing fondness for Mrs. Hayworth. She really had been so generous in her welcome and integrating Rose into the countess's household. Rose wanted nothing more than for their working relationship to flourish over time. Hurrying through the corridors and down several flights of stairs, she reached her room and quickly washed her face and hands, then donned her coat and hat. With a final pinch of her cheeks to bring a blush to them, Rose hurried from the grand house for the mews.

She stepped outside and was immediately assaulted by a blast of blustery April wind. Sucking in a breath, she ducked her head and strode quickly toward the stables, still hoping Henry would be the one to drive her so she might have the chance to encourage further friendship between them. She would like to have him as her comrade-in-arms, so if they needed each other, he would be there for her and she for him. The combination of the way she'd caught him looking at her, his quick intelligence, and that he cared enough to ask her questions about her life made Henry Ward entirely appealing… which was undoubtedly dangerous thinking.

She drew closer to the open double doors of the stables, and a cacophony of tense, raised voices and neighing filled the air. It wasn't coming from the stables, but from the area behind. Something appeared to be amiss.

Rose slowed her steps. The men's shouts flew from every direction, and they were far from happy. Nerves leaped in her stomach, but she purposefully lifted her chin. She had to face whatever happened in her future with confidence and independence. Otherwise, her mother's fears for her safety and happiness would be justified.

Striding forward, she rounded the corner and stopped.

Chaos reigned.

Men stalked back and forth, leading horses this way and that. A commotion of yelling, pointing fingers, and running was at full steam in a straw-strewn area Rose imagined was used for some sort of training or exercising.

"Can I help you, miss?" An older man stopped beside her, his eyes agitated and his brow glistening with perspiration despite the chill of the late afternoon. "You shouldn't be here."

"What has happened?" Rose stepped to the side as a groom brushed past her with a horse a whole two heads taller than her. "Why is everyone in such a panic?"

"Not panic, miss, but we are out of sorts. There was an accident just an hour past, and all work came to a standstill, so every one of us is behind in our duties. Now, what can I—"

"An accident?"

"Yes." The man hefted the bale of hay he carried, the agitation in his gaze escalating. "What are you doing here?"

Rose stared in the direction of the commotion in the strawed area, a horrible weight forming low in her stomach. "There should be a gig waiting for me. I work for the countess's dresser and need someone to take me into town." She turned back to the man. "Was someone hurt?"

"Yes." He gave a curt nod. "I'll go see about that gig."

He moved to walk away, and Rose touched his arm.

"Sir, wait."

The agitation in his eyes now bordered on outright annoyance. "I'm sorry, miss, but I really must get on."

"Who was it?" she asked.

"Who was what?"

"Who was hurt?"

He frowned, his annoyance turning to suspicion as he lowered the bale to the ground and fisted his hands on his hips. "Have you got an interest in one of the lads that works in the mews, young lady? Only cause it don't seem right that you—"

"I am merely asking out of concern for a fellow human being, sir," Rose said, tilting her chin as though utterly offended. In truth, she did have a definite interest in one of the lads who worked here. A perplexing, puzzling interest but an interest all the same.

"It was one of the saddlers, if you must know." He sighed. "One of our finest. He also happens to be a fine horse trainer but, considering the state he was in when he came to work this morning, he should not have been on that horse at all, let alone galloping her around at that speed."

Was it Henry? Rose swallowed against the dryness in her throat. "The state he was in?"

"Aye. I don't reckon he'd had more than three hours' sleep, had bags the size of marrows beneath his eyes. Henry Ward is an enemy unto himself if you ask me. Up all night gambling and Lord only knows what else, then coming in for a full day's work. He is either the most hardworking, loyal-to-the-crown man you're ever likely to meet, or he's a bloody fool hell-bent on getting himself into an early grave."

Rose's heart picked up speed. "What happened to him?"

"He was flung off and the horse fell on him, likely broke his leg, but we can't be sure. He was taken to St. Mary's Hospital about an hour ago." He lifted the bale off the ground. "Now, you stay put, and I'll see about that gig."

"Yes. Thank you."

Rose blindly stared around, images of Henry playing in her mind. She could see him smiling and that damnable, toe-curling way he had of winking at her and, no doubt, a hundred other women. The irrefutable concern she'd seen in his eyes when he'd witnessed her upset in front of her parents.

A gambler. Could it be true? Was that who Henry really was? A man like her brother? Henry had spoken of such fantastical plans for his future, whereas Gideon had always made her laugh with his insistence that the only way to live was not thinking past one day to the next. Henry's desire to travel abroad had inspired her to take her own risks, her own leaps of faith. But was he reckless rather than ambitious?

Heat seeped into Rose's cheeks and tears pricked her eyes as her potential naivete grew along with her indisputable care for a man who was little more than a stranger, yet reminded her, for better or worse, so much of her beloved brother. A man who lived to shake up the world and make the most of every minute. A man for whom her care had deepened, and her concern escalated. Now she knew what being like Gideon might ultimately mean for Henry, and what having feelings for such a man might mean for her.

Chapter Eighteen

After a few days of convalescence, which resulted in innumerable hours of boredom, Henry leaned back from the crudely constructed workbench in front of him, gritting his teeth against the slash of pain that shot up his leg, and stared at his bandaged limb. As much as he appreciated that Charles and some of the other stable workers had put the bench together so he could return to work, annoyance and barely contained frustration burned inside him. It had been just under a week since the accident—or the purposeful, bone-headed incident, as his uncle liked to call it—and he was still at Henlow House, still living down the street from Charles and his family. Everything in his life, everything in his plans, and everything in his usual routine had ground to an unceremonious halt. And it was all his fault.

Henry splayed his hand on his thigh and shifted his leg to the left, providing himself with minimal relief. Fortunately, the crack he'd heard before he passed out had not been a bone breaking, but a stirrup strap snapping. He was grateful to have avoided any broken bones, but he was bandaged up regardless. According to the doctor, the ligament damage, especially behind his knee, was severe enough that there would be no riding or training for a good couple of months. As for the beautiful, stubborn colt he'd been charged with training, he was doing just fine and dandy. The horse has gotten himself off an unconscious Henry, unaided, and was prancing around the training ring without a care in the world moments later.

Henry scowled. "Damn bloody horse. Damn bloody leg."

"You can sit there cussing and muttering to yourself as much as you want. It won't make that leg heal any faster."

Henry met Charles's gaze across the workroom. "For your information, I'm cussing and muttering to *myself*, so there's no need to bother yourself joining in the conversation."

Charles smirked and returned his concentration to his work. "I'm just saying, that's all."

A discreet feminine cough at the open workshop door turned Henry's head before his heart promptly leaped into his throat. Rose Watson stood there watching him, a soft smile playing at her lips.

He swallowed and started to stand from his chair to reach for the walking cane beside him. "Miss Watson."

She raised her hand. "No, please. Don't move on my account." She walked closer, her beautiful eyes flitting from his face to his leg and back again. "I have been meaning to come see you for days, but I either couldn't get away from my duties or fretted that my visiting might not be welcome."

Henry couldn't drag his eyes from hers as undeniable pleasure filled him at the knowledge she had thought of him—had wanted to see him. God only knew why she would ever think that visiting him would not be welcomed. She was like a breath of fresh air every time he saw her.

Exhaling, he lowered back into his seat. "A visit from you will always be welcome, Miss Watson." He coughed, immediately regretting speaking so honestly in front of Charles. He glanced at him, and his uncle flashed a knowing smile, his arms folded and an undeniable glint of amusement in his eyes. Henry snapped his attention back to Rose and tilted his head in Charles's direction. "Any distraction is welcome if it means a few minutes reprieve from *his* endless chitchat. Rose Watson, this is my uncle, Charles Summers."

She smiled. "Pleased to meet you."

His uncle touched his cap. "Likewise, miss."

Henry narrowed his eyes at Charles, willing him to wipe away his stupid smile. The man looked as if he was at a damn fairground, watching the best show he'd seen in months.

"Henry?"

He switched his gaze to Rose.

She placed her fingers on the basket over her arm. "I've brought you some lunch. Just some bread and cheese, a slice of cake. Do you have time to eat with me? I have enough for us both." She looked at Charles and grimaced. "I'm sorry. I didn't know… but I'm sure there is enough to go around." She put the basket on the makeshift worktable. "Or maybe I should leave you both to it. I only wanted to see how you were faring."

"You stay right where you are, young miss," Charles said. "Maybe you can talk some sense into him. Henry has no idea how lucky he was not to have broken his back after that fall, not to mention all the other things he should be grateful for in his life."

"I'll certainly do my best."

"That's all any of us can do by my nephew, I'm afraid." Charles turned. "And you can wipe that scowl off your face too, lad. You've got a beautiful lady come visiting with food. What more is there to put a smile on a man's face?" He lifted his hand and smacked his forehead. "How could I forget? There are far more appealing things in the world. Training horses abroad, throwing money away…"

Henry pressed his lips together, trapping the words biting his tongue. Why in God's name would he say that in front of Rose? The abhorrence in Charles's tone was palpable. Their gazes locked, the tension between them rising once again. A pulse beat in Henry's temple as his uncle's cheeks darkened before he abruptly faced Rose.

"He's all yours," Charles said.

Henry clenched his fist on his thigh and glared after Charles as he sauntered from the workshop.

"There seems to be some trouble between you and your uncle," Rose said, questions in her eyes. "Are you all right?"

"I'm fine. We were having cross words before my accident. Hence why I flew off that horse at eighty knots. But his bad temper is more about his care for me than anger."

"I see."

Henry feigned interest in the view through the open stable doors. The last thing he wanted was for Rose to witness the ugliness that stirred up in him frequently since his fall. His tetchiness was founded in the infernal pain and frustration provoked by his gammy leg, and it would be far safer for Rose to go. Except that was the last thing he wanted.

"I'd probably best leave." She sighed. "But I am not one for always doing what I should, especially when the situation involves men making decisions that result in them falling on their backsides or worse."

A smile pulled at Henry's mouth as she whipped the cloth from atop the basket and set about taking out white porcelain plates, followed by parcels of food wrapped in brown paper.

"I know we haven't known each other very long, but you've had me worried since I learned of your horse-riding shenanigans."

His smile widened. "My 'horse-riding shenanigans'?"

"What else would you call what happened? You would hardly be sitting with your leg suspended and bandaged had you shown competent horsemanship."

He laughed for the first time in days. "Ouch."

Grinning, she turned away from him and filled two plates with bread and cheese and then poured water from a bottle into two mugs. Finally, she reached into the basket and extracted a linen cloth, which she draped over her arm. She picked up one of the plates and a mug.

"Here," she said as she approached him. "Put..." Her gaze fell on the saddle beside him, and her eyes widened. "Did you make that?"

The awe in her eyes filled him with pride, and he shamelessly puffed out his chest. "I did. Do you like it?"

"It's beautiful." She stared at the saddle before putting down the plate and cup. Glancing at him again, she walked over to it and smoothed her fingers over the intricate pattern lining the edge of the brown leather. "You are an exceptional craftsman, Henry. Truly."

"Thank you."

"Who are you making it for?"

"His Lordship."

"It's wonderful." She finally met his eyes and held out the cloth from her arm. "Put that on your lap."

He took the cloth, and she walked back to the plate and cup. Picking them up, she returned to him, her eyes flitting to the saddle again. She offered him the food and drink.

"Here."

"Thank you."

Henry could not look away from her as she returned to the bench and retrieved the second plate and mug. She was a fine-looking woman, her dark-brown hair shining in the semi-lit room, her slender figure, her height, and her bosom just right.

She sat down beside him with her food. "Eat up."

They ate in silence for a few moments, their eyes catching every now and then with the odd smile. The atmosphere was surprisingly companionable, rather than awkward, as Henry had feared. She was here caring for and feeding him, and he felt a deep gratitude toward her. One he was too embarrassed to share.

"So," he said, before clearing his throat. "You've been worried about me, have you?"

"Only a little, so you can wipe that self-satisfied look off your face." Her cheeks flushed, her eyes happy. "It is somewhat confusing, but the small amount of time I've spent with you has returned to my mind more than once."

"Oh?"

"Also…"

"There's more?"

"Well, I have hardly gotten to know anyone since I've been working here, so you are good company for the time being."

"The time being? That's quite the compliment, I must say."

"It is. I especially like spending time with you because you don't expect anything from me. I don't have to pretend with you," she confessed.

"Pretend? Now there's a word that sits in my conscience quite familiarly. Sometimes my whole life feels like pretense."

She studied him with her beautiful caramel eyes. "In what way?"

"Henlow House, this work, this life… I want more than doing the same thing day in and day out. More than marriage and children."

Her gaze sobered, her eyes steady on his. "If you consider such things beneath you, I don't think you'll ever be happy. In fact, I think that's why I feel so untroubled in your company. You don't put expectations on me because you don't put any on yourself."

He laughed. "How wrong you are! I have expectations so big they cannot be contained in a single country."

"Hmm, maybe," she said, her tone sounding far from impressed by his fervent claim. "But for now, you're my…"

His heart beat faster. "Your what?"

Her eyes sparkled with clear provocation. "Light relief."

"Your…" He didn't know whether to be pleased or insulted. He wanted her to be relaxed around him, of course he did, but it would've also been nice if he evoked a little more than temporary amusement. He ripped off a chunk of bread and put it in his mouth, carefully watching her bowed head as she concentrated on her plate. "So if I'm not putting expectations on you, who is? The countess? Mrs. Hayworth?"

"Oh, the countess and Mrs. Hayworth have been nothing but kind to me. I am talking about my family's expectations, I suppose. Theirs and mine. I want to succeed here. I have to."

"You *have* to?"

"Yes." Sadness dimmed her eyes. "Especially since I've learned why it was so hard for my parents to let me come here. I owe them even more for trusting me and giving me their blessing to take this opportunity. I will not forsake them."

"I would've thought your parents would be pushing you out your shop door for such an opportunity."

She shook her head. "I shouldn't speak of it."

Henry studied her, his concern growing, but he would not press her. "Can I at least ask why you said you won't forsake them?" He ate a bite of cheese. "Because I can't see you ever forsaking anyone. You are too good. Too *loyal*."

She looked at him sharply. "You say that as though allegiance is a vice rather than a virtue."

He shrugged. "I'm just saying I can't imagine you would ever abandon or turn your back on your family."

"I definitely wouldn't." She narrowed her eyes. "Would you turn your back on yours?"

"No. In fact, when I finally manage to leave and get work, I'll regularly send money back to my family. They've been good to me—more than good—and despite my uncle thinking I'm not grateful for all he and my aunt have done for me, I am."

Pleasure softened her gaze. "I'm pleased to hear it." She looked at the saddle again, her smile dissolving. "Can I ask you something?"

He followed her gaze. "Of course."

She faced him and seemed to hesitate, a slight color coming into her cheeks. "This is a rather impertinent request…"

He smiled, entirely charmed by her uncertainty. "Go on."

"Would you…" She screwed up her nose. "Possibly consider helping me with some stitching? It wouldn't be much. It's just that my time working on my designs for the countess hasn't been what I'd hoped because of the busyness of running her apartments. You can say no, I'd completely under—"

"I can do that." He smiled and raised his eyebrows. "If you really think stitching leather and stitching silks and satins fall under the same aptitude."

She grinned, her shoulders lowering. "Oh, they most definitely do. In fact, I'd go so far as to say what I do is far easier than what you do. It won't be anything particularly fancy, but your help would mean a huge saving of my spare time, and what I can and can't get done."

"Then I'm happy to help when I can."

"That would be wonderful." Her gaze settled on his. "Thank you, Henry."

"My pleasure." He quickly looked away lest he completely fall into the beauty of her caramel eyes and never find his way back again.

"So," she said, "marrying and children isn't on your agenda?"

He met her gaze. "I've never given it much thought."

"But isn't marrying and having children why we are here? Don't you want to fall in love? Have a chance of living in a home with your loved ones, united against the world?"

The delight in her eyes, the romance in her words, poked at his heart but did not penetrate it. Could she not hear how fanciful her imaginings sounded? How unlikely such human connection between two people really was?

He lifted his eyebrows. "Don't you think you're looking at things a little off-kilter? I saw you with your parents, and you did not look as though being with them made your heart sing."

The happiness in her eyes vanished. "Maybe not in that moment, but I still love them. I still need them and will always want them in my life."

God, she was such a good person. Far too good for the likes of him.

She dabbed her mouth with a napkin, her gaze thoughtful. "I plan to work as hard as I can toward making a living by creating clothes of my design and then hopefully meet someone, fall in love, and have a family with him." She pinned him with a determined stare. "And I'll still work, of course."

"Well, of course." He forced a smile, more than a little perturbed by the unexpected jolt that ran through him when she'd mentioned meeting someone and falling in love. The jolt had felt far too much like jealousy of whoever that someone might be.

She laughed and took his plate from his lap. "Why do I get the impression you don't believe working *and* having a family is possible for me, Henry Ward?" she asked, picking up her plate, too, and returning it to the basket.

"Oh, I believe it's possible," he said, wincing as he stretched out his leg. "I believe you'll achieve anything and everything you desire."

"Good, because I have dreams, wants, and wishes, but my family is part of them too." She faced him. "I think you'll come to regret not making your family a part of your plans."

"I told you I intend to send them money, Rose." He closed his eyes, hating that once again she was making him feel inadequate, making him want to be a better man. "I'm not pushing them away." He opened his eyes. "I'm choosing to leave England. That's all."

She put the second mug into the basket and re-laid the cloth on top before hitching the basket on her arm. "Which is fine, but you should reassure your uncle that you're not leaving for good." She frowned. "Maybe someone has walked out on him before, and it still pains him."

Henry stared at her. *His father.* Could Charles fear that his nephew would also disappear and never come back? Never write? Shame twisted in Henry's chest. Of course he did. *God, I am such a blind fool.*

"I better get back to the house, but I could come back later this evening if you are able to help me with some work." She grimaced. "Too soon?"

"If anyone else asked it would be." He winked. "For you, this evening is absolutely perfect."

The blush he loved leaped into her cheeks, and she bobbed a semi-curtsy. "Then I will see you later, sir."

Henry laughed as he watched her hurry from the stables.

Chapter Nineteen

Rose emerged from the room that had been assigned to her as a dedicated workspace, a place she could fully concentrate on the countess's wardrobe whenever time allowed. Time had allowed the night before, and she'd been helped by Henry.

Her stomach gave a telling tumble. The entire time they'd been together, working side by side, talking and laughing, had been wonderful. Heat warmed Rose's cheeks—pride mixed with apprehension—and she smoothed the skirt laying over her arm.

With a quick glance at the ornate clock hanging over the fireplace, Rose gasped and hurried from the room for Lady Christina's apartments. Her Ladyship and Lord Robert were hosting a dinner for their circle of close friends, and the countess planned to wear the skirt Rose had designed especially for the occasion. It was the least formal a meal at an aristocratic residence would ever be, considering how extravagantly the earl and countess usually dressed for dinner, and Mrs. Hayworth had decided to pair the skirt with a simple ivory silk blouse.

Although Rose hoped her more elaborate pieces would soon take center stage as the beginning of the season drew closer, the skirt was her current pride and joy. Deep plum, it was decorated with hand-stitched flowers and foliage from hem to mid-thigh and finished with a flock of small birds in flight along one side. To say she was nervous for the countess's reaction was an understatement.

Stopping at the entrance corridor to Lady Christina's apartments, Rose inhaled deeply as nerves gripped her. She wanted to keep her position as the countess's garment maker more than anything else in the world, and the only way to ensure that happened was to hold fast to her courage and fully embrace her ambition. To falter in any way was not an option.

Henry's face came unbidden into her mind and Rose shook her head, frustrated that he edged into her thoughts whenever she felt the slightest cowardice. Yes, he was brave and impulsive, and, yes, that made him somewhat exciting, but he was also a gambler and undoubtedly prone to foolhardiness as much as her brother had been. Foolhardiness that had brought her feelings of fondness until she learned how Gideon really died. That same quality she had found mildly amusing in Henry before, now felt nothing short of terrifying.

No matter their mutual hankering for a bigger life, deep inside—where personal values lingered—Henry's traits were a thousand miles from hers, and there was no saying whether he ran the risk of ending up in an early grave alongside her brother. The glint in his eyes, his quick smile and devil-may-care observations stirred her more than they should, but they stirred her all the same.

She briefly closed her eyes before standing tall. Now was not the time to be dwelling on the complexities of Henry Ward. His craftsmanship on the earl's saddle had been as exquisite as it was extraordinary, likewise the work he had done for her yesterday evening. In truth, Henry was a far superior stitcher than she would ever be, and that knowledge did not offend her one iota. What offended her was his inability to love his talent; but what right did she have to name what he should or should not love? If horses brought Henry joy and fulfillment, passion and possibility over saddle work, then that was what he should pursue.

Taking a strengthening breath, Rose resumed her walk to Lady Christina's apartments.

"Ah, Watson. Good evening."

Rose started before she quickly sank into a curtsy at the sound of Lady Christina's voice behind her. "Your Ladyship, good evening."

The countess flashed a brief smile, her gaze distracted as she glanced at the closed apartment door. "I'm so glad to see you. Mrs. Hayworth was threatening to send out a search party if you were not here by the time myself and my ladies returned. Come along now." The countess led the way into the apartments, Lady Howard and two other ladies-in-waiting following behind.

Once inside, Mrs. Hayworth rushed forward, the countess and her ladies continuing past them, deep in laughing conversation. "Watson, thank goodness. You are late."

"I'm so sorry, Mrs. Hayworth. I wanted to make sure the skirt was perfect for this evening."

Mrs. Hayworth raised her eyebrows. "And is it?"

"Oh, yes. Most definitely."

"Wonderful."

Rose carefully laid the skirt on the bed and stood back, her hands on her hips. She could not have done any better. Walking to the wardrobe, she retrieved the ivory silk blouse hanging on the door.

"Oh, Watson," Mrs. Hayworth whispered. "It is indeed perfect."

Rose smiled at the admiration on Mrs. Hayworth's face.

"It's just wonderful, my dear," she said, stepping closer to touch the material. "Her Ladyship will be thrilled. I will suggest she accessorize with pearls. Yes, pearls will be perfect." Her eyes shone with happiness. "I am so glad I convinced the countess you were the right person to make her clothes this season. Opportunity should be open to all, and talent like yours deserves recognition." She squeezed Rose's hand. "Your future is bright, my dear. Very bright indeed."

"I really hope so, Mrs. Hayworth." Rose looked at the skirt, happiness swirling inside her.

"If the countess comes to wear your designs in public, who knows what the future holds for you? You could garner quite a name one day. Your talent has been esteemed by nobility, and that is something to behold," Mrs. Hayworth said firmly. "To take such appreciation for granted, to assume it as nothing significant, would be a grave mistake for anyone to make."

"Oh, I certainly realize that," Rose said vehemently, her mind once more turning to Henry. *Even if I get the impression others do not.*

"Good, because working for anyone who is part of the aristocracy almost certainly means there is a future position waiting for your children. That, Watson, is nothing to be sniffed at when poverty is such a continual threat to so many."

The chatter next door escalated, the exclamations of Lady Christina and her ladies growing louder.

Mrs. Hayworth glanced at the open door. "I should make sure Her Ladyship does not need me for anything. Oh…" She faced Rose again. "I told her how you have been working on your designs every free moment, and she has agreed that you can have an extra day or two to yourself, considering your dedication over the last few weeks."

"That would be wonderful." Rose's heart swelled at the thought of seeing her parents again. "It feels like such a long time since I've been home."

"You can leave first thing in the morning. I will remind the countess of your absence again later."

As Mrs. Hayworth left the room and Rose stared after her, Henry once again intruded on her thoughts. They were both commoners living and working in an official residence, brought together by chance, and serving two of the most eminent people in the country. They got on well, laughed often, and had big ambitions. Was it really such a surprise that she found herself so drawn to him and was growing to trust him? Or was she heading along a foolish path?

Rose fingered the intricately stitched flowers at the hem of the skirt, an audacious idea forming in her mind. He was such a talented stitcher. A master, really. He could turn his needle to anything, she was sure. After all, she had seen the whorls and swirls at the edges of the earl's saddle, and the work he had done for her the night before. Maybe he just needed some distance from his uncle for a while. Some time to really think about his next steps. Rose had planned her design aspirations at night after the shop was closed, and her parents were fast asleep. In notepads and sketch books, she had planned each step to her success until every detail was succinctly drawn, and then her life had taken the most unexpected turn.

Her idea gathered plausibility in her mind.

Surely Lady Christina would be even happier with her if she could guarantee more dresses, skirts, and jackets in less time? Rose slowly smiled, convinced Henry would come to see sense in her idea.

"Watson, quickly!" Mrs. Hayworth waved at her from the doorway. "Did you not hear me calling you? Her Ladyship would like to see the skirt. Hurry now."

Rose quickly picked up the skirt and carefully drew it over her arm before following Mrs. Hayworth into the next room.

Chapter Twenty

Henry slapped his hands together and laughed, satisfaction filling his gut even as his injured leg caused him to rise somewhat awkwardly from the gaming table in the small, dark room at the back of The Crown. His eyes were stinging from the cigar and pipe smoke hovering in long white-gray streaks around him, and his cane clattered to the floor from where it had been propped against the table.

"Thank you, gentlemen," he shouted above the din as he leaned forward to scrape his newly acquired coins and notes, the odd trinket, and a silver cigarette case toward him. "It's been an absolute pleasure."

With his gammy leg and slightly inebriated state, Henry grimaced as he struggled to keep his balance, even while relishing the groans and curses of his fellow players. He had a horrible feeling that this afternoon would be his last time at the tables for a while. It was just too damn hard when his leg throbbed with pain, and his entire body ached with the strain of sitting still and concentrating. God alive. He couldn't train horses, and now he couldn't gamble. It felt as though the whole damn world was against him.

He noticed the odd drinker looking at him with curiosity in their eyes and quickly forced a laugh. "What's the matter with you all?" He licked his index finger and made a show of counting the notes. "I've been otherwise engaged for a week. You've had as good a chance as any to win a pretty penny in my absence. But now I'm back, so you'll have to step up your game again. Simple as that."

More curses, a couple of beer mats thrown in his direction, and even a clip up the side of his head were duly distributed as the men passed him on their way to the door.

"Not bad," Henry murmured, his smile genuine as he tucked the notes into the inside pocket of his jacket and turned his attention to the decent amount of coinage still laid out in front of him. "Not bad at all."

"Think you might need an escort when you leave, my friend." Amos strolled into the room and started to clear the tankards and glasses strewn on tables and along the wooden shelving that lined the walls. "Your name is mud out there."

Henry grinned, his eyes still on his loot, the pain in his leg slowly lessening to a manageable ache. "I couldn't care less if mud is my new middle name. I've cleaned up this afternoon and would love to come back tonight for some more, but my leg is giving me aggravation like you wouldn't believe."

"Then maybe your fall has provided something worthwhile after all if it keeps you away from the tables for a couple of weeks."

Henry rolled his eyes. "If you can't share in my good fortune, go back in the bar with the rest of them."

"Good fortune? Come on, Henry. You know this is the first big win you've had in a long time."

"The past is the past and a win is a win."

"Yeah, and I'm guessing the money you gambled with this afternoon was scraped together on a wing and a prayer."

Henry tumbled the coins into a thick leather pouch he kept tied to his belt loop. "I earn a good enough wage at Henlow House, and now I'm…" He swallowed. Good God, he had nearly blurted about the one or two jobs he had worked on for Rose. That would've been a really stupid thing to do when he knew all too well how Amos and Charles liked to natter about him. If his uncle got wind of the couple of nights Rose had joined Henry after dark in the stables, he'd burst a blood vessel.

"Now you're what?" Amos asked, his brow creased with a frown.

Henry cleared his throat and shrugged. "Now I'm off my game—it doesn't mean I'm off thinking of ways to get some extra money together."

Amos sniffed. "Is that right?"

"Yes. And seeing as I won't be up to my usual form and will be stuck here in London for another couple of months, the last thing I need is you taking delight in my misfortune."

Amos put the glasses on the table. "You know as well as I do that your plan to leave England wasn't likely to happen in a couple of months, accident or no accident. It's time you settled down some, Henry. You look like crap, and half your mates are now your enemies because you've either fleeced them one too many times in a game, or they feel you owe them money. I heard you were rowing with Charles before you got on that horse. The man only has your best interests at heart, you know."

Henry silently cursed the familiar weight of his guilt and shame as it pressed down on him. Guilt and shame that once again he had given Charles reason to be disappointed. Worse, since his accident, he'd seen what he suspected to be hope in his uncle's eyes, as though he was banking on Henry's fall thwarting his plans to leave. Henry clenched his jaw. Why couldn't Charles grasp how happy horse training made him? Didn't he care beyond his plans for his nephew?

Henry made a show of examining his winnings. Anything not to have to look at Amos. "I might have taken off without thought of what an untrained horse might do, but sometimes Charles just makes it too hard for me to listen to him. Now…" He inhaled and slowly released his breath. "I think it's best I leave, don't you? Clearly, I'm not going to enjoy my winnings here."

"You can hardly call it winnings when it's such a rarity. They told me you could've broken your neck or back in that fall. You were damn lucky, yet it's not made a blind bit of difference to your attitude."

"Who's *they*? Charles?" Henry huffed and leaned down to pick up his cane, wincing when another sharp pain shot through his leg. Biting back the urge to curse the sky blue, he straightened and looked at Amos. "He'll say anything to rally your support. Ignore him. I'll be right as rain and ready to see the world come spring. You see if I'm not."

Henry held Amos's stare, not liking that his eyes were filled with pity rather than the anger Henry would have preferred. Anger from his friend would be so much easier to confront.

"Did you say you were off?" he eventually asked. "Only, I'd prefer not to see anymore of you tonight if it's all the same to you."

Henry hardened his heart against the hurt Amos's dismissal evoked. Where was the laughter they had so often shared? Why did his friend constantly look at him with frustration rather than amusement these days?

"Fine." Henry turned to the door. "I'll see you soon."

He slowly made his way through the pub, his smile and laughter forced, his chest aching as much as his leg. The fallouts between him and Amos in the eight years they had known each other had been so few, Henry doubted he could count them on one hand. He had never seen such condemnation in his friend's eyes as he had just then. What in God's name had the blokes from the yard been saying to him? Hobbling along the street, Henry glared ahead. He would return to Henlow House, confront them about their tittle-tattling and put a stop to it, once and for all.

Yet, ten minutes later, he was not heading in the direction of Henlow House, but instead he entered Regent Street, his anger cooling as he thought of Rose and her parents' shop situated on a narrow street just off the main thoroughfare. Rose had flourished in the weeks she had been working for the countess, her growing confidence clear in the way she had fewer qualms about telling him what was what. Then again, she hadn't had a problem with that the very first time they met either.

Maybe the pain in his leg was addling his brain, but Henry followed his urge to pass by her parents' shop. He would take a quick peek in the window to see how things were getting along without the daughter he sensed was beyond precious to Mr. and Mrs. Watson.

And why wouldn't she be? Henry could hardly deny Rose was becoming quite precious to him too. The couple of nights they'd shared alone working side by side only made his feelings for her stronger.

He turned into the side street but had barely taken two steps along its cobbles when he came to an abrupt halt.

Rose hurried toward him from the direction of her home, her head bowed, a handkerchief held to her face, and her shoulders shaking with her sobs.

Anger unfurled inside him. He would murder whoever had upset her. The woman was a small sliver of light in his dark, dark world—his only light alongside his beloved horses—and he would not allow anyone to extinguish what illuminated from her. Not on his watch.

Cursing his infirmity, he rushed forward as fast as his stupid leg would allow.

Chapter Twenty-One

"Rose?"

Rose sucked in a breath and stopped, hastily wiping the dampness from her cheeks with her fingers. "Henry! What are you doing here?"

"I was just… it's not important. Are you all right? Has something happened?" He looked along the street behind her. "Is it your parents? Are they unwell?"

His concern dissolved some of her previous anguish, and she shook her head. "My parents are quite well. Thank you."

His troubled gaze lingered on hers. "Are you sure?"

She lowered her tense shoulders, her attraction to him rising because of the comfort she gained from seeing his softer side. A side that had begun to appear more often and that she enjoyed immensely.

"They are still anxious about me working for Lady Christina. It doesn't matter how I try to reassure them that I am happy and well-treated, they continue to fret. My mother especially." She sighed. "Poor Florence is trying her hardest to work as I do, to bolster them, but her efforts are seemingly unappreciated."

"I see."

She looked into his eyes and saw clear interest, but no empathy or even sympathy toward her parents. Sadness twisted inside her, and she tried to harden her heart. It was dangerous to care so much for a man who chose to lead his life with such self-interest. Her parents' ongoing grief had shown her that much.

"I'm not so sure you do," she said quietly.

Hurt flashed in his eyes. "Why would you say that?"

Rose inhaled, hoping her next words did not spark a disagreement between them. "My parents mean everything to me, and I hate upsetting them. Knowing I have will bother me for the remainder of today, tomorrow, even the next day. I'm not sure you have that sort of love for your family."

His cheeks mottled. "Why? Because I wish to leave them?"

"Well, yes."

"Then you have my feelings about them completely mistaken, Rose. I love them with all my heart. My leaving is about my passion for horses and travel, not derision for them."

Shame whispered through her, and she briefly closed her eyes. "You're right. I'm sorry. I should not have assumed as much."

They stood in silence, each looking in the opposite direction, and Rose felt a sudden need to tell him about Gideon. Not only could she explain how his death had made her mother want to keep her daughter close at all times, but it would also serve as a warning to Henry to reconsider his lifestyle once he knew how her brother had so brutally died. She suddenly longed to tell him everything that bothered her heart about her family. But how could she? She barely knew him, nor he her.

He cleared his throat. "Are you headed back to Henlow House? Only…" He dropped his gaze to his feet and jabbed his cane over the cobbles.

He suddenly looked so incredibly… endearing. She bit back her smile. Was he about to invite her somewhere?

"Only what?"

He raised his eyes to hers and pulled back his shoulders as though firmly getting a hold of himself. "Only, there's a teashop around the corner. Maybe I can buy you a cup of tea and a bun? It might cheer you a little. I know I'm not always the best company, but—"

"I'd like that. Very much."

His smile was so sudden, so entirely charming that Rose softly laughed and took his offered arm, warmth in her cheeks.

"Come on, I think it best you lean on me rather than the other way around. Don't you?" she said.

"Um, I don't think so." He puffed out his chest and rearranged her arm around his. "I might be a lot of things, but I'm still intelligent enough to know it's only right that if an opportunity arises to escort a beautiful lady to tea, it should be the gentleman who takes the lead."

Smiling, Rose shook her head as Henry lifted his nose in the air and whipped his cane out ahead of them like a dandy toff heading to the West End.

"Well then, sir," she laughed. "Lead the way."

As they walked, his act dissipated and when Rose glanced at Henry's profile, she sensed his tiredness and pain. His face was far too pale, and a vein showed blue in his temple, his jaw dark with shadow when he was usually clean shaven. Even if his wit was still there so, too, was a deep melancholy. Suspecting it had been provoked by something other than the untold pain of his injured leg, sympathy twisted inside her.

They reached the teashop, the frames of the latticed window and door were painted white, and curtains of pale blue hung behind the glass panes. Henry pushed open the door, allowing her to enter ahead of him. As they waited in line to speak with the matronly, white-haired woman overseeing the shop, Rose stared blindly ahead, her mind reeling with whether or not this was the right time to share with Henry her idea of them working more permanently together.

They had slowly started to learn each other's ways over the last few weeks, and she liked to think she had a growing understanding of him. But she had no idea how he would react to her proposition.

It had grown to matter so much to her that he understood there were always other options if a person was prepared to look for them—or better still, create them. His leg was getting him down, and his fall had curbed his plans to travel abroad, which must be taking its toll. Yet if Henry was as driven and determined to forge his own path as she was hers, surely he would listen to her long enough for her to convince him of a possible alternative path that would enable him to honestly earn the money to keep him on track toward his goals. It would also distract him from his work at the stables, which was surely a constant reminder of the dream he had yet to attain.

A young waitress led them to a table for two with a white lace cloth in the far corner. Blue-and-white teacups and plates that perfectly matched the color of the shop's curtains were set out on the table, and silver cutlery glinted beneath the darts of sunshine spearing throughout the intimate space.

Rose looked around as Henry ordered tea and currant buns for them. She had to make him see the sense in her idea—had to convince him that working with her would be to his benefit and provide a more reliable income than gambling ever could, as she could pay him a proportion of her wages. Rose inwardly grimaced. Of course, it might take time for him to swallow his pride about that particular aspect, but she had to at least try.

"Have you been here before?" he asked as the waitress retreated.

"I haven't," Rose replied, plucking off her gloves. "But considering the twinkle in your eyes, you are pretty pleased with yourself that you are here now."

He grinned. "I am, as it happens. I had a good play at the tables, and a cup of tea in a place like this is no less than you deserve."

Warnings once again resonated in her head. "*A good play at the tables.*" In other words, they were dining out on his ill-gotten winnings.

She forced a smile and buried the need to lecture him. "Well, thank you. It's nice to be able to relax for a while before going back to work. I hated leaving my mother so upset, so it will be good to have some time to compose myself before we return to the house. It won't be very good if I am damp-eyed when I see Mrs. Hayworth or, God forbid, the countess."

She sighed. "My mother's worry makes me feel so selfish for staying at Henlow House, but there is nowhere else I'd rather be, and that says a lot, considering my home and the shop have always held my heart and soul. Yet neither pulls at me the way they did before."

The waitress returned to the table and laid out their tea and cakes with a flash of a smile before disappearing again. Rose poured their tea, aware of Henry watching her as nerves leaped in her stomach about her proposal. It would be imperative to carry out their endeavors in secret, and how they would manage that she did not know, but she hoped, with Henry's agreement, they would work something out. Surely, he would see sense in the arrangement. It was glaringly obvious that nothing but his freedom would give him a modicum of happiness, and she was convinced he would grasp any opportunity to help make that happen.

She placed the teapot on the table and pushed a filled cup in front of him. "I have an idea," she said quietly. "An idea I fear you will balk at, but I'd like to put it to you anyway."

"Sounds intriguing. About what exactly?"

"You and your immediate future."

"My…" A line creased his brow. "Go on."

His green eyes burned into hers with such intensity, Rose struggled to hold his gaze. She couldn't tell if he was annoyed or listening intently because whatever she had to say mattered to him. Either way, she would not be intimidated by his solemnity… or how handsome he looked. She picked up her cup, hating that her hand ever so slightly trembled, and sipped to ease the dryness in her throat. Carefully returning the cup to its saucer, she purposefully met his gaze.

"As you are unable to train horses at the moment, and things are clearly strained between you and your uncle, I thought you might consider putting your incredible stitching skills to use elsewhere."

His eyes never left hers, his tea and bun remaining untouched on the table. "Like where?"

She held his gaze, her heart thumping. "Working more often with me… on the countess's wardrobe. For a wage. Provided by her, but if not, I will pay you from my wages."

The ensuing silence was so dense, the only sound Rose could hear was her own breath. His disbelief was tangible. Feigning nonchalance, she slid the porcelain plate holding her currant bun closer, praying that she outwardly portrayed the epitome of calm, even though nerves swarmed her stomach.

"Is this some kind of jest?" he asked.

She took a deep breath and held his irritated gaze. "No, I am being sincere. It would be good for you." She pulled back her shoulders. "And me."

Another long moment of silence followed, and Rose bit into her bun, struggling to swallow the small piece as all the moisture had entirely disappeared from her mouth.

Henry laughed and took a gulp of his tea, wincing against its heat. "This is about my gambling, isn't it? You think to keep me away from the tables, the same as Charles. Albeit with a different persuasion."

"Is that so bad? All you want is to save money so you have the means to follow your dreams. This way you can replace the money you will lose not training the earl's horses and also negate the risk of losing it all once earned." Her fingers itched to take his, but she refrained. "Obviously, we will have to find a way to keep our working together a secret, but—"

"Stop."

His undisguised disdain toward her idea was clear in his eyes, and Rose's nerves hitched in annoyance.

"You don't even want to explore the idea, do you?" she said.

"What I want is for you to see how mad an idea it is." He bit into his currant bun, the crumbs dashing his lips.

She glared at his bowed head. "It could work, Henry. I want to deliver everything the countess and Mrs. Hayworth ask of me. More, if possible. As the season approaches, the pressure on me will be immense, quite possibly more than I can cope with. But with your skill and mine combined, I know we would be a formidable team."

He met her eyes, the disbelief fading and turning into something akin to curiosity. "You really are serious about this, aren't you?"

She nodded, suddenly feeling incredibly vulnerable. As though her success suddenly hung on his agreement, which was insane. His gaze slowly drifted over her face and lingered a moment at her lips.

Rose sat completely still as a strange fluttering took flight in her stomach under his scrutiny. "What?"

"Nothing." He blinked. "It's madness. I won't do it."

He might as well have slapped her, his response was so blunt, so final.

"Fine." She picked up her bun, fighting her humiliation. "Forget I suggested it. It was merely an idea."

"What made you think of such a thing?"

She glared. "You really want to know?"

"Yes."

"I care about you, Henry," she blurted. "Is that so wrong?"

Their eyes locked, but Rose refused to look away. "From what I can tell, you are in dire need of both time and space if you are ever to find the happiness you seek. The difference between you and me is that I am not wasting my opportunity for all I desire at a gaming table or ignoring the concerns of the people I love and who love me. I am working, and working hard. I am doing my best to impress the woman who could make my dreams a reality. What are you doing except sabotaging every chance you have?" Her heart beat so hard Rose feared it would burst from her chest, but she had never felt so self-assured. Let him attempt to disprove all she had alleged.

"You expect me to sew for you? Be an assistant to you?"

"Why is that so incredible?"

"Because in case it's slipped your notice, I'm a man, Rose. Not a woman and not your lackey."

"My…" Anger burned through her. "Heavens above, Henry Ward, you really are your own worst enemy." She gave a dismissive wave. "Do as you wish. If you enjoy showing your ingratitude to your uncle and long for the day his love for you devolves into something infinitely worse and irreversible, then continue as you are. It is no bother to me." She flashed him a smug smile. "Like I said, I have plans in place for my success, and they are already happening."

"As will mine."

She shrugged. "Maybe. Maybe not." Rose bit into her bun and closed her eyes as if relishing every morsel and not battling the urge to smack him up the side of his head. Infernal fool! He could stew in his own juices for all she cared. She had never felt so empowered, and his misplaced pride only served to bolster her desire to create the success that many thought impossible for people of her and Henry's class.

All it would take for her to have everything she desired was unshakable belief. And it was blatantly obvious that Henry was nowhere near as close to being in the same place as she was.

Chapter Twenty-Two

Three days later, Henry limped along the city streets toward St. Mary's Hospital where he was due for a checkup on his leg, courtesy of Lord Robert. His Lordship did not always receive the best newspaper reports about his social life, but to his staff he was often generous and jovial, which Charles took great delight in reminding Henry of as often as possible. Especially over the last couple of weeks, his uncle had stressed that the hospital care Henry had received was another benefit of a job he should be grateful for.

And, truth be told, he *was* grateful—from the bottom of his heart. God only knew what the result of his injuries would have been if tended to by some backstreet surgeon.

Two young ladies strolled past, their eyes bright with interest as they blatantly appraised him with an air of coquettishness. Henry quickly looked away, all too aware that not so long ago he would have flashed a flirtatious wink at such a lovely pair, maybe tipped his hat or even stretched to a word or two if he was confident he had gauged their interest correctly. Yet for weeks now, any semblance of toying with the fairer sex had been far from his mind. Nonexistent, even. Traits he had enjoyed and used to his advantage more times than he could count came to mean very little in light of his injury. And, of course, there was the wisdom, care, and grace of a certain lady.

He had not seen Rose since their time at the teashop, but she hadn't left his mind for more than a moment or two. He had wasted so much time milling around as though his life choices wouldn't catch up with him sooner or later—larking about and chasing money as though tomorrow would miraculously bring an influx of cash.

Westminster Abbey appeared ahead of him, its spires stretching to a heavy, gray sky, its beautiful Gothic architecture arresting and inspiring. Henry prayed the doctor would confirm his leg was on the mend and would soon be back to normal. It was certainly beginning to feel a little better, the bouts of pain not as intense or prolonged. Being trapped like a caged beast in the Henlow House stables with his uncle as his keeper steadily veered Henry ever closer to his breaking point, which he feared would mean another confrontation between them. That was the last thing he wanted and also the reason Rose's idea of them working together had become more of a possibility in his mind.

He tightened his grip on his cane and picked up his pace, his leg whispering its indignation as he thought how different Rose had been that day at the teashop. The girl he had met weeks before had evolved into a woman in charge of her destiny. It was as though being in the countess's apartments and fully embracing the opportunity presented to her had caused Rose Watson's life to take shape.

And now it seemed she wanted the same for him.

Henry drew his lips tightly together. She was a good woman with a generous heart—and way out of his league in every way. Yet… he blew out a breath. Working with her—helping her—was feasible. Yes, the thought of accepting money from her meant his pride would take a battering, but she was right. Working on the countess's clothes and helping Rose with the less complicated stitching would replace the earnings he was losing in not training the earl's horses. Not to mention, now that he had stopped gambling, his nights grew ever longer and his boredom more unbearable.

The only practical place he could work on the countess's clothes was at his lodgings. But how he and Rose would manage that when his uncle and aunt noticed his comings and goings, Henry had no idea. He smiled. But maybe they should try anyway.

The last thing Rose had said to him, before they parted ways after returning to Henlow House that evening, echoed in his memory.

"*Open your mind, Henry. Open your heart to faith. Trust that God will make what you want possible by whatever means.*"

Even though he might well misbehave from time to time and frustrate the hell out of his uncle, Henry appreciated his family's well-meant advice; however, he also wished to listen to his heart, to follow his own path. But, in truth, he was finding it damn hard to ignore Rose. To dismiss the challenge behind her questions and the excitement in her huge brown eyes. Her voice, so caring and full of belief in him, drove him to distraction. Poked at something deep in his heart too. No one had ever made him feel as good about himself, as strong and whole as Rose did, and he'd barely known her two months. She was different from any woman he'd ever met. When she looked at him, her attention was focused only on him. She listened to him as though what he said mattered to her. No one, not even Charles, had ever really listened to him. Not the way Rose did.

Bitterness that tasted far too much like fear coated his throat. His deepening feelings for her were dangerous. They had the potential to send him off course. To anchor him to a place he did not want to be. On the other hand, if he did agree to her suggestion, they wouldn't be working side by side or as closely as they had when he had helped her with the mending. If the arrangement was more long-term, there would be no reason to see her other than when she came to drop off or pick up work from his lodgings.

Stopping outside the huge iron gates at St. Mary's entrance, Henry stared at the stone building, his hand so tight on his cane his knuckles ached. Possibility and excitement simmered beneath his skin as his common sense battled the futility of his lifelong dreams. He was four and twenty with a damaged leg, a pitiful amount of savings, and—if he had the guts to be honest with himself—a gambling problem that was getting a little out of control.

Entering through the hospital gates, Henry winced against the intensified pain in his leg from the walk and pushed thoughts of Rose and her incessant positivity to the back of his mind—and heart. He would think on her proposal for another day or two and then seek her out. If he decided to agree to her plan, he could only pray he wasn't too late, her sympathy and care for him perhaps gone.

⌒

"Right, if you'd like to get off the bed, Mr. Ward, we'll take a seat at my desk." The white-whiskered doctor gestured with a wave at the chair on the other side of his desk, his expression grave. "How are you managing day to day?"

"Well, enough," Henry said as he carefully lowered his feet to the tiled floor and hobbled to the vacant seat. He sat down heavily and blew out a breath. "It's sometimes a devil to sleep at night, mind you. I'm used to moving as I want, when I want, but there has been little chance of that for weeks now."

"Hmm, well, you've got more color in your cheeks, and you've said you are taking less laudanum, which is all positive news. Now…" The doctor leaned forward, placed his elbows on the desk and laced his fingers, his blue eyes somber above his half-rimmed spectacles.

"I believe you are on the path to recovery, Mr. Ward... but a slow recovery. You must not push things."

Henry's heart beat faster and he pressed his lips tightly together as he eyed the doctor for a long moment before he dared to ask his question. "Will I be able to train horses again?"

The doctor lowered his hands to the desk. "The ligaments behind your knee are healing well, and your mobility is improving at a rate I did not expect. It's only been four weeks since the accident, but there has been good improvement. So, yes, Mr. Ward. It may be a while yet, but I believe you will once again train the earl's horses, a privileged position I imagine you are keen to hold on to."

A privileged position.

Why did everyone else view his job at Henlow House as a blessing when all he thought about was escaping it?

Henry shook his head and grinned. "The privilege is working with such wonderful animals, Doctor. The fact that I will ride and train again has cheered me beyond measure. You have truly made my day. No, my week. My year!"

The doctor smiled. "I'm glad to hear it. Just take things steady for a while yet, Mr. Ward, or you will be back to the beginning again."

Henry tried to remain focused on the doctor as he continued to talk, but he heard nothing beyond the blood thundering in his ears. Images of ships and oceans, horses and fields flashed through his mind. He didn't care if it took two months or three months, just hearing he would ride again was incredible, and he would be eternally grateful for God's mercy.

Noticing the doctor had stopped talking, Henry quickly pushed to his feet. The pain that shot through his leg was so sharp he clamped his teeth together.

The doctor stood, his hand outstretched as though to catch him. "Mr. Ward—"

"I'm all right." Henry smiled and raised his free hand to warn the doctor off, the other grasping his cane. "I need to go. There's someone I want to share this wonderful news with. Thank you, Doctor."

Chapter Twenty-Three

Rose took two pins from between her pursed lips and pushed them into the hem of the skirt she was repairing for the countess. She held it in front of the window for a closer look, but the fading light offered little in the way of illumination. She lowered the skirt and leaned across the table to draw the oil lamp closer when footsteps approached the open doorway and Mrs. Hayworth entered.

"Good afternoon, Rose. I hoped to find you here. Her Ladyship would like to see you in the nursery."

"The nursery?"

"Yes."

Rose's shoulders immediately tightened. "I've never been summoned to the nursery before."

Mrs. Hayworth smiled, her gaze softening. "Such a summons is nothing to worry about. Now, come along. It will not do to keep the countess waiting."

"Of course." Rose gathered the skirt, careful not to crush the pale-pink satin as she carried it to the table that she used to lay out any garments she was working on. Her fingers trembled, but she purposefully gathered her confidence. It did not necessarily mean something bad was afoot just because Lady Christina had asked to see her when she was with her children. Maybe she only had a short instruction or request and did not wish to leave them.

Clearing her throat, Rose faced Mrs. Hayworth and forced nonchalance into her voice. "Do you have any idea why the countess wishes to see me? She told me she was happy for me to have the afternoon to myself."

Mrs. Hayworth stored the bed linens she had been carrying in a polished walnut dresser. "You really are such a worrier sometimes, Rose. I'm sure everything is fine. Now leave that skirt to me, I am more than aware of what needs to be done with it."

Rose looked a little closer at Mrs. Hayworth. There was a definite glint in her eyes. "You're up to something."

"Up to something? Well, of all the nerve." Mrs. Hayworth laughed as she shooed Rose to the door, her hands flapping. "Go on now."

Rose opened her mouth to protest but closed it again. The amusement in Mrs. Hayworth's eyes was encouraging. Surely she would not be smiling if Rose was in trouble. After leaving the room, she walked through one opulent corridor after another, gazing at the magnificent paintings, the gleaming vases upon marble plinths filled with huge flower arrangements the likes of which she had never seen before she came to this beautiful house. From the plush carpet beneath her feet to the ornately painted ceiling, everything was so wondrous. She regularly pinched herself to make sure she was actually here, working in one of England's finest houses. She owed the countess so much for this incredible opportunity, and Rose's allegiance would forever be hers.

Once she reached the nursery, she took a deep breath, knocked on the door, and entered. Lady Christina's laughter filled the surprisingly small room, simply decorated in shades of green and ivory. Baby George, just nine months old, sat on his mother's lap as they watched his two-year-old brother, James, playing on the floor with his nanny, blocks of red, green, and blue built in a column on the oriental rug, others scattered all around them.

Rose lowered into a curtsy. "You asked to see me, Your Ladyship."

"Oh, Watson, I didn't hear you come in," exclaimed the countess with a smile before she turned to the boys' nanny. "You can leave me with the children for now. I will send Watson for you when I need to get ready for dinner."

"Yes, Your Ladyship." The nanny dipped a curtsy and nodded at Rose as she passed, closing the door softly behind her.

Lady Christina waved at the sofa opposite her. "Please, take a seat."

Rose walked to the sofa, and the moment she sat, Lord James's attention left the bricks, and his big blue eyes focused solely on her. Her heart gave a little jolt of affection when his curious frown smoothed out and he smiled. She returned his smile, battling the panic that sped her heart as he awkwardly clambered to his feet and toddled in her direction, his hands outstretched.

"Oh, I…" Rose swallowed and looked at the countess. "I don't know how—"

"Just lift him onto your lap." Lady Christina smiled. "He will either openly assess your entire face or else scrutinize the curls about your temples. Either way, he'll be delighted."

After another glance at James's heart-melting smile Rose picked him up, settling his chubby little legs on her lap. Just as the countess had predicted, he stared at her before lifting his fingers to her hair.

"So…" Her Ladyship pressed a kiss to George's head. "I imagine you are keen to know why I asked you here."

"Yes."

"Well, I hope you will be rather pleased with what I am about to say."

Rose tensed as James gave a rather willful tug on her hair.

"I continue to be impressed with your work, Watson. So much so that I would like to wear one of your designs—a full ensemble, in fact—to a public opening of a children's hospital ward here in the city. The queen was scheduled to attend the opening, but I am doing what I can to relieve her of some duties."

The entire country was aware of Queen Victoria's reluctance for public outings, and it seemed the opening of a hospital wing failed to coax her from the mourning of her husband, Prince Albert.

"It will be my pleasure," Rose said. "Do you have something in mind? A color, maybe?"

"Oh, I am more than happy to leave any such decisions to you, Watson. You have more than proven you know my taste. The only thing is…" The countess grimaced. "The opening is just three weeks away."

"Three weeks?" Rose's mind raced with how she would come up with a design, source the materials and accessories, *and* construct an entire outfit in three weeks with all the other duties she would be assigned by Mrs. Hayworth.

"I wouldn't ask this of you if I didn't believe it within your capabilities, Watson. I want you to succeed," the countess said, her blue eyes filled with fervor. "As I have mentioned before, although I am a keen painter and photographer, I am limited in my creativity and can only take the time to enjoy these pursuits as my duty and commitments allow, but your creativity and talent is a different matter altogether. I want you to shine where I cannot, and I will do whatever I can to light your path."

Joy whispered around Rose's heart, her gratitude to Lady Christina deepening. "Thank you, Your Ladyship."

"As your patron, I am determined to ensure your success. And because the press will most certainly be at the hospital, that journey will inevitably begin very soon, whether you feel yourself ready or not."

Rose's hands turned clammy. For all her dreams and aspirations, she had never considered how it would feel to see her work in newspapers and magazines. Or maybe she had not allowed herself to imagine such dizzying heights. Would she be photographed? Her stomach tightened with nerves.

"The truth is," the countess continued, seemingly oblivious to Rose's mounting apprehension, "people are becoming more and more interested in what I am wearing these days, and this event will certainly bring you to their attention. Everyone present will want to know who made my clothes."

Rose stared, only marginally aware of James clambering from her lap onto the floor. "I don't know what to say, or even how to thank you," she said, trying and failing to drag her stunned gaze from James as he dropped onto his napkinned bottom in front of his building blocks. She faced the countess. "Never in all my hopes and dreams did I think anything like this would happen to me. I saw myself making adjustments at our family shop, making occasional garments, and hopefully convincing my parents to embrace some new, exciting designs and materials in the new decade. But photographers, the press… I never dreamed…"

"Well, it is happening, Watson, and what's more, I'd like you to accompany me to the event, albeit somewhat secreted away so you are able to witness people's reactions to the clothes firsthand."

"I don't know what to say."

"It's all part of my cunning plan, Watson." Lady Christina laughed as she lifted George into the air, making him gurgle. "I intend to add to the mystique of the occasion by hinting the designer is present but wishes to remain anonymous." She lowered the little boy and her smile wavered, her eyes dimming with concern. "However, all of this will only be possible if you think three weeks is enough time for you to do the necessary work. I am sorry time is so short, but the Queen asked me to attend this event for her just this morning."

Once again, Rose's mind reeled. To be given such a monumental task was one thing, but to execute it in merely three weeks was something else entirely. Rose felt pressure building inside her, but she would not let the countess down.

"I can't honestly say it will be enough time," she said. "There will be so much to do, and I have nothing in mind in way of a suitable ensemble, but I will start work at once." She hesitated as Henry's face appeared in her mind. "Maybe if…"

Could she really suggest what she had been thinking about? Moreover, why should she when Henry had so succinctly dismissed the idea?

The countess's eyes shadowed with concern. "Watson?"

Rose met the countess's stare. "I am quite certain it will be possible if I have some help," she said. "Not with the designing—that will be my job entirely—but with the making of the outfit. You will need a skirt, jacket, blouse… I really do not think I could do everything on my own in time."

"Well, of course!" Her Ladyship smiled, her eyes shining with relief. "Do you have someone in mind? Otherwise, I am sure Mrs. Hayworth would be happy to source someone for you."

Gathering every ounce of her nerve and courage, Rose sat a little straighter. "I have a friend who is extremely talented in his—*her*—

work, and I would love to be able to send some extra work her way so she has the means of additional income. She will undoubtedly want to remain anonymous so she won't risk her other employment, but I'm sure h—" Rose swallowed. "*She* will be happy to spend some hours helping me in the evenings."

The countess frowned. "She is a friend of yours?"

"Yes."

"I see."

The countess's wariness was clear, and Rose sat a little straighter, hoping she gave an air of confidence.

"My friend is a fine stitcher, Your Ladyship, but has suffered one misfortune after another of late. I really think this work would be highly beneficial in reviving her spirits." Rose inhaled a long breath.

Deep down she doubted Henry deserved her championing him this way. Not to mention the risk she was taking by not being entirely honest with the countess about his gender and position at Henlow House. What if he agreed to help her and then let her down? Let the countess down? And Rose was forced to confess who had been helping her? She'd never forgive him if he put her in that position. So why was she risking so much for him? Well, for one, she'd seen the quality of his work, and two, this additional work would keep him on track for achieving his dreams while staying away from the gambling houses.

Lady Christina considered her, her eyes somber, before she sighed and moved George from her shoulder to cradle him, now sleeping, in her arms.

"Speak to Mrs. Hayworth. If she approves of your friend helping you, then that is perfectly acceptable to me too."

Rose nodded and crossed her fingers in her lap. "I will. Thank you."

Chapter Twenty-Four

"Go on, get out of here!" The landlord of the Royal Oak bellowed as he grabbed Henry by the back of the collar and hurled him into the street. "I don't want to see your face in my pub again. Do you hear me?"

"Loud and cle—" Henry landed with a thud to his backside on the cobblestones, his leg screaming with pain. "Oi, there's no need for that!"

He ducked as his cane was unceremoniously thrown after him, barely missing his head before it clattered to the ground beside him.

"There's every bloody need."

Henry flinched as the pub door was slammed shut with such force he could've sworn the lattice windows on either side of it shook. A low rumble of laughter started in his belly, and he dropped back and released his mirth, the cobblestones pressing into his back. He put his hands on his stomach, his joviality as heartfelt as it was ever going to be. Maybe he'd had one too many celebratory ales, but the doctor's news had been too much to contain, and he'd needed some company.

Ignoring the sickness that lolled just beneath the laughter, he turned over and pushed his hands flat to the cold, damp stones to get some traction before pushing up unsteadily to his feet. Just as he righted himself, a passerby unwittingly kicked his cane farther away from where he stood.

"For the love of God," he muttered. "Can't you look where you're going?" He narrowed his eyes and concentrated on his cane, silently willing it to conjure itself into his open palm. The mere thought of bending down made his head spin with the assured pain that would shoot from his knee, straight into his brain.

"You want some help, mister?"

Henry looked at the young boy who had appeared beside him. No older than eight or nine, his brown hair was matted with dirt, his face streaked with mud and what looked like patches of blood.

Henry smirked as he slid his hand into his trouser pocket. "And how much is this kind offer of help going to cost me?"

"Just a couple pennies and I'll have that cane fine and dandy in your hand. How will that be?"

"That would be grand if truth be told. Here." Henry dropped some coins into the boy's outstretched hand. "Good lad."

The boy duly retrieved the cane and handed it to Henry with a dip of his head. Before Henry could thank him, the urchin skulked into the busy street and was soon eclipsed by fifty other filthy bodies.

Self-loathing threatened as Henry looked around. He hadn't given a thought to the people outside the pub tonight, he'd been so intent on toasting his good fortune. He had been to this area of the city enough times to know some of these people, their misfortunes, and struggles. He usually offered a hand on his way to the Royal Oak, helping with any leather mending a family might need or fixing a broken bridle so a man might continue in his work. But he had thought about nothing besides himself earlier, his meeting with the doctor playing over and over, fueling his optimism for a future he had thought lost. What would Charles think once Henry relayed the doctor's prognosis to him? No doubt his uncle would be happy for him… to a degree. He'd also know Henry's plans to leave had been reignited.

Henry clenched his jaw and stared at the puddles glistening along the cobbled street and the people in varying stages of ragged dress—some shoeless, some not. It was no life on these streets, no life being at the beck and call of aristocracy who had no idea what truly lay past their ten-foot-high walls. Why couldn't Charles be happy for his nephew's vision of a different life? If he were, then maybe the closeness they'd enjoyed a couple years ago, before Henry had shared his global horse-training dreams with Charles, would return.

He started along the street, the stench of this part of the city clashing like night and day when he considered the gilded luxury of Henlow House. Henry reached The Crown and elbowed his way to the bar, jesting with anyone who crossed his path.

"God above, look what the cat dragged in."

Although it wasn't the most pleasant greeting from Amos, Henry was glad his friend wasn't still mad enough to take one look at him and throw him out on his ear in the same manner as the landlord of the Royal Oak.

"A pint of my usual, please, Amos." He gritted his teeth against a jab of pain in his knee and leaned his elbow heavily on the bar. "And you might as well follow that with a shot of brandy too."

Amos merely raised his eyebrows before turning to pour the drinks. "So where have you been? You smell like you've been rolling around in the gutter."

"I have. Silas tossed me out again."

"Will you never learn to stay away from that place?" Amos placed Henry's pint and brandy on the bar. "Why do you always head over there looking for trouble?"

"It isn't trouble when it amuses me." Henry took a swig from the tankard. "I've had some news. News that even the great Charles Summers hasn't got wind of yet."

Amos reached for one of the clean glasses lined up beside him. "What's that then?"

Henry repeated what the doctor had said between draining his pint and moving on to sip his brandy. "That's the long and short of it." He grinned. "So my horse-training plans are back on, my friend."

"Bloody hell, Henry, enough with the *plans*." Amos shook his head and turned away to stack the dried glasses on a shelf behind him.

Henry's gaze fell on a picture of the Earl of Bath hanging above his friend's head. Handsome and smiling in his noble finery, Lord Robert looked down knowingly, watching his subjects drink themselves into a stupor. Not that His Lordship was much different from them, truth be told. The earl indulged in a tipple with equal fervor as the working men in this fine old city of London.

Every time he came to the mews on a post-breakfast jaunt around the gardens and stables, the man was full of verve and laughter… albeit with half a canny eye looking for anything out of place. How the earl woke at the crack of dawn after being out with his friends, indulging in the high life, drinking and gaming at the clubs, meeting new people and speculating where he might travel next, Henry had no idea, but it didn't seem a bad life from where he was standing.

He raised his glass and toasted the earl. "You enjoy life to your heart's content, sir. You won't get any judgment from me."

"Are you talking to a bloody portrait now?" Amos's impatience showed in his dark eyes. "Seems to me the Lord Robert hasn't got his life any more sorted out than the rest of us."

"What are you talking about? He's an earl. 'Course he's got his life sorted out." Henry held out his glass. "Another, if you don't mind."

Amos refilled the glass and pushed it across the bar. "They reckon his wandering eye is going from bad to worse."

Of course, as well as the liquor, Lord Robert had more than a passing fancy for the ladies.

Henry sipped his drink. "Since when has royalty, the aristocracy, or others of their ilk not had extramarital activities going on?"

"That might well be, but the countess seems a good sort, and I very much doubt she is in a position to kick up a stink like other wives might. It's all about duty with that lot, and duty for a countess is pretty much to smile and wave while pretending what her husband gets up to doesn't bother her."

Henry raised his eyebrows. "Why are you paying any heed to what people are gossiping about? You're like an old woman at the Sunday market."

"All I'm saying is, if Lord Robert makes a mistake, he has people around him ready and willing to clear up any mess. You, on the other hand, would be well-advised to keep hold of your friends and family who care about you. After all, it's pretty much guaranteed that no matter what the earl might or might not be doing behind his beautiful wife's back, he's unlikely to lose her."

Henry drained his glass. "And? It's not like I've got a wife to lose, do I?"

"No, and you're never likely to have one with the way you're carrying on."

"That's the way I want it."

"Is that so?"

The way Amos asked the question raised Henry's hackles. "What now?"

"Seen any more of the young lady you couldn't help dropping into the conversation awhile back?" The twinkle in Amos's eyes would've been visible from the moon. "Rose, isn't it?"

"No," Henry lied. "Why?"

Amos shrugged. "Just wondered. The way she got you all riled up, I'd hazard a guess she's not likely to turn a blind eye to your flaws. Am I right?"

Rose's pretty face appeared in front of Henry, and he swallowed. No, Rose was very unlikely to turn a blind eye to anyone or anything that mattered to her. But did he matter to her? He took a drink of his brandy. God, he hoped so… because she was certainly coming to matter to him.

Amos arched an eyebrow, the glint still shining in his eyes. "Thinking about her, eh?"

Henry gripped his glass and held his friend's mocking stare. "So, what if I am?"

Amos raised his hands in surrender. "Nothing. If you are, that's all good by me." He grinned. "From what I can tell from the little you've told me about her and your reaction to my mentioning her, she's a good-looking girl who is perfectly content with her life and has no need for your sorry arse to be added to her day to day." He shrugged, protruding his bottom lip. "Whereas you—"

"What about me?" Henry snapped, his cheeks warm with temper.

"You, my friend, seem to be in some sort of need of her."

"You're talking rubbish." Henry held out his brandy glass. "Just pour me another drink."

Amos reached for the bottle behind him. "If this girl likes you, is willing to stand beside you and help you through this time when you are barely standing on your own two feet, don't turn her away. If you have the smallest brain between those ears of yours, you'll go back to Henlow House, straighten yourself out, and make sure she knows you appreciate her care."

"Since when did you turn into a man who cares about romance?"

Amos pushed away from the bar. "Romance? Did I mention such a thing?" He winked. "I rest my case."

"Get lo—"

But Amos had walked away, whistling to himself as he made his way farther along the bar.

"Damn idiot doesn't know what he's talking about," Henry mumbled. He got up from his stool and gingerly stepped forward, planting his cane heavily with each step he took to the door.

Rose had been too good to him to dismiss. Maybe he did need her. He drew in a long breath, then slowly released it. He would go back to Henlow House and try to get a message to her through the servants. Everything he wanted was still possible and now that he didn't feel quite so less of a man, safe in the knowledge he would be back riding and training one day, helping Rose and earning extra money felt like salvation… salvation she had provided.

Chapter Twenty-Five

Rose hurried toward the mews, her heart pounding with trepidation, but her smile wide. The countess had not completely dismissed the idea of her having an assistant and, after telling the same embellished story to Mrs. Hayworth, the dresser had given her endorsement to Rose's *friend* working with her if she found she needed the help.

Rose's smile slipped and she drew in a calming breath. Now she just had to hope and pray her and Henry's collaboration on the countess's clothes was not discovered. She didn't think they would have to work together too long, just long enough for Henry to put some money aside before he fully recovered from his accident and was able to train horses again.

A strange loss clutched at Rose's heart, and she slowed her pace, shocked by the unexpected tears that pricked her eyes. To have Henry leave Henlow House did not sit as well with her as it might have a few weeks ago. Her feelings had deepened for him, her attraction heightened… She lifted her chin. She could not—would not—think of them in any other way than friends. Doing otherwise would mean certain heartbreak further along the line.

It was clear Henry was headed on the same path as her beloved, foolish brother and she could not stand by and let something awful befall him without trying to guide him away from the card table. She had been young and innocent to the ways of the world when Gideon was killed, but now she was a grown woman and capable of helping Henry where she could not help her brother.

One way or another, she would make him see sense and persuade him to work with her.

The stables were shrouded in darkness, the cloudless black night sky punctuated by a plethora of stars. It should have been beautiful, but Rose shivered as a strange foreboding stole through her. Everything was so still…

Despite it being almost nine o'clock, she had assumed the stables would be in constant activity. Maybe they were quiet because none of the horses were needed by the family or their guests that evening. She walked through the main entrance and her gaze immediately fell on Henry's uncle. He stood in a far corner hanging a bridle on one of the hooks on the wall, his expression almost pained. Henry was nowhere to be seen.

She cleared her throat. "Mr. Summers?"

His frown vanished as he offered a tight smile. "Ah, Miss Watson. Good evening."

"Good evening. I was hoping to have a word with Henry." She glanced along the stables as though he might be hiding behind one of the horses. "Is he here?"

"Is he—hell…"

Rose flinched. "Oh."

"I'm sorry." Mr. Summers pushed his fingers into the fallen hair at his brow and held them there, his jaw tight. "I didn't mean to snap. He left for the hospital around midday for a checkup on his leg, and I've not seen hide nor hair of him since."

Immediately uneasy, Rose frowned. "But that was hours ago."

Mr. Summers came closer, lifting a rag from a workbench. He wiped his hands, his eyes boring into hers. "Why are you wasting your time with him, Miss Watson?"

"I'm sorry?"

"Surely you've learned by now that my nephew is a law unto himself. He does what he likes, when he likes, and be damned anyone who might be fretting over him."

Rose huffed a laugh. "I am hardly fretting over him."

"No?"

"No," she said firmly. "I just wished to speak with him."

"Hmm. I'll take your word for it." He brushed past her and lifted a hay fork from the floor and propped it up against the wall, then busied himself tidying other brushes and implements.

As Rose watched him, guilt whispered through her. She *was* fretting. At least, she was now that she knew Henry wasn't here, and his uncle looked fit to burst with what she could only surmise was barely suppressed fury.

"Do you think something might have happened to him?" she asked, walking closer and smoothing her hand over the soft leather of a saddle sitting atop a stand. "Could he be in trouble somewhere?"

"That, my dear, is a question neither I nor anyone else can answer," Mr. Summers said as he locked one of the stable doors. "This morning's appointment was with a good, reputable physician being paid by the earl to oversee Henry's care. And what does he do? He goes off as he should and then disappears."

His impatience was palpable, and Rose glanced at the stable entrance as though willing Henry to appear.

"I see."

"I'm not sure you do, Miss Watson." Charles let out a long sigh. "It goes without saying that most of us would be grateful for such generosity from our employer, such an expense covered, that we would keep an appointment like that and immediately return to work, ready and willing with a report should our employer come by to check on us. Wouldn't you agree?"

"Well, yes, bu—"

"But not Henry, Miss Watson. Not Henry."

"I can see that you are angry, Mr. Summers, however, do you not think—"

"Oh, I'm angry, all right."

"How do you know something bad hasn't befallen him?" Rose asked. "He is struggling with a severely injured leg, after all." Annoyed by Mr. Summers's attitude, Rose held his gaze. "He could have taken a tumble or been robbed. He is in an incapacitated state, and you know as well as I that if certain unsavory people sense the slightest weakness, they will exploit it."

He sniffed, a wry smile curving his lips. "Henry is as likely to be exploited by some chancer as I am to dress up in a frock and dance a jig. The boy is in a pub or gambling house somewhere and has probably been there since early this afternoon. I'm glad he's not found his way here, because I'll box his ears as soon as I look at him when he turns up."

"You're being unfair." The need to defend Henry reared whether it was deserved or not, and Rose looked again at the door, anxiety building in the pit of her stomach. Was Henry lying in a ditch somewhere? Had he been dragged down an alley and beaten? "He could be anywhere."

"Miss Watson, please. That boy is not worth your concern."

Rose dropped her arms and fisted her hands on her hips. "Henry might have his faults, just like the rest of us, but inside he's a good man and, as far as I know, has never intentionally meant to hurt you or your family."

The anger in Charles's eyes burned bright in the low light of the stables. "Henry has hurt my wife and family plenty with his shenanigans, gambling, and talk of leaving."

Rose's heart ached for the Summers family. She knew all too well what Gideon's way of life had done to her and her parents, but she had to stand strong.

She raised her eyebrows, her voice steady. "Just your wife and family? You feel nothing for Henry yourself?"

Their gazes locked and second by slow second, the anger in Charles's eyes lessened, replaced by sympathy as he studied her. Warmth spread up Rose's neck, rising to her jaw and then her cheeks, but she refused to look away. She had absolutely no doubt that her care for Henry was most likely misplaced, but she couldn't stem it. What if he needed her? He clearly couldn't rely on his uncle to go looking for him.

When he spoke, Mr. Summers's voice was softer. "Don't go giving that boy your heart, Miss Watson. He won't be here forever, and he'll let you down. Trust me."

Denials and protestations bit at her tongue, but how could she stand in front of Henry's uncle and say she did not care for his nephew? She did care for Henry. More than that, she liked Mr. Summers, respected him, and sensed his deep love for Henry even if he would not admit it to himself. She would not lie to him.

"I guard my heart carefully, Mr. Summers, so you have no need to worry." She forced a small smile. "Anyway, since I've known Henry, I've had his card marked, don't you worry."

He studied her before he smiled. "Now that I can believe."

Rose tried to loosen the tension from her shoulders but failed. "Let's assume he *is* in a tavern somewhere. Which one is it likely to be?"

"Probably one of the rooms at the back of The Crown or maybe The Star." He shrugged. "Maybe any tavern in the entire vicinity.

He's not particular about where he loses money." He narrowed his eyes. "I hope you're not thinking what I'm afraid you are."

"I have no idea what you think I'm thinking."

He pointed his finger at her. "Don't you go anywhere near a pub around here on your own. My nephew is not worth putting yourself at risk. Not when he's never likely to appreciate what you are willing to do for him."

"I am not looking for his appreciation, and please lower your finger, Mr. Summers. I just need to know he is all right for my own peace of mind."

Charles tutted and walked past her to a wooden workbench. "Trust me. He is not in trouble. He's just gambling away what little money he has somewhere."

Rose inhaled a calming breath. "Fine, then I'll go."

"Miss Watson?"

She stopped.

Charles approached her and gently touched her arm. "Don't do anything foolish. I love the bones of that boy, but his heart is not at Henlow House. It's not even in London and never will be. He's got ideas that involve only himself. He will hurt you in the long term, and I don't want to be witness to it."

Rose's heart ached for the sadness in Mr. Summers's eyes, but she forced a smile. "I appreciate your concern, Mr. Summers, but I can look after myself. I am not as fragile as you seem to think me. Goodnight."

She headed in the direction of the house, but as soon as she turned a corner and was out of Mr. Summers's line of sight, Rose broke into a hurried walk across the gardens to a back gate that led onto the street.

She ignored the frisson of annoyance skittering across her heart. It was clear her actions merely proved Mr. Summers's suspicions about her feelings for Henry. She did not have long before she was expected to return to her duties. But she had to at least try to find him. Or else speak to someone who had seen him and knew him to be safe and well.

She shook her head. The man was certainly trying her patience. It was madness to risk her safety this way, but still she opened the gate.

Chapter Twenty-Six

Henry swiped the perspiration from his brow and fought the horrible awareness that he'd been too weak to ignore the temptation of the tables rather than immediately return to Henlow House. He had no excuses. He could have chosen another route or, better yet, refused the challenge of the man who'd been outside the pub pushing his buttons with undiluted joy. His inability to walk away proved he did indeed have a gambling problem.

Every eye in the back room of the pub was concentrated on him and his only remaining opponent, who sat across the table, his dark eyes unnervingly calm, his forehead as dry as a bone.

The half-decent pile of money at Henry's elbow taunted him. If he put in his lot and it turned out the bastard was bluffing, the winning potential was huge… but so was the loss.

"Come on, Ward. What's it to be?"

The goad was shouted from someone standing a distance from the table, others adding in their cries of rough encouragement for good measure. Henry met his opponent's eyes and tried to gauge the worth of the man's cards, but he was as expressionless as a corpse with a stick up his back.

Henry swallowed. Every time he glanced at the inch of brandy in the glass beside him, his stomach lurched. It was time to return to Henlow House, time to finish this game one way or the other. He sat a little straighter, held his opponent's mocking stare, and embraced the steady increase of adrenaline as it pumped through his veins.

Forcing a nonchalant grin, Henry pushed away thoughts of his pathetic lack of willpower and eased his money pile to the middle of the table. His opponent's steady gaze flickered before a slow smile lifted the corners of his mouth.

"So the man has some guts, after all," he said, nodding toward the cards in Henry's hands. "Let's see what you've got."

Henry inhaled a long breath and turned over his cards, fanning them on the table.

A sharp intake of breath emanated from the motley crew surrounding him and heads turned from him to his opponent and back again. Henry tapped his good leg up and down on the sticky floor, his pulse beating hard.

Please God, let it be enough…

Reaching for his brandy, he gripped the glass so tightly he feared it might shatter beneath his fingers. His adversary leaned forward, and their eyes locked. With slow purpose, his opponent turned over his cards and laid them out for Henry and the entire room to see.

Henry looked at them before closing his eyes, as whistles and applause, backslapping and laughter erupted, bouncing from the yellow, smoke-stained walls and into his brain like a barrage of red-hot pokers. Even behind his closed lids he continued to see the winning cards spread out as though the royal family mocked him from Buckingham Palace. King, queen, knave…

"Well, Ward, I guess tonight is my night. Too bad, my friend."

A slow hum started in Henry's temple, and he squeezed his eyes tighter, his hand once more gripping his glass, his knuckles aching. Over and over, fingers prodded him, hands ruffled his hair, laughter and stinging comments rang all around him as the thrum in his head grew louder.

He abruptly stood, sending his chair clattering to the floor behind him as he wobbled left, then right, trying to get some stability on his one serviceable leg. "Why don't the lot of you just pis—"

"Henry!"

Rose's voice cracked like a whip, slicing through the relentless jesting with such indisputable authority that the entire space descended into instantaneous silence. Henry's gut knotted with shock and then undeniable pleasure despite the fact that this was the last place in the world a woman like her should be. Half of him wanted to kiss her firmly and with shameless possession; the other half wanted to scoop her up and carry her out of this godforsaken cesspit.

She stood a few feet away, dressed in a gray wool coat, red cloth hat, and black boots, her dark curls framing her pink cheeks. She looked like an ethereal hallucination as she approached him. One by one, the men afforded her a pathway without her having to raise her hand. On each side of her, men stared agog, their eyes wide and their mouths open as Rose strode between them with blazing eyes on Henry's, her mouth a thin line.

"I dare you to say another word," she said quietly as she gripped his elbow. "I have been all over town looking for you, and here you are throwing your money away as though there is plenty more where that came from."

She was a woman and a half.

Willing his larynx to function, he glanced around, torn between snatching his arm from her grasp and demanding to know who the hell she thought she was—dressing him down in front of his peers—or bursting into laughter and pulling her firmly into his arms. Instead, a third option thankfully came to mind, and he looked down at her lovely face, just about level with his shoulder.

"I was merely passing the time until you got here, my love. Now that you've arrived, we can leave this fetid hole and go dancing wherever you see fit. My evening is yours." He picked up his hat from the table and put it on, dipping his head to his opponent and a few other gentlemen before returning his attention to Rose. He chose to ignore the fire flickering dangerously in the depths of her caramel eyes. "Shall we?"

She opened her mouth, then snapped it closed and studied him. A second or two ticked by, then she slowly smiled, even if none of the anger left her eyes. "Well, that would be grand."

He walked confidently forward, his cane firmly striking the floorboards as he led her from the back room of the pub into the main bar. There, women were almost as commonplace as the men, but not women who looked and spoke like Rose, and certainly not women who worked for the Countess of Bath. His initial shock at seeing her had given way to amusement, but now volatile protectiveness pumped through him, and Henry steered her through the crowd as quickly as possible, forcing himself to rise above the sneers and unceremonious ribbing he sustained along the way.

Once they were outside, he stopped and breathed deep, drawing in great lungfuls of air as if he could somehow wash away the night's fiasco and start again. He faced Rose, ready to tell her how bad of an idea it had been for her to be inside that pub alone, but the way she glowered at him froze the words on his tongue.

"Have you anything to say to me?" she demanded, seemingly oblivious to the men ogling her backside from where they leaned against the pub windows behind her. "Or is it usual for you to have women fetch you out of gambling dens?"

He glared at the men over her head until they turned their backs and resumed their conversation, then he slid his gaze to hers. "I've plenty to say to you, but I refuse to talk out here in front of all and sundry. Come on." Without waiting for her agreement, Henry took her hand and led her along the street with as much authority as he could muster with a gammy leg.

God only knew what he must look like to her. She could drag him any way she chose, if truth be told, but he sensed she would never do that to him, would never humiliate him that way or any other. Over and over, he cursed his damaged leg and how it stopped him from walking at the pace he desired. Rose Watson was far too good to be here. Far too special. She did not belong in this part of the city. Not by a long shot.

"How much further do you intend to drag me until we talk?" she asked, abruptly snatching her hand from his and stopping. "I refuse to walk any more. I am so mad I could hit you."

He turned around to face her. "Hit me?"

"Yes, Henry. Hit you."

He clenched his jaw and gripped her elbow, then made a pathetic attempt to march her into the nearest alleyway. Releasing her, he hobbled deeper into the dark, damp space to make sure they were alone. Satisfied they were, he returned to her.

"So," he said, fighting the urge to lift his hand to her hair and brush back the curl that had fallen from beneath her cloth hat onto her cheek. "Why are you—"

"I'll tell you exactly why I'm here and exactly why I will be gone in less than two minutes." She planted her hands on her hips, her eyes flashing with dangerous irritation. "I went to the mews looking for you only to be told by your uncle—"

"For the love of God—you spoke to Charles?" He pushed his hand into his hair and blew out a breath. "Well, that's him trying to put me in my place again when I get back."

"You're worried about what your *uncle* might say to you?" She glowered. "He should be the least of your concerns right now. Let me tell you something. You are selfish and unreliable. You are a fool, a—"

"Enough," Henry snapped, his pulse beating hard as she continued to glare at him, seemingly unaffected by his tone. No one, including Rose Watson, hurled insults at him without expecting some choice words in return. "You do not get to stand there—"

"I get to stand here and do whatever I like when I have been trying to help you, spending my time running all over town while you sit in a stinking pub's back room gambling away your money. Money I would have thought precious to you. Your poor uncle—"

He laughed. "My poor uncle? There is nothing poor about—"

"See? Selfish."

"Rose…" He purposefully lowered his voice and battled to keep a hold on his temper. "You need to stop talking to me that way and calm down."

"Is that so?"

"Yes."

"Well, too bad. Not that he would admit it, but your uncle is sick with worry, having not heard a word from you since you left for your doctor's appointment." Her eyes bored into his, her disappointment and anger palpable. "There are people looking out for you, caring for you, but no, the great Henry Ward thinks he is better than everyone else, so he pays them no mind. I, and most likely Mr. Summers, have tried to talk some sense into you and all you do is—"

He crushed his lips to hers and the sudden silence was golden, yet that indulgence was fleeting as Henry fell into the bliss of her lips. He cupped her jaw in his hands and her stiff body slowly softened until he slipped his fingers from her face to her waist. He pulled her closer, relief washing through him when she gently gripped his shoulders, urging him closer, rather than pushing him away. Their kiss deepened and grew a little rougher as each fought for dominance, control, or whatever it was they seemed to want.

Far too soon, she stepped back.

She slid her hands from his shoulders and pressed them firmly to his chest. They looked into each other's eyes, their breaths harried, but their tempers spent. Slowly, she dropped her hands and took another step back, looking at him as though she had no idea what he might do next.

"Well." Henry cleared his throat and gestured with a nod at the entrance of the alley. "We'd better get back to the house. Don't you think?"

Her fingers trembled as she touched them to her lips before snatching them away, her gaze instantly turning defiant. "Yes. I agree that would be the best course of action at this juncture." She brushed past him, her nose in the air.

Henry bit back his smile, feeling a million times better than he ever had at the gaming tables.

Chapter Twenty-Seven

As she and Henry walked closer to the back gates of Henlow House, Rose willed the trembling in her body to abate. Never in her life had she imagined a kiss could be so thrilling, so passionate, and so frightening. Although she had sneaked the odd kiss with three or four suitors who had passed briefly through her life over the years, she had barely made time for romance, instead concentrating on honing her design skills. Her kiss with Henry had been something entirely different.

Dangerous.

Exciting.

Rousing.

Their passion had been matched. Not just physically, but mentally—through their souls—an assured communication despite their mouths being far too busy to talk.

"Penny for your thoughts?"

She blinked and cleared her throat, forcing her eyes to his lest he detect the mayhem tumbling around inside her. "I was considering your insistence on continuing to gamble."

He smiled that slow smile of his, the one that made her stomach quiver.

"*That's* what you were considering?" He raised his eyebrows, his eyes glinting with amusement. "Well, I can't think for the life of me why that should make you smile and blush."

She pinned him with a glare and stepped up her pace, knowing it would annoy him. "I don't have to share my thoughts with you," she said over her shoulder. "But as you've asked, despite you so roughly stealing a kiss from me, I—"

"I'm not sure you can call it stealing," he said, deftly stepping up beside her. "If you take into consideration your response."

Choosing to ignore his retort, Rose slowed, unable to taunt him so unfairly when she was grudgingly impressed that he had managed to keep pace with her. "I came looking for you because I was worried, and now there is every possibility I will be reprimanded by Mrs. Hayworth for my absence."

"Rose, that's the last thing I want. Stop a moment. Please." He gently touched her arm, his gaze somber. "You should not have been in that pub tonight. A fight could've broken out. Glasses could have been thrown." He slipped his hand from her arm and pushed it into his pocket. "I don't want you worrying about me, and I don't want to have to worry about you."

Rose's heart stumbled. Not only had he unwittingly voiced the potential danger of a fight breaking out in a pub under similar circumstances to the one that had resulted in Gideon's death, but the unexpected turmoil etched on his face was impossible to ignore.

"Oh, Henry." She sighed. "Why do you fight the fact that it is natural and good to care about someone and have them care about you?"

He slowly searched her face, lingering a moment on her lips. "It's not that I fight it, Rose."

"Then what are you doing?"

"Allowing myself to care for people too much endangers my ambition, and I won't allow that to happen. I have wanted the freedom to travel the world, doing what I love, for too long for it to fall by the wayside because of something entirely emotional."

Confusion and selfish disappointment whispered through her. "I think you're wrong, Henry. Or making excuses. I have opened my heart to family and friends my entire life and look where I am now."

His frown only deepened, his eyes shadowed with what looked to be regret. "Then maybe I am selfish… just as you said at the pub."

Shame enveloped her, and she looked at the ground. "I didn't mean that."

"Yes, you did, and you were right."

She met his eyes. "No, I was wrong. You are…" *Wonderful.*

"Charles and my aunt took me in as a child." He exhaled a shaky breath and looked along the street. "I was barely four years old when my mother died, and my dad disappeared shortly after." He faced her. "Charles taught me to read and write, laugh and cry, and eventually brought me to Henlow House and taught me all he knew about saddling."

Her heart twisted for the young boy he once was. "And the horses? Who taught you to ride?"

His eyes filled with undisguised pride. "The horses are all me, and now the doctor has confirmed I will ride again one day soon—"

"What?" Rose stilled, joy warming her. "The doctor said that? Your leg is getting better?"

He grinned. "Yep. In fact, I wanted to see you to tell—"

"Oh, Henry, this is such wonderful news." Her entire being yearned to kiss him, hug him close, but she refrained and instead focused on how much easier it would now be to press her proposal for them to work together. "You must be elated. I am so happy for you."

They stared at each other for a moment, their eyes locked, their smiles matching. Rose's heart hitched with her care for him, and she quickly looked away, afraid to acknowledge that what she was beginning to feel for the man standing in front of her had somehow bypassed friendship and ventured toward something much deeper and more worrying.

She cleared her throat. "So assuming your plans are still at the forefront of your mind, you need money, and gambling isn't the way forward. Deep down, you must know that."

He sighed. "Fine. It's not the way forward." He flashed a brief smile. "Unfortunately."

Her stomach knotted at the sight of that smile, the one she feared would become her undoing. "Then why not take advantage of any alternate opportunities that present themselves? Why immediately reject them without exploration?"

He pushed his hand into his hair, looking past her along the street. "I don't need to be a genius to guess what opportunity you are referring to."

"I spoke to Lady Christina about employing someone to help me with her wardrobe."

Surprise widened his eyes. "You told her about me?"

"Well, no. I think if she knew I was suggesting you, the request would be swiftly refused."

"Well, it's a relief you realize that, at least. What did you say exactly?"

"I kept as close to the truth as possible."

"Meaning?"

"Meaning I told her I had a friend, a very skilled friend, who is need of extra income and would willingly help me work on her

wardrobe in the evenings. That way, it will help both me and *her*…"
She grimaced. "Or rather, *him*. You."

Although impossible to decipher them, Rose watched in
fascination as myriad thoughts flashed through his wonderful
green eyes.

"You really are one of the gutsiest women I've ever met," he said.
"Do you know that?"

Pride whispered through Rose as she fought her smile. She had to
remain serious in her expression or risk him thinking her incapable
of subterfuge on this scale. She had to do this. Wanted to do this.
How else would she be secure in the knowledge she had done all she
could to keep Henry safe and help him toward his dreams?

"Well?" She raised her eyebrows. "Will you do it? Can we find
a way to make this work?"

"I was actually planning to get a message to you before I… got
distracted at the tavern."

"You were?"

"Yes. I was going to tell you that if you give me a second chance
at your proposal, I'd like to agree."

"Well, that's very good news." She smiled, but nerves took flight
in her stomach. "But I need you to understand how important it is
that our working together remains undiscovered. Everything that
has led to me being in the countess's service, of living and working
at Henlow House, is in jeopardy if we do this, Henry. You do
understand that?"

"Of course, and I will be careful. Everything we do—everything
I do—will be under your direction."

Absurdly pleased, Rose smiled, her thought to remain grave
entirely abandoned. "Well, in that case, I am sure everything will
work out perfectly."

His gaze bored into hers, then traveled lower to her mouth. "There's one more thing."

Rose frowned. "Which is?"

"I won't take your money, Rose. That is not going to sit well with me at all. If you can persuade the countess to pay an extra worker, that's all well and good, but—"

"I will, don't worry about that." *And if I don't, you'll never know.* "So we're agreed?"

He smiled and lifted his hand to gently cup her jaw. "We're agreed. You truly are so good to me. I want you to know I appreciate all you are doing to help me."

She swallowed, her heart searching his in a way that felt so very wonderful in that moment. "You're welcome."

His hand slowly slipped from her face as a slight color darkened his cheeks. "But it's not just the countess or her staff we need to worry about uncovering our secret."

"Oh?"

"Under no circumstances can Charles find out about this. I do not want to give him even the smallest indication there is hope of me staying in London."

Disappointment—or maybe loss—twisted her stomach. "Then you have nothing to fear, because I would not want him to have false hope either. Not him or... or anyone else who cares about you."

He nodded. "Good."

A telling pain jabbed at Rose's chest. He seemed entirely oblivious—entirely unaffected—by her or her insinuation that what she felt for him had deepened.

She glanced toward the house. "I should go, but before I do, do you have a pencil and a scrap of paper?"

"Why?"

"I intend to speak to the countess as soon as I can to secure her agreement for me to employ some help. With that done, if I have a note of your address, I'll come by your lodgings with some of the work I need to get done the night after tomorrow. Would that suit?"

He frowned and rubbed his hand along his jaw. "Your plan is to come to my lodgings? I had thought the same, but—"

"Isn't that the best way?" Rose stepped back. "I must hurry, Henry. Mrs. Hayworth is bound to ask questions as to my whereabouts when she sees me. Do you have a pencil? Some paper?"

He reached into his pocket and pulled out a stub of pencil, sending her an uncertain glance before retrieving a small notebook too. He scribbled down his address and ripped the page out, then handed it to her. "Here. You'll need to be careful. Charles and my aunt live only a few doors away."

She slipped the paper into her skirt pocket. "I will. Don't worry. Good night, Henry." Rose quickly turned, fighting every treacherous instinct in her body to kiss him as they had kissed before, but she would not do that when his feelings did not seem to be in the same place as hers.

The trouble was, how was she to close her heart when it had at last been well and truly opened?

Chapter Twenty-Eight

Rose opened the countess's traveling trunk and reached for the first of the two capes Mrs. Hayworth had asked her to pack. The queen had summoned Lord Robert and Lady Christina to Buckingham Palace, requesting that they spend a few days with her. Rose suspected neither the earl nor the countess was particularly thrilled by the prospect, having overheard them several times lamenting over the austerity and lack of entertainment at Victoria's court. Their time at the palace would undoubtedly be profoundly more sober than the jolly hours the earl was used to at Henlow House.

Running her fingers over the cape's black velvet collar, Rose considered whether velvet would work as a trim on the jacket she had designed that was almost ready for Lady Christina's endorsement.

"Is everything well with you, Watson?" Her Ladyship asked as she stood from her dressing table. "You seem rather distracted this evening."

Rose met the countess's gentle gaze and purposefully buried the guilt that niggled at her. "Not at all, my lady. I was just admiring the velvet on this cape and wondering if I might add a length to one of the jackets I have created for you."

"Oh! Does this mean you might soon have something new for me to try on?" The Countess grinned as she picked up a book and handed it to her maid. "I will take this one, Harris, thank you." She turned her attention to Rose. "You have been so tight-lipped about what you are working on for the hospital opening that I've barely given it much thought. I assume all is in hand?"

Rose stared at the cape rather than the countess. It had been a few days since she'd spoken to Henry. Now would be the perfect time to remind Her Ladyship about her request for additional help.

"Watson?"

Rose pulled back her shoulders. "Everything is in hand to a point, but I worry I may soon fall behind schedule without additional help. The ensemble I want to create requires quite a lot of work, and—"

"You are still thinking you need assistance."

There was a harshness to the countess's tone, one that reminded Rose that Her Ladyship might be friendly and kind to her overall, but they would always be aristocrat and servant.

Rose swallowed. "Yes. It would be wrong of me not to admit everything is taking longer than I anticipated. Or that I wouldn't appreciate an extra pair of hands."

"I see. And you have spoken to this friend of yours? She knows who the clothes will be for? The due diligence and care needed when working on such expensive fabrics, et cetera?"

"Yes. I have also told her what it means to me to be working for you, and I expect the same commitment to excellence from her that I expect of myself."

The countess gave a satisfied nod. "Very good."

Rose glanced at Mrs. Hayworth, who was lightly running a brush over the shoulders and neckline of an ivory silk evening dress. "I have spoken to Mrs. Hayworth, and she is in agreement, as I have confirmed I am happy to work in the evenings, and it will not affect my duties here."

"Well, considering I already allow you as many evenings as I can spare you to work on my new clothes, I concur." The countess frowned, her thoughts seeming to drift momentarily before she smiled. "In that case, why don't you ask Mrs. Hayworth to devise a suitable wage for your friend, and it can be added to my household accounts in due course."

Rose resisted the urge to dance a little jig. Taking money from her wages had been Henry's only resistance, and now that problem had been resolved. "Thank you, Your Ladyship."

"You're welcome. Now…" Lady Christina glanced at Harris, and the maid quickly dipped a curtsy and moved away, leaving Her Ladyship and Rose relatively alone. The countess leaned in close and placed her hand on Rose's forearm. "I am going to share something with you that I trust will go no further."

Rose stood completely still despite the fluttering in her stomach. "Of course."

The countess's eyes darkened with undisguised resentment. "The earl's eye is wandering to a degree that I know the time is nigh when he will take a permanent mistress. One I can only hope he keeps private rather than claiming openly, leaving me no choice but to remain silent."

Protectiveness for the countess and scorn for the earl stirred inside Rose. "His Lordship…" She paused, the title tasting bitter in her mouth. "Surely will not expect you to—"

"Oh, but he will." Lady Christina briefly closed her eyes before opening them again, her gaze fiery with determination. "Before this possible revelation comes to light, I intend to make myself matter to the people, Watson. I want to matter to England. After all, I am a part of this great family, this mighty institution. If he has more interest in women than in this wonderful country, then I shall pick up the mantle rather than allow him to inevitably drop it."

Rose looked deep into the countess's eyes and saw nothing but fierce pride and sincerity. Did Lady Christina love her husband?

Sadness and sympathy over her mistress's plight knotted Rose's stomach.

"I will do everything in my power to support you, my lady. And if that support comes in the form of the clothes you wish to wear, I will work day and night to ensure they are ready for every occasion."

Lady Christina tightened her grip on Rose's arm and offered her a brief smile. "Thank you. Truly. But…" She dropped her hand and once again glanced around the room. "It is my cross to bear. Now, why don't I join you and we'll talk to Mrs. Hayworth about your friend together?"

Sending up a silent prayer that she would soon be able to set Henry to work, Rose followed the countess across the room.

"Mrs. Hayworth," the countess called. "Might I have a quick word?"

Mrs. Hayworth looked up from the emerald-and-diamond tiara she was inspecting. "Of course, Your Ladyship."

"I understand you are happy with Watson's request to have her friend assist her with my wardrobe."

"Yes, Your Ladyship."

"I am so pleased as it is my deepest wish that Watson has the required time and resources to make me a wardrobe that will astound the press and public alike, beginning with the hospital ward opening in just two weeks. If Watson believes this friend is the right person to help her, then I wish to make her employment possible immediately."

"Of course, Your Ladyship."

"Wonderful. Then I shall leave it with you to determine acceptable payment in addition to Watson's income."

"Of course, my lady." Mrs. Hayworth faced Rose, her brow furrowed. "Are you absolutely confident this friend of yours is up to such a task? The work needed on the countess's wardrobe must be some of the finest in the country, as you know."

"My friend is highly skilled, Mrs. Hayworth. Her work is exemplary. More than that, she needs this opportunity and will work hard to prove herself, I'm sure." Rose stepped forward, inwardly pleading that the countess's dresser understood how much this mattered to her and how much trust—albeit quite possibly misplaced—she had in Henry. "I promise she won't let me, you, or Her Ladyship down any more than I would."

Silence fell and sickness rolled through Rose's stomach as the countess and Mrs. Hayworth looked at her with mixed expressions of surprise and curiosity. Had she been too exuberant? Her feelings for Henry were clearly becoming harder to conceal, which only spelled trouble if she did not appear unemotionally attached. Rose tried her best to remain still under their scrutiny. Should she have made such a promise when Henry could once again flee Henlow House in search of a gambling den at any given moment?

Mrs. Hayworth cleared her throat. "You certainly seem to have a lot of confidence in this young lady to give her such advocacy. Have you known her long?"

Warmth slowly spread over Rose's neck, and she flitted her gaze between Mrs. Hayworth and the countess, who both watched her with interest. "A while, yes."

"A while?" Mrs. Hayworth narrowed her eyes. "As in… a month? Two?"

Rose hesitated. In truth, she had known Henry only a short time, yet she felt as though she had known him forever.

"Well, Watson?" Lady Christina frowned. "Is this woman known to you personally?"

Rose kept her gaze firmly on the countess's as she lifted her chin, intent on forcing as much authority into her voice as she could muster. "She is, and I know her to be a hard worker, committed, and talented. However, she has become unsure of her place in this world or what the future might hold. Something… happened, and she has been unable to work as she once could, but…" Rose pressed her lips together, battling to calm her racing heart. "I'm convinced this opportunity will be the making of her."

The challenge in Mrs. Hayworth's eyes, and the uncertainty in Her Ladyship's threatened to weaken her, but Rose stood tall. She must instill faith in these women that she knew exactly what she was asking and what would be expected of her in return should her request be granted: hard work, commitment, and delivery of the countess's garments perfectly made and on time.

"The employment of your friend clearly means a lot to you, Watson," Lady Christina said. She inhaled a heavy breath and walked across the room to her dressing table. She picked up a bottle of scent and smiled at Harris, gesturing with a dip of her head for her maid to add it to her case. "I trust that you know the right people you would like to have working with you." She then addressed Mrs. Hayworth. "I ask that you agree to Watson's request. It is important that all the outfits she has in mind for me are complete and exquisite in every way, and if Watson would be happier having this young lady working alongside her, so be it. I wish to be admired by the people of London for the right reasons. Reasons that have nothing to do with the earl. I know I shouldn't say such things, but trust that my motivation and motives are just."

Rose stared at Lady Christina, care for her unfurling in her heart. She recognized the hurt and frustration on Her Ladyship's face. She was unappreciated and vexed—the earl's philandering and late-night outings caused his wife unfair distress. So much so, the countess felt the need to strike out alone and ensure the British public see her for herself and not just as the Countess of Bath or Lord Robert's consort. Rose admired her immensely.

She met the countess's eyes. "And they *will* look at you that way, Your Ladyship. In another week or so, you can examine the first few outfits I have made. Everyone will be looking at you and only you, I promise."

Lady Christina smiled. "That makes me very happy." She faced Mrs. Hayworth. "You will ensure Watson's friend is made welcome to my service?"

Mrs. Hayworth nodded, but her jaw was tight. "Of course."

"Very good."

Lady Christina beckoned Harris closer and as they began to talk, Mrs. Hayworth gripped Rose's elbow and drew her away, past the cluster of dogs sitting in front of the hearth and into a corner of the room. She feigned inspection of two dresses hung up in front of her and Rose did the same, her heart beating fast.

"Is everything all—"

"Have a care, Watson," Mrs. Hayworth whispered, her gaze resolute. "I have no idea how well you know this friend or why you seem so determined to have her work with you. The entire situation is extremely unorthodox. You are taking a great risk. If this leads to even a single mistake as far as the countess's wardrobe or her expectation of you is concerned, it will mean the end of your time here."

Dread rolled through Rose's stomach, but she remained stalwart. "I understand, but I have every confidence in her work," she said quietly. "I just want to help her put her skills to good use."

"That's all well and good, but from the first time I saw your work, I believed your future could be quite extraordinary." Mrs.

Hayworth's eyes hardened. "I hope I am not proven wrong. Your time here is precious, Watson. Don't be foolish with it, and do not look elsewhere for company if you find yourself growing lonely. You can talk to me whenever you need to."

"Thank you."

"You're welcome." Mrs. Hayworth stepped back, her eyes dark with warning. "Remember, there are a hundred and one other girls who would give their eyeteeth for the extraordinary life you are currently living."

Mrs. Hayworth walked away, and an inexplicable mix of excitement and fear filled Rose. Excitement for the opportunities ahead, and to be working with and helping Henry. Fear in case her plan failed, or she was found to have lied to her superiors. Despite the risk, Rose couldn't help but smile. She had no idea why, but suddenly she felt as though she stood on the precipice of something remarkable—something that had much to do with Henry being by her side.

Chapter Twenty-Nine

Henry laid down his pliers and awkwardly pushed to his feet, pleased that his damaged leg had not overly pained him, considering he had been at work for almost two hours. He shifted from side to side to stretch out the knots in his lower back and then hobbled to the open front door of the stables.

A week had passed since the night Rose instigated his abrupt removal from the pub, and he'd spent the same amount of time wondering if he would be working with her on the countess's wardrobe. The late-afternoon sun hung low in the sky, bright with the welcome promise of summer. A season that was always pleasing for him and the rest of the house's outdoor workers. He walked to the training area and leaned his forearms on the fence surrounding the large circular lawn. Yearning pulled at him, and envy coated his throat as he watched another worker put a young colt through its paces.

Henry narrowed his eyes and contemplated how he would have done things differently, how he would have directed the horse this way and that. It wouldn't be long before he was back working with these phenomenal animals and now, with Rose's generosity, he had every intention of saving his money. No more gambling. He clenched his jaw, fighting his dastardly impulses. That part of his life was over.

Footsteps approached, and Henry turned to see Charles walking along the graveled pathway that ran from the back of the main house. He led the earl's horse by its bridle, its master absent.

Henry eased away from the fence as his uncle came closer. No matter how much it might rankle, it was time to admit temporary defeat and offer Charles an olive branch. Henry blew out a slow breath. He was man enough to admit he was currently the underdog in the ongoing battle between them and, for now, he was staying in England, in London, and at Henlow House. His dreams of living across the ocean had been curtailed for the time being and, if he was going to work with Rose in secret, he needed to ensure he gave Charles no reason to find fault in his nephew or—God forbid—keep a closer eye on him.

Forcing a smile, he raised his hand, and Charles nodded in acknowledgment. Henry limped toward him, pleased that the need for his cane lessened a little each day. He ran his hand over the horse's velvety muzzle, and the animal snorted a greeting.

"How is His Lordship?" Henry asked.

"In a buoyant mood. Too buoyant." Charles slapped the horse's shoulder. "He's been parading around the park all afternoon and just announced he'll be out on the town again tonight. Lord only knows what that will entail. I got the impression he felt as though he'd been locked up in a dungeon while visiting the Queen. You'd never think he'd been waited on hand and foot, his every whim catered to."

Henry gave a wry smile. "I imagine the Queen's idea of a good time doesn't quite match that of the earl's."

"I have no doubt you're right." Charles studied him through narrowed eyes, his shrewd gaze running over Henry's face before he looked him straight in the eye. "How are you faring? You look a little less melancholy than you have of late."

"I'm feeling the best I have in a good while."

"Well, that's good news, son. I'm pleased for you."

Henry focused on the horse, smoothed his hand along its forelock. "Not only is my leg on the mend, but I finally understand something you've been saying."

"Oh?"

"The gambling, Uncle. I'm giving it up."

The incredulous look on Charles's face came as no shock, but the jolt of unexpected yet strong determination that immediately shot through Henry upon seeing it was certainly a surprise. He held Charles's disbelieving stare.

"I'm leaving the tables behind for good. I've had enough of my finances seesawing back and forth. It's time I grew up."

"Good God."

"I can't deny that Rose's words, added to yours, has made me see sense." *Not to mention that I want to make her happy, to have her smile at me.* He swallowed. "I'm speaking the truth. It's over."

"Well…" Charles slapped his hand to Henry's shoulder. "I'm as pleased as punch, son. I really am."

Henry looked into his uncle's eyes, and the pleasure there was most definitely edged with a hint of skepticism. But he could hardly blame Charles for that.

"So I'll keep working and saving."

Silence fell and Henry waited.

And waited some more.

Charles sighed. "Well, it gladdens me to hear you say it, even if I'll always prefer you to stay here with your family. But if you must go, I'd rather you went on money earned than on winnings." He gave a considering nod. "The genuine way is better. It shows you have an idea of how people really get on in the world."

Battling to remain calm and not have the slight ignite another row between them, Henry purposefully adopted a passive expression and kept quiet.

"Maybe," his uncle continued, "you'll start to see the benefit of standing on your own two feet and earning a living you can be proud of. Of building something to pass on to your family one day, just like I wanted to pass my work on to you."

Habitual guilt twisted through Henry's gut. "*Wanted* to? Is that particular wish no more?"

His uncle's eyes sobered. "I'm not getting my hopes up anymore that you will find happiness here, Henry. Or that you will accept that working at such a revered house, making the finest saddles in the country, isn't such a hardship."

Henry closed his eyes. "I'm sorry, Uncle."

"Sorry?"

Henry opened his eyes. "Sorry I'm not who you need me to be."

Now that he'd spoken honestly, he felt purged of a burden that had been eating away at him for two long years. He wasn't who his uncle wanted him to be, but that was no more his fault than it was Charles's.

Regret flashed in Charles's eyes, and all his previous anger and frustration seemed to seep away as his shoulders dropped. "All I want now is for you to keep away from the gambling houses. Nothing more, nothing less." Charles studied him before he nodded and tugged on the horse's bridle. "Right, we'd better get on." He moved forward and then stopped. "One more thing. I highly recommend you take special care of Miss Watson, son. She is a kind and considerate soul. She has an aura about her that speaks of loyalty, honesty, and openness, traits that are hard to come by and once found should be cherished."

Henry clenched his jaw, defensiveness simmering beneath his skin. But deep down, he knew he'd not done anything in a long while to earn Charles's trust in him to do the right thing—by Rose or anyone else.

"I'll take your advice, Uncle," he said quietly. "Don't you worry about that. Rose—Miss Watson—has made me see that you talked some sense over the years about family and friends." He rubbed his hand over his jaw, glancing along the pathway. "She has made me want to explore a different avenue… or at least try one anyway."

"Good. Then I'll see you later."

Charles walked away, leaving Henry staring after him, hoping against hope he kept to all he had damn near promised.

Chapter Thirty

Rose inhaled a strengthening breath as she entered the street housing her parents' shop. She had not been home to visit in over a month and, despite thinking of her parents daily, she would be lying if she said her return home filled her with anything other than trepidation. Her newfound independence, the people she had met, and the sights she had seen in and out of Henlow House had shifted something inside her. Something exciting, something empowering. A strong sense of possibility had awoken in her that she never wanted to lose. Yet whenever she returned home, the idea that she might one day soar was shadowed with feelings of guilt and selfishness.

The pain in her mother's eyes the day Rose first left to work for the countess and the one time she had returned since, still haunted her. She had no reason to believe this visit would be a happy one either. Stopping in front of a shop window, her back to the street, Rose tried to steady the erratic beat of her heart. She was so strong and in control when she was working in the countess's apartments or discussing designs and outfits with Mrs. Hayworth.

She looked at the box she carried. Heavens above, she had even found the strength to take a risk—a big risk—for Henry. Would she not be delivering these two skirts for him to alter following her visit home? But now that she was here, she felt herself regressing to little more than a grown daughter still under the management of her parents.

Rose stared at her reflection and stood tall. No. This time would be different.

Spinning around, she planted one foot in front of the other until she reached her parents' shop and firmly pushed open the door.

"Good evening, Mama."

"Rose!" A long piece of cloth dropped from her mother's hands to the counter as she rushed forward and enfolded Rose in a firm embrace. "You're home."

Relief melted Rose's heart as she put the box by her feet and squeezed her mother back with equal vigor. Could her fears be entirely unfounded?

"I am, but just for a little bit, I'm afraid." She smiled. "I must get back to Henlow House before eight o'clock."

Tension immediately stiffened her mother's body, and she stepped back, her smile dissolving.

"You know it must be so, Mama."

"Well, of course." Her mother's smile was strained, the momentary delight that had flashed in her eyes vanishing. "Why else would you be here if not for duty's sake? I daresay the countess is far more important to you these days than I could ever be."

"Mama…"

Her mother returned to the counter. "Why don't you go through and greet your father? He will be happy to see you."

Sadness pressed down on her as Rose stared at her mother's turned back. "I am glad to be home, however briefly, Mama. I wish you believed that."

When no response came, Rose looked around her, struggling to think of something more to say. "Is Florence not here?" she asked.

"No, she is off visiting her aunt and cousins for the evening."

Her mother's back remained turned, so Rose picked up her box and walked behind the counter. She pushed aside the curtain separating the shop from the back rooms. As she walked to the kitchen, she heard some bustling and the slow murmur of her father's voice as he spoke with their maid.

"That's fine, my dear. You get yourself to bed for the night. I'm sure Mrs. Watson and I can see to our dinner."

Rose stood a little way back from the doorway and when Sarah turned and saw her, her eyes widening with surprise, Rose put a finger to her lips. The other woman smiled and slid out of the room, giving Rose's shoulder a squeeze as she passed. Humming happily to himself, her father moved around the room, checking the kettle on the stove before walking to the drawer where the cutlery was kept and taking out knives and forks. Rose smiled and stood a little straighter, knowing he would turn at any moment.

"Rose!"

Tears leaped into her eyes as pure, unadulterated pleasure lit her dear papa's face, the cutlery clattering to the tabletop before he rushed to embrace her.

"You're home."

She laughed and quickly put her box and reticule on an empty chair at the table before hugging him. "I am, Papa. Just for a little while."

He grinned, pressed a firm kiss to her cheek, and then held her at arm's length. "Well, a little while is better than not at all. Come, sit. Sit."

Rose sat before removing the pins from her hat. "You are looking well, Papa."

"I am well," he said, his eyes soft with love as his gaze wandered over her face. "And you?"

"Very well." And she *was*. Happy, in fact. And with the news that she was to create an entire season's worth of clothes for Her Ladyship that she was desperate to share with her parents—the people she loved most in the world—she may even be surpassing happiness. "In fact—"

"In fact, you are so well that you cannot possibly afford your parents more than an hour or so of your precious time." Her mother swept into the room, the heels of her shoes tip-tapping across the floor tiles as she snatched her apron from a hook on the wall. She tied it at her waist, her movements sharp before she met Rose's eyes. "Is that not what you were going to say?"

"No, Mama. It was not." She held her mother's awful, hurting gaze and fought the horrible knowledge that it was she who caused her such pain. "Please, stop this. I love you and I want to visit, but you are making that very difficult."

"Is it my fault that this is only the second time we have seen you since you ran off to Henlow House without so much as a backward glance?"

"I am in service to a countess, Mama. My time is no more mine than it was when I worked here. I have rules and restrictions to abide by just the same."

Silence fell and Rose fought the urge to explain herself further even as the weight of her subterfuge with Henry and how much she wanted to help him pressed down on her. "Even when I leave here, I have to run an errand. My life is busy, but I am happy."

Being dutiful and compliant to her parents made becoming who she wanted to be all the harder. It hurt to cause them pain, and it jarred her to defy them, but she was enjoying becoming her own woman, her own person. She would not give that up easily. Maybe if her mother believed her that her life was no more hers now than when she had been home, she might be a little more merciful.

"The only thing that has changed," Rose said, "is that I am able to make decisions with regard to the clothes I make. I am building an occupation that might be more financially fruitful than any of us could have believed, Mama. And for that I am grateful and always will be."

"Clementine, my love." Her father's voice was quiet in the thick stillness of the room. "Stop this. Rose is home. Do not waste this short time together on words and emotions you will regret once she is gone again."

A single tear ran over her mother's cheek and Rose's heart jolted painfully. She quickly stood, the legs of her chair scraping over the floor.

"Oh, Mama. Please don't cry." As a horrible racking sob escaped her mother's throat, Rose pulled her close and kissed her hair. "I am learning so much, and everyone, the countess included, is treating me so kindly." Rose stepped back and thumbed the tears from her mother's cheeks and gently cupped her jaw. "She even wants me to design a whole ensemble for her to wear. She is determined to be seen not only as the wife of the earl, but as herself, as Lady Christina." Rose smiled, tears pricking her eyes. "She is such an inspiration to me, and I want nothing more than to work for her and learn from her for as long as I can. She is wonderful, Mama. Truly."

"Oh, Rose… I do love you so." Her mother shook her head and stepped away. She sat down at the table and took her husband's hand. "I'm sorry."

Rose's heart ached to see her mother, a woman usually so determined and unbreakable, suddenly look so small.

"There is no need for you to apologize. I cannot imagine how you have borne the loss of Gideon. And I understand how much you love me, I really do. But everything about working at Henlow House feels right. It's as though I belong there."

Silence ensued, and Rose could hear her pulse beating in her ears.

"More than you ever did here?"

She faced her father, surprised he had asked the question rather than her mother. "No, Papa, not more. I belonged here all my life, but then this opportunity came along, and I took it gladly. The future looks bright for us all. I am able to send you money. You have all you need?"

He nodded, his fingers tightening on her mother's. "Yes, my love, we do."

The sadness in her mother's face slowly lessened and her eyes, so like Rose's, brightened a little. "We have all we need, darling. Except for you, of course. But…" Her voice cracked before she smiled. "I will try to live with your absence and embrace your presence whenever you are home."

Rose looked at each of her parents and thought of Henry and how she wanted to make him as happy as she was. "So much good can come from taking chances and trying new things. In fact, I intend to use this opportunity to help others too."

Her father frowned. "But surely you are in no position to make decisions concerning others at the house?"

"I didn't think so, but…" Rose hesitated. Mentioning Henry to her parents suddenly felt like telling them of her growing feelings for him. She cursed the heat that rose in her cheeks, knowing she so rarely blushed and her father was sure to notice it. "The countess has already allowed me to choose an assistant to help me. That is a sign of her fondness and trust in me. Don't you agree?"

The doubt and suspicion in her parents' gazes burned into her, but Rose remained stalwart under their scrutiny.

"Then you are revered indeed, my dear," her mother finally said as she rose from the table and walked to the stove. "You have my blessing, and I promise to welcome you home with open arms from now on, but…" She turned, her gaze worried. "I want you to be careful, Rose. Always."

"I will. I promise." She looked at her father, relief tentatively encircling her heart. "Papa?"

He studied her, his brow creased. "An assistant, you say?"

Once again, heat seared Rose's cheeks. "Yes, Papa."

He continued to look at her, and Rose tapped her foot beneath the table until he gave a satisfied nod.

"Then there is not much to say other than to echo your mother's warning. You have my blessing too."

Rose forced a smile, not particularly enjoying what pursuing her happiness and satisfaction felt like in that moment. She had no doubt her father knew she had not told them the entirety of what was happening behind the high walls of Henlow House, including her new, innovative designs that she now felt at liberty to indulge in… or that every day it grew harder for her to deny that she was falling in love with Henry Ward.

Chapter Thirty-One

Henry stood at his front room window and looked left and right along the street, willing Rose to appear so he could get her into the house as quickly as possible. Normally, he moaned about renting the two ground-floor rooms of the three-bedroom townhouse because the upper floors were almost certainly lighter and airier, but tonight was different. Tonight, he was thankful because the moment Rose appeared, he would be able to go straight to the front door and—

There! Was that her? He squinted. Yes, it was!

His heart thumping, Henry rushed to his door and stepped into the hallway, praying his landlady didn't make the unusual decision to leave her nightly tot of brandy to come see what he was up to.

He pulled open the front door, then stepped out onto the pavement and lifted his hand to Rose as she came closer. His heart stumbled. God, she was beautiful.

She reached his house and stood in front of him, tendrils of dark hair blowing about her cheeks. "I'm sorry I'm later than promised."

Blinking out of his momentary stupor, Henry shook his head. "No need to worry. Come on…" He took the box she carried and ushered her ahead of him into the house. "Mine's the first door on the left. Go on in."

He waited at the front door and watched her until she was safely in his room before he carefully and silently lowered the box to the floor. He straightened to close the front door when—

"Hello, Cousin Henry."

His heart leaped into his throat. *No, no, no...*

He eased the door back on its hinges and stared, dread knotting his chest, into the bright blue eyes of his young, ten-year-old cousin, Martha.

"What... what are you doing here?" He looked over her head. God, were his uncle and aunt behind her? "Are you alone?"

"Yes." She frowned. "Why are you whispering?"

"You need to go."

"What?" Martha narrowed her eyes, her intelligent gaze intent on his. "Why? You always let me come see you when I'm bored. Why not now?"

"Because—"

"Henry?"

Henry squeezed his eyes shut as Rose spoke behind him.

"Oh, hello. And who might this be?"

He could hear the smile in her beautiful voice. One more minute—one more person—and Mrs. Baxter would be out her door, rolling pin in hand.

Snapping his eyes open, he gripped the front of Martha's cardigan and more or less propelled her into the house.

"Quick," he hissed, picking up Rose's box and gesturing them forward with a frantic nod. "Both of you into my rooms. Now."

Rose looked at him, her eyes flashing with annoyance and an almost certain preparation to defy him. But then she looked at Martha and clearly—thankfully—thought better of it.

"Come along, darling. Let's do as the moody man says."

Martha giggled and happily followed Rose into his room, damn near closing the door in his face if it hadn't been for the box in his arms stopping it. He shouldered the door ajar, put the box on the floor, and then eased the door closed as quietly as possible. When he turned back into the room, Rose and Martha stood side by side, staring at him with infuriatingly similar expressions of barefaced amusement.

Ignoring Rose, lest she weaken him with those ridiculous eyes of hers, Henry pinned his cousin with a stare. "As you can see, I have a visitor. Therefore—"

"Rose, I know. She already told me her name." Martha grinned and nodded at the box on the floor. "She said she's brought some skirts you are going to alter for her. That's a very nice thing to do, Cousin Henry. It's good that you're being good. Mama often says you are far from good."

Rose chuckled.

Henry snapped his gaze to hers, heat rising in his cheeks. "It's not funny."

"No, of course not." She rolled her lips tightly together.

"So…" He picked up the box and carried it to the low table in front of his settee. "What do we have?" He glanced at Martha. "Clearly, my cousin has no intention of leaving us until she sees what's inside this box."

Martha grinned.

Henry glared at her, trying his best not to let his love for her influence him. "If I show you what is in this box, you are not to say a word—not a single word—about the clothes or Rose being here to anyone. Including your ma and pa. Do you understand?"

The little girl's smile faltered. "It is bad, then?" She looked back and forth between him and Rose. "Are you up to something naughty?"

"Naugh—" He looked at Rose, his gut clenching with fondness when he saw the two spots of color on her cheeks. He smiled. "I can't say it's naughty exactly and, as much as Miss Watson tries to lead me astray from time to time—"

"I do no such thing!" Rose whispered urgently. "Henry, do not tell the child such things."

He shrugged. "As you wish." He faced Martha, her canny gaze sliding between the adults. "Do I have your word? Do you promise you will not say anything about what happened here tonight to your ma and pa?"

She pressed her hand over her heart, her gaze solemn. "On my honor, your secrets are safe with me."

Biting back his smile, he faced Rose. "What do you think? Can she be trusted?"

She stared at him, the worry in her eyes slowly softening to something that made Henry's heart beat a little faster. Her beautiful lips curved into a smile, her gaze moving over his mouth before she met his eyes.

"I think she can."

Henry tried and failed to drag his gaze from hers. Admiration, care… attraction… that was what he had seen in her eyes, and it suddenly felt like months since he'd kissed her.

He abruptly cleared his throat and faced his cousin. "Right. Miss Watson has given her approval. If you tell your parents what you saw here tonight, you won't just be letting me down, but Miss Watson too. Understood?"

Martha lifted her hand to her brow in a sharp salute. "Understood."

"Right then." Henry gave a curt nod and opened the box, then pulled out a midnight-blue, satin-silk skirt. Martha's gasp filled the room, but Henry's appraisal remained focused on the material he would be working with, his mind intent on the task ahead of him. "What's wrong with it?"

Rose joined him at the table and maneuvered the material in his hands until she found the seam she wanted altered. "This. It needs taking in where I've tacked. The same on both sides. There is also this…" She eased the skirt from his hands and pointed to the embellishment along part of the hem. "It needs taking back and re-stitching." Her eyes met his, her brow slightly creased. "It's the same problem on both skirts. It would be fabulous if you can do this for me, Henry, and have them ready for collection in two nights' time."

He smiled at her. In that moment he would have given her the world. "Consider it done."

"Thank you."

Their eyes locked, their smiles wide.

"Oh, no…" Martha murmured. "Are you going to kiss now?"

Chapter Thirty-Two

"Oh, Watson. It's beautiful!"

Rose swelled with pride as Lady Christina held her latest creation in front of her before the full-length mirror in her bedchamber.

"You are beyond talented," she exclaimed. "I will have the press's entire focus. Mark my words."

Smiling, Rose stood beside her and studied the countess's reflection, overjoyed that the gleaming dark-blue satin impeccably enhanced her mistress's hair and eyes, just as Rose had envisioned. "You will look wonderful, Your Ladyship, and I have specifically ordered sunshine all day, which will make this dress sparkle, making it impossible for guests not to gasp with delight when they see you."

Lady Christina laughed. "You are incorrigible, Watson. It is for the press I will preen, not the guests. The journalists persistently see me as nothing more than a woman following her husband rather than as a member of a noble family in my own right. Moreover…" Her jaw tightened. "They see me as a woman the earl has every right to treat as he chooses."

The light in the countess's eyes dimmed as she stared at her reflection, the joy that had lit her entire being now snuffed out, leaving only wisps of sadness suspended around her. Rose silently cursed Lord Robert and the way he continued to spend night after night away from Henlow House, doing what no one in Her Ladyship's household knew for sure, but could certainly guess. It was so wrong, and Rose hated that she was useless to do anything to curb his conduct or ease her mistress's distress.

Desperate to buoy her, Rose purposely stood between Lady Christina and the mirror, her smile forced as she eased the dress from the countess's hands. "Well, this dress and the other I showed you are now complete and with my new assistant's employment, I'm sure I will have not one, but two more ensembles to show you in a week or so."

Her Ladyship took a seat in front of the fireplace. "That is very welcome news, Watson, especially as..."

Foreboding whispered through Rose.

The countess grimaced and glanced at the door. "I was going to wait for Mrs. Hayworth to return from her meeting with my maids, but it will do just as well to speak to you alone." The countess picked up her embroidery from a small table beside her and plucked out the threaded needle. "Although my husband only takes occasional notice of what I am wearing, it is a credit to your skill that he has remarked favorably several times when I have been wearing your designs."

"He has?"

"Yes." Lady Christina smiled tightly, her eyes filled with more annoyance than pleasure. "So much so that he has insisted on meeting you to talk about your work and plans for future garments."

Uneasy, Rose laced her fingers tightly together in front of her. "I see."

"Do you, Watson? Because I do not. I have no doubt he is merely causing trouble for his own amusement, and I wish I had not indulged his questions about you at dinner last night." The countess studied the embroidery in her lap, her shoulders high. "Clearly, my declaration of happiness and satisfaction with you and your work is insufficient for my husband, Watson. He likes to be involved in all that I do, think, and say, I'm afraid. At least, he does for the time he is not distracted elsewhere." Lady Christina sighed.

"So, to that end, the earl has made room in his diary to briefly speak with you this afternoon." She glanced at the tall clock in the corner before laying down her work and finally meeting Rose's eyes. There was no mistaking the apology in her gaze. "In the next half hour, I'm afraid. But rest assured, he will not call a halt to my plans for the hospital ward opening, so do not worry. My husband just likes to assert his majesty…" She shook her head. "Over us all, it seems."

Rose stared at the countess, trepidation twisting inside her, Lord Robert's reputation around women echoing in her mind.

"You are a wonderful addition to my household, Watson. I enjoy having you here. Please don't forget that no matter what the earl might say or how he might make you feel." She smiled. "Now, put that beautiful dress away. I will pass on what is happening to Mrs. Hayworth shortly, and she can escort you to my husband's apartments."

Rose swallowed against the dryness in her throat. "Will I… be alone with the earl, Your Ladyship?"

The countess's gaze snapped from her embroidery. "Oh, do not worry. I will join you in my husband's apartments when you meet him."

Relieved, Rose released her breath. "Thank you, Your Ladyship."

As Rose followed Mrs. Hayworth through the corridors to the earl's apartments, she nodded hello to one or two familiar servants who carried messages to and from the mews. The number of servants and upper servants, guests, and gentry they passed as she strode behind Mrs. Hayworth through the countless corridors, landings, and hallways made her head spin. Not to mention the décor. Gold glinted, silver shimmered, and precious stones sparkled. Huge paintings with great golden frames hung on the walls, and gigantic chandeliers ran along the center of every ceiling as they left one grand area to enter one even more opulent.

It was so lavishly decorated it was clear why the earl and countess chose to carry out the majority of their entertaining in this part of the house. Rose could not imagine what it was like inside one of the Queen's palaces.

They turned into a narrow, wood-paneled corridor and Mrs. Hayworth stopped and turned to Rose, her eyes widened with warning.

"Next, we'll enter His Lordship's apartments." She glanced along the hallway. "Just be grateful the countess is in there with him. The earl is much harder to please in his own territory."

"You sound as though Lord Robert might eat us for supper," Rose said with a smile.

Mrs. Hayworth raised her eyebrows. "Something I think completely possible. However, he can be jovial enough when he chooses to be."

Rose's smile wavered as she glanced at the door. "I really hope so. Designing and creating the countess's wardrobe is a dream come true, and I would hate for the earl to be dissatisfied with my work. I never would have imagined I would find myself here, like this... with you, but here we are, and I have no desire to leave."

"Then we will make this meeting with Lord Robert successful for us both," Mrs. Hayworth said.

Her conviction was contagious, and Rose straightened her spine.

After walking through an anteroom and then a receiving room, they stopped outside a dark-wood door. Mrs. Hayworth glanced at Rose over her shoulder, gave a curt nod, and then pushed it open.

They had barely stepped over the threshold when Mrs. Hayworth dropped into a curtsy. "Your Lord and Ladyship."

Rose quickly followed suit beside her.

Rising, she looked across the room and stiffened. The earl stood at the fireplace, one hand on the mantel as he puffed on a cigar. The countess sat on a white-and-gold brocade sofa opposite him, holding a small glass of wine.

"Ah, you're here." The earl walked to the middle of the room and eyed Rose through a mist of cigar smoke. "Thank you, Mrs. Hayworth. You may go."

"Yes, sir." Mrs. Hayworth curtsied and then looked at Rose, her gaze kind and encouraging, then she turned and left the room, quietly closing the door behind her.

Rose battled her rising panic at losing Mrs. Hayworth's company.

The earl appraised Rose from head to toe. "Well, it pleases me very much indeed to finally meet you, Watson."

"Thank you, sir," Rose said, struggling to hold his intense blue gaze. She did not like the way Lord Robert leered at her or how his voice was laced with undisguised flirtation. Clutching her hands tightly in front of her, she fought to keep her face impassive, a treacherous tremor shaking through her knees.

"Well then, Watson, I want no modesty," the earl barked. "We are here for the sole purpose of my meeting you to find out what you have planned with regard to my wife's wardrobe."

"Yes, sir."

"Oh, Robert," the countess admonished, her cheeks pink. "I asked that you not tease her. Watson, come closer. Do not look so concerned. My husband enjoys his own wit. Often at the expense of others' ease."

Rose walked closer to the couple as Lord Robert continued to stare at her before his mustache lifted above another smile.

"So Watson, I understand you are not only making my wife's clothes, but you have also persuaded her to employ an assistant for you. Is that right?"

Rose's heart picked up speed. Did he know one of his staff was working on his wife's wardrobe? Was this the moment when her entire world came crashing down? Henry's smiling face appeared in her mind and the trembling in Rose's knees grew stronger. Both she and Henry would be dismissed. Maybe she had a modicum of hope with the countess, but the earl would never accept one of his household deceiving him.

"I…"

"Robert, please." Lady Christina put down her glass and stood, her face etched with clear annoyance. "You assured me you would not behave this way." She turned to Rose. "I'm sorry, Watson. I very much welcome the new addition to my staff considering the way it is helping you produce such beautiful clothes in an extraordinarily timely manner."

"Thank you, Your Ladyship."

"Why don't you tell my husband your plans for my wardrobe this season? I fear if we do not move on to the reason we are gathered, he will dismiss your intentions altogether."

Rose shakily cleared her throat and glanced at the earl, suspecting he entirely enjoyed her discomfort. His gaze ran over her from head to toe again, his eyes lingering a moment too long on her bosom. He would not intimidate her. She stood tall and strong, her body unmoving and her gaze firmly locked on him.

"As the first event the countess will attend this season is a garden party, I have already created…"

The room was silent but for her voice, and with each passing moment Rose's confidence returned, blurring the lines of her concern for her and Henry's positions with the certainty that their work was exemplary. She had no doubt the earl barely listened to what she said, his interest much more in Rose herself than on her work. The lechery in his gaze made her skin crawl, but her voice was firm and steady, her tone holding just the right amount of enthusiasm as she spoke of her knowledge of clothes, material, and design.

"I very much hope Your Lordship approves of the garments as much as the countess," she finished.

The room lapsed into a silence that felt charged with words unspoken. Rose wondered that the birds chirping outside the open window did not clamp their beaks shut too.

"Well…" The earl smiled, his eyes roaming over her whole body once more. "That all sounds most impressive, Watson, and you make a clear case for why you require an assistant."

Rose dipped her head. "Thank you, sir."

The countess stood in front of Rose, her gaze full of pride. "Watson, my husband saying your plans sound impressive is the most we can hope for by way of approval. So from this day forward, you can relax into your work with your friend alongside you." She pointedly looked at her husband and faced Rose once more. "Assuming you are still happy to work in my household after the earl's inquisition?"

"Of course, Your Ladyship."

The countess smiled.

"Your lady friend is to be envied, Watson!" Lord Robert exclaimed as he walked to a decanter and glasses on a bureau at the side of the room. "She will be working with you and a harem of other lovely ladies, I suspect." He poured himself a glass of claret, the red liquid almost reaching the top of the glass. "I have no issue with that. None at all. However..." He turned and sipped his drink before pinning Rose with an unwavering stare. "I do have issue with what my wife might or might not wear."

"Oh, Robert, really!" The countess admonished. "Watson just explained everything to you, and you did not say a word of disapproval. Now you decide—"

The earl sharply raised his hand. "I would like you to bring each design to me for endorsement before you proceed to buy material and so forth. Is that understood?"

"Robert," Lady Christina protested, "this is too much!"

"It is the way I wish it." The earl's tone broached no argument. "Watson? Is that understood?"

"Yes, sir." Rose cursed the crack in her voice as it echoed throughout the room, a sound she was certain she had never produced before and one she never wished to hear again.

"I will send my secretary for you in a few days to see what you've come up with." Lord Robert drained his glass before nodding at the door. "You may leave."

Rose curtsied and left the room as quickly as was decently possible, her dislike of the earl having increased exponentially.

Chapter Thirty-Three

Rose stood in the middle of Henry's living room, smoothed the sheets of parchment she had glued together, and studied her finished sketch. With swatches of material attached to one side next to drawings of the hat and accessories she would source for the ensemble, she prayed that this one and the two others she had ready, met with Lord Robert's approval when she saw him in less than two hours. Trepidation rolled through her stomach. The man made her want to dress in workman's clothes and an overcoat, his eyes hovering on her bosom more often than her face whenever she found herself in his company, which had been suspiciously frequent since their first meeting. She gripped the table, her dislike of the earl beating alongside the erratic thrum of her pulse. She just prayed he never suspected Henry was her assistant.

Rose swallowed. Bearing Lord Robert's lechery was a small price to pay in the scheme of things she had to concern her. The more days that passed, the more work Henry did for her, the more they talked and laughed, the more her feelings for him grew. But his leg was almost healed, his money pot was growing, and so his inevitable leaving came ever closer.

Wiping the back of her hand across her lightly perspiring brow, Rose inhaled a steadying breath. She had worked fourteen-hour days for the last three, ensuring all the duties allocated to her by

Mrs. Hayworth were completed before returning to work on Lady Christina's wardrobe. She turned away from the table, once again marveling at the way her life had changed. It really was as though she had been struck by a miracle.

In the corner of the room, Henry sat hunched over a great swath of material that would become a skirt Her Ladyship would wear to an upcoming charity event. He looked up and her heart jolted as their eyes met, his brilliant green gaze intense, yet softly admiring—a combination that became harder and harder to resist. He rose from his chair, his eyes still on hers as he came toward her, his limp barely visible. She dabbed the back of her hand under her chin and along her jaw, all too aware she must look a fright. Curls that had fallen from their pins tickled her temples and, despite the impropriety, she had undone the top two buttons of her dress for fear of self-combustion in the stuffy room.

"How about we take some fresh air?" Henry stood in front of her, his voice low. "I'm sure your designs are perfect and nothing more can be done to improve them today." He glanced at the window and the dusky evening sky beyond before touching his fingers to hers, his gaze filled with care. "Are you all right?"

"I'm fine," she lied, her cheeks warming at the thought that he might detect her body's reaction to him. "Why do you ask?"

"Because I was watching you before, and I would bet my good leg that your thoughts veered toward the earl rather than your work."

Rose lowered her shoulders. "I can't deny it."

"Then let's go outside. Our work is almost done. Your designs are like nothing I have seen before. You are going to make Lady Christina a countess who sets trends in fashion whether you take a break or not and, for now, my concern is your happiness."

Rose smiled. "She is already hailed for her dress sense. Any recognition on that score won't be my doing."

"I beg to differ, but I'm happy to wait until my predictions are proven true." He winked. "What do you say? Will you accompany me on a short outside walk, Miss Watson?"

"I'd love to, I really would, but there is still so much to do, and—"

"Won't there be even more to do once the earl approves your next designs?"

"*If* he approves them."

"He will."

Rose closed her eyes, hating the hint of self-pity in her tone. She could not abide her weakness, her fear. Worse, she could not afford to be weak or fearful in front of Lord Robert. Ever. He was most certainly the sort of man who thrived on female fragility.

She opened her eyes and eased her hand from Henry's. "I was so convinced my confidence in my work would win the earl over, but it clearly did not when he continues to insist that he approve each design individually. I thought I had achieved some small victory by asserting myself, proving how much my self-esteem has grown since I first came here. But now that I've seen how he treats women, I revel in the blessed freedom I have from him where the countess does not."

"I suspect Lord Robert's insistence of looking over your work has a lot more to do with the sort of man he is than with your abilities."

"But don't you see?" Frustration wound tight in Rose's stomach, and she stepped back, pushing her unruly curls behind her ears. "If he ever disapproves my designs, if he ever discovers we are working together, he and the countess could easily dismiss us."

Henry stepped back, concern etching his face. "I have thought more about that as we've worked together, but we won't have to for much longer."

"What do you mean?"

"I have been saving hard, Rose. I won't allow you to carry on the deception any longer than necessary. This has always been about me saving the money for my passage abroad. Right?"

Her heart sank. "Right."

His gaze bored into hers, his passion palpable. "We have been playing a dangerous game, and it must end before you lose everything." He studied her a moment before grasping her hands, his gaze dropping to her mouth. "I will not allow that to happen."

Heat crept into Rose's cheeks as the urgency of their kiss came rushing back to her, and suddenly she wanted nothing more than to feel his mouth on hers again.

She tried to break free before she acted on her desire, but he tightened his grip. Rose glanced behind her. "Henry…"

"Listen to me, Rose. You are an amazing designer. The materials you select are the finest; the colors beautiful and dynamic; the textures luxurious and original. Everything will be all right. You need to start making yourself a priority and stop worrying about a hundred and one other people." He touched his fingers to her chin, looked deep into her eyes. "If you are that worried about our working together being discovered, I will call a halt to it. Today."

"No." Unexpected panic rushed through her. "I don't want that."

"It's the right thing to do."

A knock sounded at the door.

Rose flew away from him and ran for the settee, scurrying as fast as she could behind it.

Henry cleared his throat. "Who is it?"

"It's Mrs. Baxter. I have your young cousin here," his landlady called from the other side of the door. "I'm surprised you didn't hear her knocking."

Rose closed her eyes as Henry's footsteps sounded across the rug and floorboards to the door. "Ah, Martha. Come on in. Thank you, Mrs. Baxter."

"Oh, you look busy—"

The door slammed closed.

Rose stood. "Henry, that was not nice."

"She's as nosy as they come." He faced his cousin who looked white with worry. "What is it, Martha? What's wrong?"

Rose came out from behind the settee and approached the young girl. "Are you all right, sweetheart?"

The young girl's eyes darted between her cousin and Rose, her mouth opening and then closing.

"He knows," she blurted. "Pa knows."

"Knows wh—" Henry stopped, his cheeks mottling. "He knows about Rose and me working together?"

"Yes." Martha's eyes filled with tears, her bottom lip trembling. "It slipped out. I'm so sorry."

Henry closed his eyes. "What happened?"

"He was talking about you, and I said you really like Miss Watson, and after all the time you spend working together, it's no surprise that you are falling—"

Henry grabbed her and pulled her tight against his chest. "It's all right. Don't you worry. Everything will be just fine. Hush now. No more chatter."

Rose met his eyes above Martha's head, her heart treacherously swelling with hope. Was Henry falling in love with her? She blinked.

What was she thinking? The important thing right in that moment was whether or not they were about to lose their positions.

"Henry…"

He shook his head, his jaw tight. "Everything will be fine, Rose. I promise."

Chapter Thirty-Four

Mrs. Hayworth knocked on the outer door of the earl's apartments, and Rose stared resolutely ahead, trying to control her pounding heart. She had to pull herself together or everything good she and Henry had done for each other over the last few weeks would come to a very abrupt and premature end. All night, she had tossed and turned, worrying his uncle might feel compelled to tell the earl of his nephew's clandestine work. Mr. Summers's loyalty to his employer was unbreakable, according to Henry. Then her fretting would turn to Henry's insistence that their stolen time together was over, filling her with dread that he would leave soon—possibly forever.

Mrs. Hayworth cleared her throat and bristled, "It seems Lord Robert is in no hurry to admit us."

She knocked on the door again, and Rose continued to stare ahead, her mind still reeling with worry. She must focus on this moment and not allow Henry to overtake her thoughts. All that mattered for the immediate future was that Lord Robert approved her designs, and she could continue to serve the countess.

At last, the door was opened by a liveried servant, who dipped his head in greeting, his thin face solemn.

"Miss Watson to see the earl," Mrs. Hayworth said, her chin high.

The servant offered another curt nod and stepped back.

Mrs. Hayworth turned and gave a faint but encouraging smile. "Off you go, Watson."

Swallowing hard, Rose walked past the servant into a dimly lit, wood-paneled anteroom, the only light coming from the wall sconces and a jewel-colored lamp on a circular table in the middle of the room. She looked at the landscapes and hunting scenes on the walls, at the mammoth chandelier hung above a highly polished table holding a vast bowl of the most wonderful arrangement of varied blooms she would have no hope of naming.

"If you'd like to follow me…"

She started at the servant's voice as he brushed past her, walking to a closed door.

"His Lordship has requested your company in his sitting room."

He pushed open the door and Rose followed him into a room decorated in shades of cream and dark blue. The wood paneling on the walls, dark furniture, and blue damask settees made what should have been a comfortable room feel decidedly eerie and imposing.

Sensing someone watching her, Rose turned, and her gaze met Lord Robert's.

Dropping into a low curtsy, she gripped her rolled designs and material samples so tightly her pulse thumped in her fingers. When she straightened, the earl's eyes were alert and bright above the gold-rimmed coffee cup he lifted to his lips.

"Miss Rose Watson, sir."

The servant's pronouncement seemed ridiculously superfluous when it was clear the earl knew she was there and exactly who she was.

"Thank you, Hughes. You are free to leave."

"Sir."

Rose stood stock-still as the servant retreated across the thick oriental rug and the door clicked shut. She had been concentrating on a spot just above Lord Robert's head, not sure he would condone her looking directly at him—the opposite of what his wonderful wife encouraged all her staff to do, as well as asking them to speak openly and as informally as protocol allowed. Conversely, the earl blatantly basked in his position and importance, and loved adulation to be slathered upon him as frequently as possible.

Bitterness coated Rose's mouth, her disdain evoking the strength she needed. She was at Henlow House in service to Lady Christina and hoped to remain here for a long time yet. What she wanted more than anything in the world was to continue playing her part in making her mistress the most beautiful and confident countess Britain had ever seen. If she was to do that, she had to get Lord Robert to like and respect her work. She had to focus on her commitment to the countess rather than her feelings for Henry.

From the corner of her eye, she watched the earl put his cup on a side table and settle back against the settee cushions.

"So here we are, Watson." He grinned. "Alone at last."

Gathering every ounce of her determination, Rose ignored the insinuation of intimacy and faced the earl directly. "I have three designs to show you, sir, along with the materials I would like to use and the accessories that will complement—"

"I hadn't finished speaking."

Rose flinched, her enforced bravado melting into a puddle at her feet. He hadn't shouted. Instead, his tone was chillingly quiet. Fear tiptoed along Rose's spine, her mouth draining dry. What was wrong with her? She knew the protocol. She knew not to speak until invited to do so. He had not asked her a question nor shown the slightest want of her response. She bowed her head, her hand tightening around her designs once again. Lord only knew how crumpled they would be if the earl eventually asked to view them.

The silence stretched.

"I understand it was my wife's dresser who discovered you," the earl said at last. "Considers you something of a talent. Is that right?"

"Yes, sir."

"And before coming to Henlow House, you worked at your family's shop?"

"Yes, sir. I worked with my parents and one other employee."

"And now you are here. Working for the Countess of Bath, no less."

The trembling she had fought so hard to suppress threatened to break free on a gargantuan scale. The earl's eyes were filled with lecherous intent, his lips shining from where his tongue wetted them with horrible frequency. It was imperative she showed absolute confidence and commitment to her task, otherwise she suspected her weakness would be the fodder Lord Robert needed to torment, or worse, dismiss her.

She held his unwavering gaze. "Yes, and I have never felt more honored. It is my sincere wish that you approve my work. I want nothing more than to help the countess flourish with confidence in her duties. I truly believe clothes are a contributing factor to anyone's self-esteem, and I wish nothing more than to ensure your wife's."

He lifted his coffee cup and sipped, eyeing her carefully over the rim. He sipped again before returning it to the table. "That is all well and good, but my wife is a revered member of England's nobility. If you make a singular mistake and persuade her to wear a badly selected choice in public, the press will have a field day."

"I understand. However—"

"I very much doubt that, Watson. What could a girl like you know of public expectation, newspapers, or anything people in the public eye must endure?"

"Nothing at all, sir, but—"

"But?" he sneered, his eyes gleaming with sardonic amusement. "There is a 'but'?"

Heat crept into Rose's cheeks, but she straightened her spine. "Alternatively, if one of my designs is a public success, then the press will talk about it positively for days, maybe even weeks."

His smile slowly dissipated, and he narrowed his eyes. "You are clearly no fool, Watson."

Determined that once the earl saw her work, he would understand she only had Lady Christina's popularity, influence, and happiness at the forefront of her mind, Rose stood a little taller. Yes, she still held deep ambitions, but other factors had come into play since she'd arrived at Henlow House. Loyalty, fondness, and care for Lady Christina's staff and the countess herself. Sometimes her ambition even became secondary when members of the countess's household shared personal and familial moments with Rose. No matter how much she admired the countess or how much she wished to serve and protect her, there were other things in life that a person should desire to achieve too.

She glanced at a wide, empty table at the side of the room. "Allow me to show you what I have designed, sir. They might encourage your belief in me. I would be glad for you to look."

He stared at her before the abject amusement in his eyes changed to something more akin to genuine interest. "As you wish."

Rose walked purposefully to the table and removed the tie from her rolled designs and carefully laid them out on the table. "May I?" she asked, nodding toward a paperweight and a leather-bound book.

The earl gestured with his hand. "By all means."

Rose pulled them closer to her and used them to anchor opposite corners, before inhaling a steadying breath. She glanced over her shoulder only to witness the earl's eyes lingering on her bottom. She stayed perfectly still until he slowly raised his gaze to hers. He grinned, his eyes bright with delight, neither embarrassed nor ashamed to be caught appraising her in such a way.

Sickness unfurled in her stomach. "Sir," she said stiffly and gestured at her designs with her outstretched hand. "If you would."

He came to stand so closely beside her that his arm brushed against hers, and the nauseating stench of cigar smoke and strong coffee evoked a sudden need to gag. She stared at her design and gathered every ounce of her passion for her designs and dreams. She would not fail now, no matter how much Lord Robert tested and tortured her.

"This is the first design," she said, splaying her hand on the parchment. "I envision the countess wearing this when she attends..."

Rose continued in her explanations and visions, relieved when the earl remained silent, which she hoped indicated his interest. Otherwise, wouldn't he command that she stop talking and leave his apartments?

"I believe the countess will attract both public and media admiration, sir. It is my motivation and wish every hour I work that she shines as the Countess of Bath and your wife."

His gaze wandered over her face before traveling lower to her bosom. Rose's chest tightened, her palms growing clammy, but she did not move and did not drop her gaze from his face.

With no idea what he had in mind to do next, she forced herself to speak. "Your wife's happiness is most important to me, sir. I do not wish her humiliation in any guise." She lifted her chin, her body trembling with a simmering anger rather than fear. How dare he assess her in such a way. How dare he do such a thing behind Her Ladyship's back. Shame threatened that it was somehow her fault that the earl looked at her with such lust. She cleared her throat. "And I'm sure you do not wish to humiliate her either." Her words were laced with clear accusation, and Rose stepped back lest he shouted or, God forbid, struck her.

But he did neither.

Instead, the lust in his eyes turned to annoyance and tension enveloped them. Finally, he glanced over the designs before abruptly leaving the table and returning to the settee. He picked up a silver box on the side table and removed a cigar. Rolling it back and forth in his fingers, he met Rose's gaze.

"Fine. You may continue to work for my wife. Your assistant too. But know this, Watson, my relationship with the countess is ours alone and needs no interference. Especially from her household, and that includes you." His gaze was ice-cold, any inkling of his lust had vanished.

"How I choose to live my life is my business, and if I suspect you of whispering poison against me to my wife, you will be gone from Henlow House, carrying such a black mark against you that your design aspirations will be well and truly over. Do I make myself clear?"

Rose nodded, her heart racing. "Yes, sir."

"Good. Now gather your papers and leave."

Turning to the table, Rose bit back a victorious smile as she quickly pulled her things together, returning the paperweight and book to their original places. Her risk to be insolent, to stand up for herself and Lady Christina had seemingly reversed the earl's attitude toward her, and she could not be happier. She would much rather he disliked her, was suspicious of her, than found her in any way attractive.

Chapter Thirty-Five

Henry locked gazes with his uncle, inwardly concerned that Charles might burst into flames, judging by the scarlet red of his face.

"You need to calm down," he said. *You're going to set the damn stables alight.* "My work with Rose is over. Finished."

"Does *she* know that?" Charles demanded, pushing his fingers into his hair and holding them there. "Because you are a damn fool for even agreeing to this, Henry. God above, I wish you'd stay in good, honest work as much as Miss Watson, but for her to risk her position for you like this? You never should have allowed it. Whatever your circumstances."

"I know."

"You know? Then why did it bloody well happen?"

"Because..." Henry's heart pulsed in his ears, his hands curled into fists at his sides as he tried to keep a hold on his temper. "I was in a bad place, Charles. A really bad place, and when Rose convinced me that I would be helping her more than helping myself, I believed her."

His uncle glared. "You only do what benefits you, Henry Ward. I know that and so do you. Now that girl is at risk of being in trouble with Lady Christina and you with the earl. God only knows what his reaction would be upon discovering you have worked for both him and his wife. The households are kept separate for a reason."

Henry pressed his lips together. He refused to keep going over this. He had said he was finished working with Rose, and he meant it.

Charles dropped his hand from his hair and crossed his arms. "Have you told her?"

"Who?"

"Miss Watson. Have you told her it's over between you?"

Henry stilled. The awareness in Charles's eyes, mixed with his undisguised anger, was unmistakable. This wasn't just about his fear for Henry and Rose's positions. It was about his belief of intimacy growing between them, and that Henry was only capable of hurting her.

And he would… but for her own sake in the long term.

He tilted his chin. "I will tell her as soon as I next see her."

"You tell her today." Charles leaned down and picked up the saddle that had been lying on the ground beside him. "Today, son, or so help me God, you'll have the wrath of your aunt to deal with on top of mine."

"Does she know?" Henry asked, hating the thought of having to bear his aunt's disappointment too.

"Not yet. Luckily for you, Martha let slip what she knew when it was just me and her alone." He stepped toward the stable doors. "Sort this out, Henry. I mean it."

Henry watched Charles until he was out of sight and then walked back to his workbench, grateful his leg was at least healed… even if cracks had slowly begun to creep across his heart.

He picked up his needle and tried to focus on his stitching, but his mind continued to reel, and his heart beat itself into a mess. The fear and worry in Rose's eyes when she'd left his lodgings had harangued him relentlessly until Henry feared he would roar out loud, his cries echoing from his living room walls.

There was no use fighting it any longer. He had fallen in love with her but wanted nothing more than to have her free of him and every misplaced obligation and feeling she might have toward him. The disappointment in her eyes when he'd tried to tell her their association had to end had been hard to handle, but it was even harder that each day they worked together, though their feelings for each other increased, so did the risk of her dismissal from her dream position creating garments for the countess. What in heaven's name had he been thinking, agreeing to work with her in the first place? Charles was right. It had been downright selfish and knowing he had caused her distress twisted painfully inside him. Complete contentment was all Henry wanted for her, and if that came in the form of him traveling to the other side of the world so she might soon forget him, so be it.

He laid down the saddle and stared through the open stable doors. She had hinted now and then that she saw changes in him since they'd met, but little did she know how fear grew wilder in his heart every day. Fear he could no longer contain. He loved her, but deep in his heart he knew his leaving was inevitable. He would never be contained in a single place, his love of horses and his need to see the world had not entirely diminished, no matter the peace he felt deep inside whenever he was with Rose.

He walked to the stable entrance, looking out into the yard, and breathed in the fresh June air. He could not stay here. He had to leave Henlow House. For as hard as he had tried to embrace the steadiness of his new position, working and not gambling, and fought to silence the whispers in his head urging him to get back to the card tables, back to what he knew best, he had to leave. The notion that the rest of his working life would be spent here, working side by side with his uncle, or even Rose, had proven beyond him.

Worse, he had begun to suspect Rose hoped his new position of working legitimately and saving up would eventually quiet his need to leave England and seek his fortune abroad. The way she sometimes looked at him told Henry his suspicions were merited, and even if she did not entirely believe he would settle here, or anywhere else for that matter, it was what she wanted from him. But such a wish was futile, and although hurting her would cut a wound deep in his heart, he had to set the record straight and leave.

But how he was to do that when quashing her optimism would destroy the wonderful light in her caramel eyes? How could he do that when he yearned for the feel of her skin under his fingertips? To know the taste of her lips over and over again?

Henry closed his eyes and tipped his head back, planting his hands on his hips.

The sound of rapid footsteps over gravel broke through his thoughts, and he opened his eyes. His stomach lurched at the sight of Rose approaching as quickly as her crinoline would allow, smiling so beautifully his heart burned with regret.

"Oh, Henry, thank goodness you are alone!" she said, her cheeks pink. "You will never guess what just happened—what I just said to the earl."

Henry stared down at her, words sticking in his throat. She was right. He would never guess because everything she did amazed him.

He forced a smile. "Whatever you said clearly gave you satisfaction, judging by the mischievousness in your eyes."

She laughed and grasped his forearm. "Oh, it did."

Her touch yanked at his heart, and Henry covered her hand with his. "What did you say?"

"Well…" She slipped her hand from his and narrowed her eyes. "He had the audacity to insinuate that I might put Lady Christina in a position of possible humiliation, and—"

"You would never!"

"Exactly! But trust me, there is no need to look so offended on my behalf. I managed the situation well enough."

Henry glanced at the house, debating whether to stride through the corridors to the earl's apartments. "I have no doubt."

She touched her finger to his chin, turning his face to hers.

"I told him… in a much more subtle way, that it was not *me* he had to worry about humiliating the countess but someone else entirely. And, what's more, I believe he understood I was talking about him, and that I am all too aware of how he treats Lady Christina and how he hurts her."

Concerned for her, Henry glanced at the house again. "If he thought that, he would have dismissed you on the spot. Be thankful he didn't understand your implication. You cannot test a man like Lord Robert, Rose. He won't tolerate insubordination."

"But he did." She grinned and whirled away from him, turning in a circle as though she danced in a ballroom rather than conversed with him in a stinking stable yard.

She had never looked more beautiful, and Henry's guilt deepened. She looked so happy, so completely luminous and trusting that she could confide in him, which only made Henry fear he was a contributing factor to her elation. He never should have allowed them to become so close.

"Rose…" He closed his eyes. "We need to talk."

"About what?"

Henry slowly opened his eyes, and when he looked into her excited gaze, his heart sank like a lead weight. He had to tell her now. Had to make it clear that his feelings about training horses overseas had not changed and likely never would.

"Rose…" He pushed his hand into his hair. She had come to mean more to him than anyone ever had, and although his yearning to live abroad had certainly lessened, it had not ceased altogether. Neither had the knowledge of how much his desires had the potential to hurt those he loved.

"Henry, what is it?"

She stepped closer and he instinctively stepped back lest she touch him. Thank God she had not come to feel for him what he felt for her. The light in her eyes dimmed, her smile vanishing.

Self-loathing burned inside him, but he forced himself to step closer and take her hand. "Rose—"

She snatched her hand away, her beautiful eyes darkening. "Tell me what's wrong. I've seen that look on your face before, and I think I know what you are about to say."

His gut wrenched.

Come on, you coward. Damn well tell her.

Henry lifted his chin. "Working here like this for the countess is *your* destiny, Rose. It isn't mine."

"I know that. You have never lied to me about how you would like your life to be."

"Maybe I haven't, but that does not make it any easier to insist our working together must end. Today. I'm too afraid of what would happen if the countess or earl found out what we have been up to."

A flicker of distress sparked in her eyes. "I understand, but—"

"No buts. Charles is angrier than I have ever seen him." He gave a wry smile. "And that is saying a lot, believe me. It's time for me to leave."

"Leave?" She crossed her arms, her gaze searching his face.

Whatever she sought, Henry knew deep in his gut that he couldn't give it to her—that he was utterly incapable of giving her all she deserved.

"I have enough money now for a passage abroad. I have to go."
He hitched his shoulders against the weight of his arrogant selfishness. "I need to see the world, discover all it has to offer, and I'd be a fool to allow my feelings for you to stop me from doing that."

"Your feelings for me?" The skin at her neck moved as she swallowed, her cheeks tingeing with color. "Our feelings for one another are by the by, Henry. You and I have wishes and dreams beyond feelings. By giving you extra work, I wasn't trying to cling to you. To hold you here. Maybe you thought I was waiting for you to ask for my hand in marriage?" She huffed a laugh and pushed a curl behind her ear. "When I care for someone, I do all I can to see them happy, fulfilled, and unafraid. That's why I wanted to do this for you, so you could earn money and save it, not lose it." She planted her hands on her hips. "Your leaving isn't about hurting *my* feelings or yours. It's all you've ever wanted to do."

Henry pulled back his shoulders, purposefully hardening his heart, just as he believed her to be doing. Did she know her words were like a knife blade in his gut, a hammer to his heart? Either way, he would endure it because he must.

"Then we understand each other."

"Of course." But her smile was strained. "I must return to the house. You won't leave without saying goodbye, will you?"

Before he could respond, she turned and strode along the path, leaving him standing alone with loss aching deep in his chest, dragging him down so low it was a wonder he wasn't flat on his back on the ground.

Chapter Thirty-Six

Angry that her heart still felt bruised a whole four hours after speaking with Henry, Rose marched along the pathway that led to the servants' entrance at Henlow House. She was not used to brooding over a man or having something bother her so much that she felt she might not manage to eat for the rest of the day... or week.

She had known this day would come. After all, the arrangement between her and Henry was only ever meant to be temporary. He was never going to help her forever. But to have him so easily bring a halt to their burgeoning romance had hurt.

Which was why she had walked away from him and not looked back. Otherwise, she might have reached for him, kissed him, tried to convince him to stay.

She was so glad Mrs. Hayworth had believed her story of needing to urgently go into town for some additional embellishments for the dress the countess would be wearing to a literary reading next week. Mrs. Hayworth had shooed her to the door, telling her to make sure nothing else was overlooked. Of course, nothing *had* been overlooked. Rose simply needed an escape so she could walk off her annoyance—her pain—that she meant very little to Henry if he could so easily leave Henlow House—leave her—after all they had shared together.

And even now, upon her return to the house, her heart continued to ache.

The stupidity of losing it to the man was of no importance. What *was* important was that she buried her feelings for him and fully concentrated on her life and ambitions once more. Tears pricked her eyes, and Rose hastily blinked them back as she entered the house. It wasn't her fault he couldn't see that their growing feelings weren't something to be feared. That they might have found the start of something special and were meant to meet that day at her parents' shop. That they had been brought together for a reason.

Cursing her silly, romantic heart that had become Henry Ward's, Rose stopped at the bottom of the staircase and gripped the banister. She had to get a hold of herself. What did it matter that he was leaving? She had helped him as she'd been unable to help Gideon. That had been her goal, and that was what she had achieved. Henry now had the money to leave. Yet sickness unfurled inside her that the ache in her heart was of her own making.

Taking a strengthening breath, Rose purposefully ascended the stairs. The truth was, the mere thought of their fledging relationship leading *somewhere* had excited her, had sent the most delicious tremors through her body whenever she imagined them together making plans, thinking of the future, making love. Her cheeks heated and Rose quickly pulled back her shoulders. Well, whatever they might have been together was no more. Snuffed out like a candle.

She entered the red-carpeted corridor that led to the countess's apartments, and when she pushed open Lady Christina's bedroom door, she was greeted by Mrs. Hayworth rushing back and forth, arranging a shawl and shoes against a beautiful ivory silk jacket and skirt laid out on the bed.

The dresser turned; her face flushed. "Oh, Rose, you're back. Very good. Her Ladyship told me just half an hour ago that some unexpected guests are arriving this evening. We're all-hands-on-deck, I'm afraid. Your other work will have to wait."

"Of course. What would you like me to do?"

Mrs. Hayworth studied the ensemble, her brow creased. "Yes, I think this will do perfectly for this evening's dinner. I will just take this skirt to the laundry. There is a small spot I'd like removed." She picked up the skirt and carefully arranged it over her arm. "If you could find two selections of jewelry to suit, that would be wonderful. The countess can choose which she'd prefer to wear."

"Of course."

Mrs. Hayworth walked toward the door and stopped. "Oh, before I forget, I was asked to give this to you." She pulled an envelope from her pocket and held it out. "I believe it's a message from someone who works in the Royal Mews." She arched an eyebrow and pinned Rose with a pointed stare. "As I have warned you before, Rose, be careful what choices you are making."

"Oh, I am." Rose looked at the envelope and regret twisted inside her as she recognized Henry's handwriting. "And I will. Always."

"I'm glad to hear it."

Mrs. Hayworth left the room and Rose quickly slid her finger under the envelope's seal and opened the single folded sheet of paper.

Dear Rose,

I have no doubt you will think me a coward, but you must understand it would have been too hard to part in person a second time…

Rose lowered the letter and glared blindly ahead. The nonchalance of the man! Slowly, she counted to ten then returned to her reading.

Therefore, this is my goodbye.

Please do not worry about me or waste time thinking of me. After we spoke, I realized that I am merely delaying the inevitable by staying here and will leave England's shores within the next day or two, if possible. I am confident Charles will be keen to see the back of me once I tell him I am leaving.

I have every faith in the great future ahead of you, Rose, and I know with absolute certainty you will ensure Lady Christina's happiness as much as you possibly can.

Farewell, beautiful lady.
Henry

Rose lowered the letter as profound sadness and loss whirled inside her, a horrible knot growing tighter in her stomach.

Mrs. Hayworth hurried back into the room and rushed to the bed, picking up the jacket. "I think maybe I should take this—" She halted on her way back to the door and looked at Rose, concerned. "Is everything all right?"

Rose forced a smile and held the letter behind her back. "Yes, of course."

"Then step to it. We do not have time to dawdle this evening, Rose."

Mrs. Hayworth flew from the room a second time and Rose swallowed. Were her feelings for Henry etched on her face for all to see? Quite possibly, considering she had lit up like a gas lamp whenever she was around him. She looked again at the letter, battling her desire to run to the stables to see if he was there, and if he wasn't, to scour every street, tavern, and market until she found him.

Slowly, she crumpled the letter in her fist. She would not follow him. He had his dreams. And she had hers. She would not rely on Henry Ward to help her accomplish them. She could do that herself.

Pushing the balled-up letter into her skirt pocket, Rose marched across the room. Ignoring the treacherous tear that rolled over her cheek and dropped onto the dressing table's surface, she drew in a deep breath and was about to open one of the drawers when she heard a discreet cough behind her.

Rose spun around and quickly dropped into a curtsy. "Your Ladyship."

Lady Christina smiled, her ladies-in-waiting hovering at the door. "Watson, how are you? I am looking for Mrs. Hayworth. I have no idea where she is, which is very unusual."

"She has gone to the laundry, Your Ladyship. Would you like me to take a message to her?"

"No, no. I'm just conscious of the extra work I have given you both this evening and wanted to stress that you don't have to worry too much about what I will wear to dinner. It is very informal."

"Oh, it's all in hand." Rose's voice cracked, and unexpected tears leaped into her eyes. Mortified, her cheeks burned hot. "It's no bother at all."

The countess's blue eyes widened in surprise and then care. "Can I ask that everyone leave Watson and me alone for a moment?"

No, no, no. Rose's heart beat so fast she swore Lady Christina could hear it. This was too awful. The entire staff would be talking about her being singled out this way.

The door quietly closed behind the last lady to leave.

"Your Ladyship, please. There is no need—"

"This will take just a minute, Watson. You are clearly distressed about something. Are you able to tell me what it is? Your happiness matters to me very much, you know."

"I promise, it's nothing."

"Watson, it is not nothing," the countess said sternly. "Clearly something has upset you, and I do not believe it has anything to do with my clothes, considering how pleased you must be that the press is clamoring over one another to find out more about you. Now, I would hazard a guess that it involves something of a romantic nature?"

Rose silently cursed Henry to high heaven for putting her in such an unprecedented position when it meant so much to her that Lady Christina continued to hold her creative credibility in such esteem. She lifted her chin. "Yes, Your Ladyship, but I will be right as rain in no time. There really is no need for your concern. I am perfectly all right."

Lady Christina walked closer and took Rose's hand. "Disappointment and heartbreak are not prejudiced. High class or low born, we are all open to pain and humiliation."

Rose nodded, unsure of what to say when it was clear the countess spoke of her husband.

The countess sighed. "My current humiliation is my sincere belief the earl will soon take a permanent mistress, and I will have to abide by his wishes."

"Oh, Your Ladyship... I am so sorry."

"I just want you to understand how important it is that women not lose their hearts completely to any man, Watson. No matter who he might be or the position he holds. Do you understand?"

Rose nodded, filled with sympathy for her mistress for being trapped in a dynastic marriage with such a brute of a husband. The situation must be torturous more often than it was happy.

Her Ladyship smiled even as her eyes remained shadowed with sadness. "Good, because your talent and all you have done to help me feel that I have more to offer this country than being the earl's wife means everything to me, Watson. Everything. You are a success. A designer. A clothes maker of the highest caliber. I know that, the press agrees, and you should too."

Rose swallowed, pride filling her heart. "Thank you."

"No gratitude is necessary, Watson. I just want you to see that you shouldn't allow anyone to take you for granted. To trample on your dreams and desires. You are too good, too lovely, too talented for that to happen." Tears glazed the countess's eyes. "Now, I will bother you no longer. If you could find Mrs. Hayworth and ask that she please come to my chambers straightaway, I would be obliged."

"Of course."

Rose stood stock-still until the countess left the room and then released her breath, her heart thundering. Never would she have believed such words would be spoken to her by a countess. A member of England's most noble family. Exhaling a shaky breath, Rose turned back to the dressing table, opened one of the drawers, and carefully selected two of the countess's favorite sets of jewelry, one of emeralds and diamonds—which only served to make her think of Henry's eyes—and another of sapphires and diamonds—which reminded her of the recent sad and blue state of her heart.

She swiped at the treacherous tears that slipped onto her cheeks as prisms of light danced from the jewels. From this moment forward, she would banish Henry from her heart and mind. Henlow House was where she belonged, and if she was to be there without him beside her, so be it.

Chapter Thirty-Seven

"Are you pulling my pecker?" Henry glared around the table at the other gamblers, entirely ashamed that he'd lost at least half his savings.

"Maybe it's time you called it a day." His opponent's yellow-white teeth glinted in the dim, semi-darkness, his eyes alight with triumph as he scooted forward and enveloped his winnings with a purposeful slide of his open arms. "We don't need any histrionics, Ward. It is what it is."

Henry continued to glare at him. *What the hell have I done?*

Gathering up the pitiful number of notes and coins in front of him, Henry emitted a parting snort and left the table. He weaved through the room, past the bar and croupiers dealing cards until he reached the front door of the gaming house and stepped outside. He squinted against the bright, late-afternoon sunshine. God only knew what time it was or how long he had been at the tables, but it had been a darn sight less bright when he'd entered.

He walked slowly, ignoring the whores who tried to catch his eye and purposefully turned away from the open doors of the taverns and gaming rooms. Why in God's name had he resorted to a quick fix in a bid for some extra cash? Hadn't he learned anything? Didn't he know by now that gambling always led to loss for those who chose to repeatedly partake in it? He needed the money he had left for a bed tonight, or he'd be sleeping in another doorway. Dossing on the street was what it had come to after leaving Henlow House two weeks before with all the nonchalance and arrogance of an imbecile.

"Any spare change, sir? A penny or two to help a boy trying to do some good for his ma?"

Henry's heart ached for the lad who held out his cap, his face caked in mud, the whites of his eyes gleaming, his teeth brown. The poor urchin could have done with a fortnight's feeding. God only knew how far the few pennies Henry dropped into his cap would stretch.

"Here. Now get yourself back to your mother," he said, glancing along the street and catching the eye of an older bloke, dressed in a black hat and suit, his gaze on the boy rather than Henry. "You don't need to be hanging around here. Go on, get out of here."

"Thanks, mister."

The boy ran off and Henry held the man's gaze until he flashed a grin and walked in the other direction. Anger writhed in Henry's gut as he continued walking. The streets were full of predators and pickpockets, lowlifes and thieves. Why was he choosing to be here when he could still be working side by side with Charles? Why was he here when he could have kept a hold of any modicum of respect his uncle might have had for him before he left the Henlow House mews without as much as a backward glance?

Pride was most definitely one of life's deadly sins.

He narrowed his eyes against the soot and filth, the stench of horse muck and rotting food. Good God, it was shameful the stories he told himself and others because he had fallen so utterly in love with Rose and feared he'd never be able to keep her happy. The truth was, he could train horses right here. In England. He no longer needed the excitement of the Mediterranean. He needed to be with Rose. To build a life with her.

And for that to happen—for there to be any chance of her considering him romantically again—he must find a way to prove himself worthy of her love and trust.

As he joined the throng of people walking back and forth along the cobbled street, the sun did little to brighten the gray-and-brown canvas of poverty everywhere he looked. Didn't he deserve to be here after the opportunity he had thrown away? Lowering his gaze to the ground, Henry walked on, feeling as though the eyes of the city watched him.

Judged him.

Laughed at him.

Scorned him.

Nothing about the game had felt the same today—not the rush of winnings he'd achieved early on, the pursuit of the next game, the idea that he might one day be in a faraway country working with some of the best horses in Europe.

None of it lifted his mood as it had before. The whole fantasy was pathetic. His fear of not being enough for Rose, and his innate selfishness had led him to losing a chance at real happiness. He knew that now, but what the hell was he supposed to do about it?

Henry blew out a breath. He had no choice. He needed to see Charles. Beg his forgiveness and for another chance. His last chance.

He headed across town and eventually reached Henlow House.

Sneaking through the staff gate, he made for the mews.

The familiar smells of leather, glue, and burning metal enveloped him as he walked through the arched entryway and into the stables. His uncle was leaning over a saddle on one of the workbenches, his brow glistening with perspiration.

Inhaling a long breath, Henry gathered his fortitude. "How are you, Uncle?"

Charles stilled, his hand not moving from the tool he held, his eyes remaining firmly fixed to the saddle.

The seconds beat out like minutes…

Henry stood his ground and fought the weight of intimidation and shame that shrouded him.

Charles straightened and slowly turned, his gaze hard. "You're back."

"I am."

"I wonder why that could be. Did you not find what you were expecting at the gaming tables?" Charles smirked and tossed his tool on the workbench, its clang echoing sharply. "I would have thought by now you'd have learned that you're not going to find anything worth looking for in one of those places."

"You've got every right to be disappointed in me," Henry said, walking closer. "I'm disappointed in myself, but—"

"You promised no more gambling, Henry."

He swallowed. "I know I did, and I failed. I'm sorry, Charles. I really am."

His uncle's jaw tightened, his gaze showing his hurt. "What am I supposed to do with that apology, son? Add it to the list of the ones you've given me before?"

Henry closed his eyes and swiped his hand over his face, self-loathing sitting like the devil on his shoulder. Opening his eyes, he sighed. "If you can find it in your heart to give me one last chance, I will prove myself to you this time. No more empty words or promises, just deeds. I am done with messing about and playing the fool."

"Why should I believe you? How many times have I heard this before? What's different this time?"

Henry pulled back his shoulders. "Rose."

"Miss Watson? This turnaround is because of Miss Watson?"

"Yes."

"That girl doesn't need the likes of you hanging around her." Charles snatched up a rag and wiped his hands. "She's doing well enough on her own. The clothes she creates are causing a sensation. More than that, they are adding to the countess's prestige and popularity. That, my boy, is how talented Miss Watson is; how important she has become to Her Ladyship. She does not need you."

"I know she doesn't need me." Henry's heart beat faster, his annoyance growing. "I left because she doesn't need me."

"Is that so?"

"Yes."

"Good, because she deserves a man who will adore her, who will support her talent and kindness to her mistress." Charles's eyes flashed with protectiveness. "Miss Watson is excelling in her work for the countess, and she doesn't need complications from you ruining that for her."

"I've no intention of approaching Rose for a long while, Charles. Not until I've got something to offer her."

"Something to offer her? My God, son, she didn't want anything more from you than to be able to trust you not to let her down. She risked everything for you, and you walked away."

"But I won't again. Please, Charles, let me have my saddling job back, and—"

"Whoa. What are you saying? You've given up the tables *and* horse training? But I thought your leg was healed."

"It is."

"Then why are you giving up the horse training?"

"I'm not. That might or might not come. In time. For now, I want to work here by whatever means. Sticking with what I know will keep me close to Rose. I want a future with her, Uncle. I've got to prove to her I'm not going to leave her again."

His uncle stared at him, his brow creased and his gaze hard. "So you feel no differently about saddling?"

"No, but I'll do it if it means there's a chance Rose will want to be with me."

"Why have you not thought of the earl's horses? I don't want you in the stables with me if you are thinking about what is out in the field."

Henry stared at his uncle, possibility burning in his chest. "You think I should speak to the earl's Master of the Horse about training permanently? He's never offered me more than the occasional job before now."

"Have you ever asked him for more?"

"Well, no. I always assumed—"

"Assumptions get people nowhere in this world, Henry. Why don't you take a leaf out of Miss Watson's book and start putting yourself on the line for what lies in your heart? Stop being so afraid to make yourself vulnerable. Just because you've decided to stay at Henlow House does not mean I am jumping up and down with pleasure to have you work with me. Go after the horses, Henry. Stop looking for a fast result for once in your life and go out there and do something to make us all proud of you."

Charles turned back to his work, and a smile pulled at Henry's lips. His uncle had hit the nail on the head. It was time to lay himself bare and go after what he wanted—the hard way. Only once he had succeeded and landed himself a position training the earl's horses, no matter how long that might take, would he court and woo Rose. He had to have something of his own, something to show her he had changed, in order for her to consider him as her beau.

Chapter Thirty-Eight

Rose turned onto Regent Street, humming to herself.

Her happiness was complete.

That is, if she continued to tamp down her thoughts about a certain vagabond gambler. Or should she say returned horse trainer? She had not believed the tittle-tattle she'd overheard in the servants' hall almost three weeks ago, her hardened heart refusing to let the news of Henry's return to the mews hurt her.

Yet after catching glimpses of him in the yard and training fields from the upstairs windows of the house, she had waited another day, another week, and now a third week with a shameful hope that he might seek her out to speak to her. To tell her why his plans had changed. At this point it was clear his return to Henlow House had nothing to do with her. She shouldn't even be thinking about him, much less caring why he hadn't gotten on a boat bound for the Mediterranean.

It seemed he had listened to her somewhat. At least now he was working with the earl's horses rather than with his uncle. That was something that made her proud of their time together if nothing else.

And then there was their kiss, of course. Although the memory that thought evoked hurt so much more than her dented pride, it represented what she had hoped was the beginning of something beautiful between them. Now she knew that would never be.

Well, men had no place in the lives of women who sought their own happiness. After all, if Lady Christina could hide her hurt over her husband's blatant philandering, then Rose's struggles with Henry were pitiful by comparison.

She resolutely turned her mind to the money tucked inside her purse. She could not wait to give it to her parents. It was her first visit in over a month, and in that time she had been paid her weekly wages and two extra payments the countess insisted she accept when Rose unveiled two new dresses. It felt wrong to take the money when she would have toiled for free, but she needed to bring something worthwhile to her parents—her mother especially—if she was to finally quash their worries about her safety.

She strode farther along the street and then stopped, transfixed by the three gentlemen banging on the door of her parents' shop, peering through the latticed window and brazenly braying at the door. What on earth?

Clutching her reticule, Rose rushed forward. "Excuse me, what are you doing? Get away from there right now!"

The men turned and one of them grinned. "It's her! It's her!"

Rose pressed back against the door of the shop and glared at the men in turn. "Who are you?"

"We're reporters, Miss Watson," one of them said. "We're hoping for a few words from you about your position with the countess."

"It must be quite the step up from working here, eh?" another asked, his mustaches twitching.

"Just a quote or two from you will suffice, miss."

Sickness unfurled in Rose's stomach. The article in *The Queen* had been published yesterday. It had been a small piece where Rose's name was made public on the countess's urging, believing it would lead to bigger and better things for Rose in the future. Had her parents been suffering harassment ever since?

She abruptly turned to the door. Despite knowing it would be locked, she tried the handle. Nothing. She cupped her face to the glass, ignoring a reporter's fingers that patted her shoulder. "Miss Watson? Any comment?"

Were her parents even here?

But then relief washed through her. Through the glass, her father's eyes never left hers as he walked to the door, reached up, and pulled back the top bolt, then the middle bolt, and finally turned the key. Bracing herself, Rose thrust herself through the door the moment he opened it. He slammed it closed, threw the bolts into place, and turned the key.

She faced her father, and the sadness in his eyes wrenched her heart. Helplessness swam through her blood, turning it icy cold. But no matter what her success might have brought to her parents' doorstep, she would not regret it. How could she when she had never felt so accomplished? So sure Henlow House was where she belonged?

Culpability enveloped her. What kind of daughter was she to feel that way? What kind of woman?

"Papa, I am so sor—"

Bang! Bang!

She spun around and glared at the reporter who slapped his palm against the window, his eyes downright maniacal behind wire-rimmed spectacles. "Just a comment, Miss Watson. One comment and we'll leave you be!"

Anger rose hot behind Rose's chest. "How dare you harass my parents this way!" she cried. "My work has nothing to do with them. Go away!" She snapped the curtain over the door closed and then strode to the window and pulled the curtains there too. She turned around just as her mother emerged from the back room and came to stand beside her husband. Her parents joined hands, their expressions unreadable.

"Mama, Papa…" She shook her head. "I'm so sorry."

"What are you sorry for?" her father asked quietly. "We are shocked by the press attention, Rose. Of course we are."

"But we're also pleased that the countess has acknowledged your work this way." Her mother smiled. "I assume that in order for the article to be published, she must have authorized it?"

Rose slumped her shoulders with relief. "You're not angry?"

"We were more than a little taken aback when the first reporter arrived, but now you're here, and looking so well, it doesn't seem quite so bad."

"But still." Rose glanced toward the front door, guilt pressing down on her. "I never could have expected such interest."

"The Earl and Countess of Bath are news. Will always be news. For the rest of their poor lives. Are you happy, Rose?" her father asked, staring at her intensely. "I believe I see sadness in your eyes, my love. Something inside of you is missing."

Her heart treacherously ached. *Someone* is missing…

"Nothing is missing, Papa." Rose walked closer to her parents, opening her purse. "Here." She held out an envelope containing more money than she had ever seen at any one time. "Take this. I will earn more and will soon have enough for you to employ another girl to work alongside Florence, or even a young apprentice tailor if that is what you want. Eventually you will be able to retire. Don't you see? My position could change everything for us. All of us."

Her father took the envelope and peered inside, his jaw tightening before he met Rose's eyes. "This is a lot of money."

He passed the envelope to his wife who also looked inside, a small gasp escaping her before she turned, wide-eyed, to Rose. "This is… too much."

"I work hard, Mama." Rose smiled and walked forward to squeeze her mother's hand, appealing to her heart and praying she heard her. "I deserve this, and I refuse to feel guilty about it. I make the countess happy with my designs, and she deserves to be happy more than I can say. This isn't just about designing anymore, Mama. This is about leading a life that I love and knowing you are happy for me makes that so much easier."

Knock! Knock!

All three of them jumped at more banging on the door. Rose turned on her heel, muttering a low curse. The softening in her mother's eyes, in her demeanor, had been the glimmer of hope Rose needed and now a journalist had most likely destroyed that momentary peace. Well, if he wanted a comment, she would give him a comment he wouldn't forget in a hurry.

She yanked back the bolts and flung open the door. "Will you just—Henry!"

Chapter Thirty-Nine

Henry held out the bunch of roses he'd purchased from a nearby stall and flashed Rose what he hoped was his most charming smile. "For you."

She glanced at the roses, her lips pinched into a thin line before she lifted her icy gaze to his. "Come inside. Quickly." Wrapping her fist around his lapel, she yanked him forward, and unceremoniously pitched him behind her. She faced the reporters in front of her. "If you don't leave right now, I will send my friend for the constable. Good day."

Henry glanced over his shoulder and grimaced at Rose's parents. They looked at him with curiosity before looking at each other. The front door slammed, and they all snapped their attention to Rose. Her bosom heaved as she glared at him, her hands fisted on her hips, her eyes flitting over his face. Her expression told him well enough that she was far from thrilled to see him.

He held out the flowers a second time. "For you."

"I do not want your flowers, Henry. You need to go."

"I attempted to get a message to you at the house."

"I don't care, Henry. Go away."

He looked into her angry, beautiful caramel eyes and stood tall. "No."

Her cheeks flushed pink. "What?"

"I said no." He looked again at her parents, their interest flitting between him and their daughter. Assuming it a good sign that neither of them had staged an intervention, Henry continued his entreaty. "I came to congratulate you. I'm not leaving until I've done what I came here to do."

"Congratulate me?"

"The article. In *The Queen*. You are on the rise and—"

"You saw that?"

"Yes. It was pasted to the window of the boutique that—"

"Stop." Her cheeks darkened as she flicked her gaze to her parents and back again. "Give me those flowers." She snatched them from him, her throat moving as she looked at them. "They're lovely. Thank you." She lifted her chin. "I was just about to leave anyway. You can walk out with me." She faced her parents. "Mama? Papa? This is Henry Ward. I'm not sure that you remember him from the last time he was here. He is easy enough to forget, after all. It's for the best that I leave now, lest he decides to speak to you. Believe me, anything he says will hold little sincerity."

Henry narrowed his eyes at her turned back, a sharp retort biting his tongue. He opened his mouth to defend himself, but then caught the look of love and amusement in Mr. Watson's eyes as he watched his daughter. Such open enjoyment of Rose's derision and tetchiness surely meant this side of her was something her family witnessed often and with love. A side that rolled off their backs as inadvertent and words said in irritation, nothing more.

Henry smiled, his stomach quivering with suppressed laughter, and his heart only growing with love for her.

"Rose?" Mr. Watson's voice was firm, and Henry's urge to laugh vanished.

"Yes, Papa?"

The tension left her face and her eyes filled with such a depth of love that Henry's heart picked up speed. *What it must feel like to have her look at you that way…*

"Mr. Ward is clearly not your favorite person, but your mother and I raised you better than to talk about people like that. Especially young men who come calling with congratulations and flowers." He faced Henry. "Now, Mr. Ward, it is a surprise to see you again. Do you work alongside my daughter at Henlow House? See each other from time to time?"

Henry nodded and looked Mr. Watson in the eye. "We did, sir, but I left for a while."

Rose emitted a rather inelegant snort, her body rigid. "A while, indeed."

Henry looked at her. "What?"

"Oh, nothing." She gave a dismissive wave, her gaze cold. "Please continue."

"I will continue, if you don't mind, daughter," her father said. He turned to Henry. "And now you are once again part of the earl's household?"

"Yes, sir." Henry pulled back his shoulders. "I am training his horses, sir."

A flicker of respect widened Mr. Watson's eyes, and he glanced at Rose, who steadfastly stared at a floral print on the wall, before facing Henry again. "Are you indeed? Well, there is something to be said about that, young man."

"Thank you, sir."

"Well, Rose," her father said, turning away. "I suggest you leave with Mr. Ward now, and we will talk again very soon. Clearly, now is not the best time."

Two spots of color darkened Rose's cheeks. "Yes, Papa."

Sensing a moment to themselves was needed between Rose and her parents, Henry nodded to Mr. and Mrs. Watson. "Goodbye. I hope to see you again."

He waited at the door, surreptitiously watching Rose as she kissed her parents' cheeks and squeezed their hands before she walked toward him. He opened the door, pleased that the press had come to their senses and disappeared.

They walked a short distance along the street before Henry spoke. "Can I walk you back to the house? I assume that's where you're going."

She stopped, her gaze dropping to his mouth for a second or two before she lifted her eyes. "Why are you here?" She looked at the flowers. "Why give me flowers? After the last time we spoke... your letter..."

"I was wrong to leave you a letter rather than..." He clenched his jaw. "I'm not the best of men, Rose. You know that."

"Yes, unfortunately, I do." She drew in a breath, then slowly released it. "Let's have a cup of tea somewhere. We need to talk."

Relief whispered through him, and he held out his elbow.

She hesitated before sliding her hand into its crook.

The teashop was quiet and due to close in the next half hour. With only two other tables occupied at the far end of the room, Henry relaxed a little, grateful for the lack of curiosity that might be directed his way if Rose reacted to his return in a way that would almost certainly draw attention.

Once their tea had been brought to the table, Henry took a sip from the china cup and leaned forward, intent on delivering another apology for disappearing without talking to her properly as she deserved.

But she spoke first.

"Just now on the street you said you were wrong," she whispered. "That you're not the best of men."

"I did."

"But that is hardly an explanation for vanishing the way you did."

He stared at her, words utterly failing him as his heart grew heavy with regret. "I left as I did because I knew how much it would hurt looking in your eyes again, knowing that with one word from you, I would stay, but I couldn't do that."

"Because?"

He swallowed. "Because all the worst parts of me were the same, Rose, and until that changed—*I changed*—then…" He shook his head. "My leaving had nothing to do with us, nothing to do with how I feel about you." He bowed his head, his heart hammering before he forced his eyes to hers.

"I was too afraid of our working together being uncovered, and it leading to your dismissal. You risked that happening for me, something I will never forget, and the only way I could truly show you the same care was to leave, in the hope that my absence would be enough to prevent the earl or anyone else from learning what we had been doing behind his and Her Ladyship's back." He slid his hand to hers where it lay on the table, but she pulled it into her lap. His heart stumbled. "I admit I felt I had to leave for reasons of my own, too. I thought…I needed to go, pursue what I've always dreamed of. I'm so sorry I hurt you, Rose. Truly, I am."

"That may be so, but now you're back, which means your logic about preventing discovery of our subterfuge makes no sense."

"But it does."

"How?"

"Because you no longer need me to work with you. The urgency for the countess's season wardrobe is over, and you are becoming more and more established in her household. If there is ever another time you need help, you will be given a seamstress of your choosing." He grimaced. "A seamstress who doesn't need your help to keep them from throwing away every penny she earns."

Her gaze locked on his and shame engulfed him when tears sprang onto her lashes before she hastily swiped them away and jutted her chin. "Well, what is done is done. I've moved on, as I am sure you have." She picked up her teacup, and the liquid ever so slightly trembled as she brought it to her lips. "So you liked the article? In *The Queen*?"

He forced a smile despite wanting to touch her so badly it physically hurt. Did she not hear his insinuation that his feelings for her had changed what he needed to do? Did she not realize that she was now part of the dream he wanted to pursue? "Yes. I'm so proud of you. The world is ready for Rose Watson, mark my words."

She laughed softly, warmth seeping into her eyes. "Thank you. I cannot deny that things are going extremely well for me at the house. Lady Christina loves my designs, and the clothes give her such confidence. Where have you been, Henry? I thought your absence meant you were halfway around the world on a journey of feckless gambling and goodness knows what else. I was clearly mistaken."

"It was I who made the mistake, Rose."

She stared at him, her mouth a straight line and her gaze resolute.

"I made a mistake leaving Henlow House. Leaving you."

She studied him, her gaze unreadable before she looked past him, her cheeks flushed. "Yes, I think you did."

He reached for her hand, and this time she didn't pull away. After a few seconds, she faced him.

"I'm back for good," he said. "Training the earl's horses is something I did not even consider because of my desire to travel, but my desires have changed. It's you I want to be with, you I want to build a life with. Here. In London."

Her eyes told him nothing. What lie in their brown depths could be distrust or maybe hope. He couldn't be sure.

She shook her head. "Desires don't just change, Henry. You have told me how much traveling the world means to you a hundred times. A yearning like that doesn't just disappear."

"No, it doesn't, and that is why I could not have been more thrilled when I asked the earl's secretary if, as well as training the earl's horses, I would be taken into consideration to accompany the earl when he travels overseas to buy and sell his horses."

"And he said yes?"

"Yes." Henry smiled, encouraged by the softening in her eyes. "But it only happens three or four times a year. I hope both of us will be happy with that."

Her gaze moved over his face. "Well, that sounds wonderful, but…"

"But what? Rose, ask me anything. Say anything you feel, please."

"What if it happens again, Henry? What if you leave without a backward glance? Then what?"

If she had taken a knife to his chest, her distrust would have hurt less, but he should have known it would take more than a few heartfelt words to win her trust back—to win her back. She had too much self-respect to forgive him that easily.

He drew in a long breath. "I've learned a lot over the last few months, but what I know for sure is that you and I were meant to meet, meant to be together at Henlow House serving the earl and countess in ways that are special to each of us. I want to be with you, Rose, to earn a proper, legitimate wage and be of service to the earl. My days at the tables are over. Forever. And if you can find it in your heart to give me a second chance…" He briefly closed his eyes, then opened them again. "I promise I will prove my conviction, my love for you and, God willing, regain your trust. If I manage that, I will protect it, cherish it, forever."

She studied him, her brown eyes burning into his. "Do you really mean that?"

"With my entire heart."

The seconds ticked by like minutes.

She exhaled a shaky breath, lifted her teacup. "I suppose a second chance won't be too hard to agree to… considering all that has happened… all you have said. But I warn you, Henry Ward, one more seat at the gaming tables, one more broken promise, one more leaving without a word, and I will not be held responsible for my actions."

"Does that mean…"

She smiled, her eyes almost laughing. "One more chance."

Relief and joy washed through him, and Henry smiled. "You really are the best thing that ever happened to me. Do you know that?"

"Oh, I know." She lifted her eyebrows, her eyes glinting with love that pierced his heart. "But it's nice that you finally do too."

A Letter from Rachel

Thank you so much for picking up my novel, *Dressing the Countess*. I hope Rose and Henry's story filled your heart with love and possibility while immersing you in the charm and history of Victorian London.

If you'd like to know when my next book is out, you can **sign up for new Harpeth Road release alerts for my novels here:**

www.harpethroad.com/rachel-brimble-newsletter-signup

I won't share your information with anyone else, and I'll only email you a quick message whenever new books come out or go on sale.

If you enjoyed *Dressing the Countess*, I'd be so thankful if you'd write a review online. Getting feedback from readers helps to persuade others to pick up my book for the first time. It's one of the biggest gifts you could give me.

Until next time,
Rachel x

Acknowledgments

First, and foremost, I want to thank the founder of Harpeth Road and all-round amazing lady, the fabulous Jenny Hale! When the acceptance for *Dressing the Countess* dropped into my inbox, I literally screamed with joy after wanting to work with Harpeth Road for over a year. Since I signed the contract, everyone I have worked with on this book has been amazing, and I have learned so much from genius structural editor Karli Jackson and wonderful line editor Jodi Hughes. Thank you so much, ladies, for making this book the very best it can be!

I also want to thank my amazing writer friends from the Romantic Novelists Association, others online and beyond for all the encouragement, belief, and commiserations you've given me over the years. I don't know where I'd be without you, but I'm pretty sure I would not be writing.

And finally, a huge thank you to my long-suffering husband, the unbreakable Mr. B and our wonderful daughters, Jessica and Hannah—I am so sorry, but Mumma's started writing another book…

Printed in Great Britain
by Amazon